FAERIE CURSE

THE CHANGELING CHRONICLES: BOOK FIVE

EMMA L. ADAMS

1

Everyone in the supernatural world knew never to mess with a witch. Everyone, apparently, aside from whoever had had the audacity to steal from the coven's warehouse in broad daylight.

"Someone has a death wish," I remarked, surveying the closed doors to the warehouse. The shimmering wards were back in place, but this time the thieves had even had the nerve to leave graffiti behind. The text, smudged by rainwater, stood out above my head in glittering ink. I tilted my head, trying to read the words, but the language was unfamiliar to me.

"Oh, they'll wish for death when I'm done with them." Isabel cracked her knuckles and placed a tracking spell on the ground. "Let's see what we have here."

At one time, I'd pretended to be a witch to hide the fact that I'd stolen my magic from a lord of Faerie. I didn't need to lie any longer, but I was still more than happy to give Isabel a helping hand when it came to such matters as punishing thieves foolish enough to cross the Laurel Coven.

That they'd done so three times in a week merited consequences on a level with one of Isabel's high-grade itching spells.

"The thieves struck a couple of hours ago at most." Isabel dropped to a crouch. "That means the tracks will be fresh."

"Unless they covered their traces." Stealing from the witches' storeroom in the first place suggested they knew how to avoid detection, especially as a significant number of the spells inside the store were used to erase evidence. "Want me to try one, too?"

"Sure, go ahead."

I pulled out a tracking spell of my own. Trackers were more precise when they locked onto a specific person, but the thieves hadn't left any physical evidence behind, so we'd have to cast the spell on the area directly in front of the warehouse and hope that nobody else had walked past in the time that had elapsed since the robbery.

As green light swirled up both my arms, my vision tunnelled, and then the warehouse reappeared in monochrome. One disadvantage to tracking spells was that they played like old movies with no sound, so the thieves could be having a full-volume discussion of their nefarious plans in the background and I wouldn't be any the wiser.

As I watched, four figures walked out of the open door. All four wore black, down to the masks beneath their hoods that concealed their features. I hadn't expected them to come out wearing name tags, but come on.

Swearing under my breath, I withdrew my hands from the tracking spell, and the circle collapsed into fine powder.

Next to me, Isabel shook spell residue from her own hands. "See anything useful? I didn't."

"Nope." I rose upright. "Just four hooded figures in black masks. Not faeries, and probably not shifters either. I'd say human."

But why—and how—would non-supernaturals, humans without magic, steal supplies from the coven? They hadn't even used magic openly, as far as I'd seen, though the trackers only afforded us a glimpse into a few recent moments of time. The further back you tried to reach, the fuzzier the results would be.

"Same here." Isabel ran her heel over the remnants of the tracking spell, smudging the dust into the pavement. "I didn't see how they broke in."

"Lock pick?"

"We have booby traps." Isabel pointed to the faint glyphs painted on the walls on either side of the door. "I found them disabled, just like the last two robberies. Whoever our thieves are, they know how to detect and negate spells."

"Do they have a dispeller?" The device revealed and negated certain spells, but the only one I'd seen was Vance's custom-made model, and they weren't easy to come by.

"If they did, they likely stole that, too." Isabel's eyes gained a steely glint. "I'm going in to see what they took. Cover for me?"

"You sure?"

"Nobody's inside. Shana and I already reset the wards."

"All right." My eyes followed the movement as she unlocked the door, and the dark, wide room lit up in a blaze of fluorescent light. One of my hands rested on the sword strapped to my waist and I unsheathed it a couple of inches, but no blue glow warned me of faerie magic.

Boxes and crates filled most of the space inside, packed with spell ingredients ranging from leaves and herbs to less pleasant items like dried insects and powdered bone. Their herbal scent wafted over me as I planted my feet in the doorway, watching Isabel search behind the boxes for attackers. If an aggressor waited inside a room full of deadly spells, they'd be in for a nasty surprise if they tried to jump Isabel, but robbing the coven three times was not an act of someone who feared retaliation. If anything, they were begging for a chat with my sword, Helena.

Once I'd verified there weren't any hidden attackers behind the boxes and crates, my gaze panned over the wards at the entrance. Standard security wards, which detected threats and prevented anyone from passing by who wasn't a witch. In fact, they'd gone one step further. When I rested my hand over the ward, I met an invisible barrier coating the wall beneath. When the wards were fully functional, nobody aside from a select few—presumably coven members—could walk through the door into the warehouse without meeting resistance. An iron barrier was also set in place to keep the faeries out, and there'd be more wards concealed around the immediate area beneath shadow spells.

That the thieves hadn't used shadow spells themselves was another sign of their sheer boldness. Shadow spells reduced the person wearing the charm to, well, a shadow. Handy for thievery, at least for most people. Though my magic was only visible to those with the Sight—in other words, anyone with faerie blood—it blazed like a neon-blue beacon even when I employed a shadow spell to hide myself. I suppressed a groan when a passing piskie spotted me and zipped over, drawn by the low-level glow of my magic.

"Shoo," I muttered, waving a hand.

The piskie ignored me, buzzing around my head like an oversized fly, and inadvertently flew straight into the invisible barrier on the warehouse door. There was a popping noise, and the small creature shot into the air like a cork from a champagne bottle. *So much for not drawing attention.*

Piskies were small fry, but I sometimes missed the days when I'd been able to slide under the radar. Until last year, I'd primarily made a living by killing any rogue faeries out to cause trouble but never acquired a reputation among the lesser fae. Now, though only a handful of people knew the story of how I'd acquired faerie magic as a regular old human, the newfound notoriety was a constant thorn in my side. Literally, in some cases.

Ugh. Don't think about thorns, Ivy.

Though the piskie took the hint and didn't come back, my sword continued to emit a faint blue halo warning of faeries somewhere nearby. The sword, which I'd christened Helena, was a replacement for Irene, my old iron blade. Forged in the faerie realm from one of their ancient trees, this blade was the physical manifestation of the magic I'd stolen from a Sidhe lord. In addition to boosting my speed to levels that rivalled the supernatural grace of a faerie, the talisman was stronger and sharper than any other blade I'd seen and had the extra bonus of being impervious to damage. I rested my hand on the hilt and drew the blade a couple of inches, revealing shimmering glyphs and a brightening glow that pointed to a shifting shadow behind me, hidden by glamour it thought I couldn't see through.

"Nice try." I spun around and fully drew the blade, decapitating the imp before it could conjure up a flame. Fire imps were fairly harmless as far as faerie pests went, but they travelled in packs. As I'd expected, the noise brought five more imps scurrying out. When they saw my glowing sword up close, they turned tail and legged it for the nearest alley.

"Oh no, you don't." Plenty of non-supernaturals lived nearby, and I knew from experience how fast an imp's fire could spread. With a quick glance behind me to make sure none were in the warehouse, too, I ran in pursuit.

Entering the alleyway, I lifted a hand and sent a controlled burst of magic that slammed into all five of them at once. I'd toned the attack down, but the blast still sent them flying in all directions. One flung a fireball past my head, which I deflected, forming my magic into a shield between me and the miniature faeries. They might be small, but the buggers packed a hell of a magical punch, and on one memorable occasion, a group of the little shits had skipped past the wards on our flat and had set Isabel's flowerbeds on fire.

Apparently not taking the hint, a fire imp leaped into the air, brandishing a knife the length of its arm. I used my shield to knock the blade from its hand and caught the imp on the end of my sword. Magic burst outward, sending the imp's head flying into the air and spraying gore all over the alley wall. I took down the other imps in three swipes, my blade humming with both pleasure and impatience, wanting a real challenge. When there was only one imp left, surrounded by the bodies of its fallen companions, it let out a shriek and flung a last fireball.

I flicked my blade and deflected the flames right back at its owner. The imp howled, its papery skin caught afire, and I shook my head at it. "You'd think Faerie would have given you fireproof skin. Guess that place screws all of us over, huh."

I finished the creature off with a quick stab to the throat and checked myself for injuries. None, aside from a shallow cut to the back of my hand, which I'd absently wiped on my leg and left a crimson smear behind. Might get some stares, but at this point, I'd perfected the denim-and-blood aesthetic. My lifestyle didn't offer many chances to make fashion statements.

"Ivy?" Isabel approached me from behind, taking in my dishevelled state and the bloody mess smeared on the wall. "I left you for five minutes and now you're bleeding in an alley surrounded by bits of dead faerie. Honestly, Ivy, I think you have issues."

"You think?" I pulled a cleansing spell out of my pocket to get rid of the bloody smears on the alley wall. "Find anything in there?"

"No." She threw in a cleansing spell of her own, while I picked up each decapitated imp's body and deposited them into a dustbin. I'd call cleanup to come and collect them later. "I checked, and it doesn't look as if they took anything dangerous. I keep all the experimental stuff at the flat anyway, but I'm pretty sure they stole nothing aside from a few trackers and cleansing spells. It's bizarre."

"You mean to say they robbed the witches' most secure store and didn't steal anything important?"

"Yeah." Isabel's lips pursed. "If I didn't know better, I'd wonder if their only objective was to draw the coven's attention. They left enough traces for us to know they were here, but not enough for us to follow them."

"Yeah, that's sketchy." I thought. "Maybe they're selling the spells for profit on the side and picked ones that wouldn't be traced back to the coven."

"That's a possibility, but I can't believe they've done this *three* times and not got caught." Her tightening jaw betrayed her annoyance. It wasn't every day that Isabel's top-notch spells failed to turn up answers. "I'm still lost on who they even were. Only a witch would know how to get past our wards. Or a mage, but the mages' headquarters is where half the deliveries are bound for in the first place."

"It won't be a mage." They didn't do petty thievery. "Any rival witches in the area?"

"No, and no coven member would have any reason to steal supplies. We're allowed to take as many spells home as we want to, *and* we have keys to the storeroom anyway." Her forehead creased. "I'm missing something."

"The graffiti?"

"The what?"

I closed the dustbin lid on the fire imps' corpses and strode back to the warehouse, pointing out the neon words shimmering before our eyes. "That."

"What am I supposed to be looking at?"

"The words. I can't read them, but… wait. You don't see it?"

"No. I don't see any writing."

"Damn." If she couldn't see it, that meant the writing was glamoured. A faerie, somehow, had left that text. Did that mean the fae had been responsible for the thievery? *Those hooded figures… they weren't fae. Right?*

Isabel met my gaze for a long moment, her expression reflecting a chain of thoughts that mirrored mine. Then she looked away. "It might not have been the thieves who left the message. There'd be no point if none of the witches can see it."

Unless it was for me. I had more enemies than I could count, especially amid the fae, but my ability to see through glamour didn't extend to reading whatever gibberish they'd scrawled on the wall. "I can't read it either."

"Fae language, do you think?" Isabel swivelled to the alleyway. "Did those faeries who attacked you…?"

"Nah, fire imps can't read or write," I said. "Not sure if they knew me or if they just wanted to cause trouble."

No faerie would have any reason to steal from the witches. They had their own spells and human ones often flat-out didn't work for them. As for the other supernatural groups, the mages and necromancers had arrangements with the local coven to receive the best spell supplies before they went on sale to the public, while shifters rarely bothered with spells at all unless in situations of dire need. Which left regular, mundane humans as the most likely suspects. Mercenaries, perhaps, though I'd assumed even they would have more sense. Most had no magical talent, either, and whoever had disabled the wards must have had at least some level of skill. Hmm.

I pulled out a small notebook to copy down the text scrawled on the wall. Then Isabel and I turned our backs on the warehouse and left for home.

My phone buzzed in my pocket as we reached our flat, located on the bottom floor of a two-storey semi-detached house at the street's corner. By habit, Isabel and I checked on the wards etched onto the garden wall on either side of the gate and the tripwire spells on the inside, positioned to offer maximum discomfort to anyone who had the misfortune to enter the house intending harm. Potential clients didn't fall into that category, but nobody lurked in the flowerbeds today. Our flat also doubled as the office for the freelance business we shared and we'd had to give Erwin a stern lecture about dropping glitter spells on our clients' heads.

"Ivy!" The piskie flew out of the upstairs window to greet us, perching on the door frame. "No bad faeries today?"

"Good. And you didn't drop glitter on anyone?"

"No, definitely not."

Isabel grinned. "See, told you he'd remember."

I made a sceptical noise. After years of reluctant cohabitation with our winged squatter, Isabel and I had long since given up on trying to evict him and it had been Isabel who'd suggested employing him as a security guardThe piskie might have less brains than a gnat, but I'd reluctantly conceded that it wasn't a bad idea to have one of the faeries watching for trouble when Isabel was alone in the flat. Unlike me, she couldn't see through glamour.

Which made me wonder, once again, who'd left that message at the warehouse. If I went with the paranoid conclusion that the person responsible wanted to find *me*, they didn't need to go to that much trouble. Pretty much every faerie in the city knew our address already.

And our current immortal enemy made the witches' highest-grade security wards look as flimsy as cobwebs.

True, I hadn't seen Fionn, former commander of the Wild Hunt, since he'd disappeared after Calder had woken him up six months ago. Those of us who knew of his existence were working under the assumption he was enjoying freedom in the Grey Vale too much to come back and destroy humanity for kicks, but I of all people knew how tenuous human existence was compared to the callous immortals who saw us as little more than playthings. I also knew better than to assume he'd forgotten about me, the sole human who'd witnessed his rebirth.

My phone buzzed again, and I pulled it out, skimming through my messages.

"Vance?" Isabel said questioningly.

"Yep." I read the text on the screen, a smile forming on my lips. "Date night."

"Nice." She unlocked the front door and looked me over. "You aren't wearing those jeans, I hope."

"Nope." I entered the flat and headed to my room to change out of my bloodstained clothes and into something nice, which admittedly had a high chance of acquiring its own set of bloodstains by the night's end. Even when I wasn't on duty, being the faerie killer came with its fair share of hazards, and my skills had never been in higher demand.

Despite my ex-boss's attempts at sabotage, Isabel and I had done just fine since I'd quit working for Larsen. Around half our jobs came from from the mages, thanks to Vance Colton, head mage and my long-term partner, and the rest from independent clients. We split jobs evenly between us most of the time, though I sometimes volunteered to go solo due to her being busy with her duties as the second-in-command of the Laurel Coven. I normally stayed out of coven business, but I was more than happy to lend my sword to help her with this current outbreak of thievery, and I had little doubt that Isabel and I would catch the sticky-fingered intruders whether they were fae or human.

Once I'd changed, I left the flat for my second home, the manor belonging to the local mage guild and the property of Lord Vance Colton.

2

I hovered in mid-air, pinned in position by a ferocious air current that held me ten feet off the ground with my legs dangling beneath me. Vance, the culprit, grinned up at me. "Do you give up yet?"

"Hell, no." I should have figured the tricky bastard would be waiting to take advantage of any gap I'd left in my magical shield, and I wasn't at my sharpest at this hour of the morning. Even on a nice day like this.

The manor's sprawling lawns were damp with the early summer rain from the previous night, but the sky today was clear with bright rays of sunlight gilding the vibrant flowers arranged in neat beds around the patio. Not many people were around yet, which was why I'd reluctantly dragged myself out of bed early for a bout of magical training, but I was starting to regret giving the Mage Lord permission to unleash the full force of his displacement ability on me. It took a hell of a lot of focus to move the air around with enough precision to levitate a human off the ground, and the slightest lapse in attention on his part would end in a swift fall and a hard landing.

Luckily, I had a trick or two of my own. A shimmering blue magical shield visible only to me hovered in front of my hands, and as I focused, the shield expanded, pushing against the air holding me in place.

Vance peered up at me as though trying to figure out what I was doing, but he was unable to see through the glamour. *Here we go.*

I took a deep breath, then gave one final push with my shield. Vance's hands fell to his sides, the air stopped holding me up, and I dropped like a stone.

Or I would have, if I hadn't angled myself so I'd fall forward as the dispersing wind current hit me from behind. I crashed straight into Vance, tackling him to the ground. He wasn't easy to knock over, but he hadn't expected an Ivy-shaped bullet to hit him from ten feet in the air. We slammed into the lawn, my knees resting on his chest. He shifted on his back, trying to throw me off him, but I used my shield as a solid force that pinned his arms down like an invisible concrete block.

"Give up, Lord Colton?"

"You're stronger." Approval resounded in his voice.

"Only you could take me trouncing you as a compliment. Maybe you're just growing soft."

Lightning-quick, he wrenched one arm free. "I wouldn't be so sure."

I'd asked for it. Vance's hand shot out and flipped me over onto my back. An instant later, he'd pinned my arms to my chest.

"Damn you." I twitched my right hand and mimed stabbing him in the chest. "If I had a dagger, you'd be dead."

He laughed. "If you did, I'd have finished you ten minutes ago."

"Oi." I turned the stabbing motion into a punch. My fist bounced off hard muscle. Ow. I flexed my throbbing hand

and allowed the tiniest bit of magic to flow over my skin, forming a shield between me and Vance.

"Don't think I can't tell what you're doing," Vance said.

"Never said you couldn't." I shoved my shield outward, hoping to unbalance him, but he sprang to his feet instead.

Sparring with Vance forced me to think about fighting in a different way than I'd been accustomed to as a mercenary. I'd learned to strike hard and fast before the enemy got the upper hand, but I was always up against people of the same skill level, and even the faeries living here were weakened shells of their counterparts in the faerie realm.

None of my usual methods had much effect on a foe who had literally centuries' more training than I did, and the last Sidhe I'd fought had only spared my life because of the novelty factor of witnessing a human wield a talisman that had once belonged to one of his fellow Sidhe lords. There was no guarantee he'd do the same during our next encounter, and the lack of any willing Sidhe to use for target practise had sent me searching elsewhere for worthy opponents. The mages made duelling into a sport as much as a survival tactic, and the most skilled of their number could rival a faerie for sheer destructive power.

Case in point: the mage in front of me, who lifted a hand and displaced the air, knocking me flat on my back. "Ow."

"Need a hand?" Vance reached out, a smirk on his face,

"Nice try." I pulled my shield into place, blocking another displaced air attack from behind. Unlike some other mages, Vance didn't rely on his magic and trained equally hard at swordplay and hand-to-hand, a habit he'd placed a particular emphasis on since we'd both got stranded in Faerie a few months ago and he'd found himself without access to his abilities. But he went all-out when duelling with me, and it took all my efforts to fend off his attacks until I was within striking range.

Then I let go of the shield and released the magic into twin streams of energy. Vance blocked one, but the other knocked into him from behind. He staggered, catching his balance before he slid over.

"That was supposed to knock you on your face, dammit." I'd made a habit of toning down my powers during training sessions to avoid causing unnecessary damage to the garden, but it didn't have quite the same visual effect.

"Let's assume it did, if I were a faerie." He stretched, giving me an appealing view of the defined muscles of his chest through his T-shirt.

I jumped to my feet. "If you were a faerie, you wouldn't be walking."

Vance's phone appeared in his hand. "I also wouldn't be babysitting the necromancers again."

"Again? What is it this time?"

"Minor spell backfiring. They need a witch to keep an eye on them, if you ask me."

"No ghost-related trouble?"

"No, it's not that." The soft, reassuring note to his voice indicated he'd picked up on my thoughts. Months had passed since I'd wiped Calder's memory and his ghostly allies had departed this realm in droves, but the nightmares had taken much longer to fade. The necromancers had it worse than I did, as their leader's death had left their ranks in disarray and nobody had been willing to step in and take Lord Evander's place. The mage council had taken unofficial leadership instead, which was probably for the best, but it was frustrating when their apprentices insisted on calling Vance over the most minor issue.

"Do you want me to come with you?"

"I'll only be ten minutes or so," said Vance. "We can pick this up later."

"Yeah, you're not off the hook yet."

Less than a year ago, I'd have laughed if anyone told me the sight of the Mage Lord's smile would send happy tingles through my whole body. When we'd first met, he'd thought I was a troublemaker plotting against him, while I'd thought he was an interfering, stuck-up mage hellbent on making my life as difficult as humanly possible. Yet somehow, after several narrow brushes with death and a few misunderstandings along the way, we had the kind of stability I'd never thought I'd ever have in a relationship.

"You can practise with Drake," said Vance. "There he is."

The fire mage walked out the conservatory door, accompanied by Wanda, Vance's frost mage assistant, and older woman leaning on a cane. Lady Harper. *Oh, great. Just who I wanted to see.*

Vance displayed no surprise at his former mentor's unannounced arrival. "I've been called to the necromancers' headquarters. Drake, do you want to take over my match with Ivy?"

"Oh, I'm game." Drake grinned at me, though he kept a notable distance from the sturdy old woman who walked alongside Wanda. It had been months since my last encounter with Lady Harper and I'd given up on expecting her to apologise for using her mage powers to break into my mind during our first meeting in order to discern if I was conspiring against Vance. Not to mention insinuating that I wasn't good enough to stand at the Mage Lord's side. I was far from the first to fall on the bad side of Vance's former mentor, and anyone with a smidgen of sense was scared shitless of her.

"Lady Harper," I said, putting on the excessively polite voice I typically reserved for council meetings. "Nice to see you again."

She didn't need to be a mind-reader to know I was

silently telling her to fuck off, but her only response was a slight narrowing of her eyes.

I offered a smile to Drake and Wanda. "Ready?"

"As I'll ever be." Drake beckoned to Wanda. "C'mon, we'll make it a three-way fight. It'll be fun."

Lady Harper, for her part, planted herself in one of the deck chairs on the patio. "I'd like to speak to you when you return, Mage Lord."

"If you like." Vance disappeared. Literally. The Mage Lord defined the word 'dramatic', though I wouldn't have minded having access to an easy way to escape Lady Harper at a moment's notice either.

Drake approached the lawn, lazily tossing his coat aside. The mages typically wore formal attire, coupled with their distinctive knee-length black coats, though Drake's untucked shirt and unruly copper hair were a stark contrast to Vance's usual impeccable appearance. At a guess, he'd just come back from sending out patrols. Vance had tripled the manor's guards in recent months and had also made the slightly questionable decision to put Drake in charge of the rota. Drake's reputation as a matchmaker also extended to organising patrol teams with the sole purpose of setting up his fellow mages on dates, but in fairness, he was also Vance's closest friend among the mages and took his job as second-in-command seriously despite his tendency to act the fool on a regular basis.

As a powerful fire mage, he wasn't a bad fighter either, though fire mages were a little more predictable than those with rarer talents like Vance. Lady Harper, too. As far as I knew, nobody else among the mages shared her gift for extracting and influencing thoughts and memories, and while while the former head mage hadn't laid a hand on me since our first meeting, I sincerely hoped she planned to stay on the sidelines rather than joining in our three-way bout.

"Are we fighting with magic, or weapons, too?" Wanda asked. The kind-faced young woman was a frost mage apprentice who also worked as Vance's assistant, as well as carrying the dubious honour of being Lady Harper's one surviving relative.

"The usual. Just give me everything you've got."

Drake grinned. "You might live to regret that request."

Within ten seconds, I was running for my life. Half the lawn was ablaze, flames chased Wanda and me across the grass, and while I'd conjured up a magical shield around myself, the flowerbeds were in severe danger of catching afire.

"Did you forget I'm supposed to be fighting you, not the grass?" I puffed out, shooting Drake a glare. The fire mage stood watching, arms folded and a smirk on his face. "You're not even trying."

"Oh, I'm just enjoying the show."

I flipped him off and put on a burst of speed to evade the flames licking at the edges of my shield. Wanda, without the benefit of faerie magic-enhanced speed, stood with her back to the fence, unable to run any further. "A little help, Ivy?"

"All right, you asked for it." I spun around and reverted my shield into an attack, aiming not at Drake but at the flaming torrent rippling across the lawn. A burst of blue light seared through the oncoming flames and drove them towards their owner. Drake jumped, comically, but was too late to avoid being caught in the path of his own attack. While the flames licked harmlessly at his skin, his trouser legs were were soon singed and smoking, and he yelped, kicking off his burning shoes.

Wanda doubled over in silent laughter at Drake's predicament. I'd been a little overenthusiastic, and now a wall of rippling flames circled the fire mage.

"Cut it out!" he yelped.

"They're your flames." I folded my arms and mimicked his previously casual pose. "Vance isn't here to displace the fire this time, and there aren't any water mages around. Hmm. Does anyone have a hosepipe?"

"Quentin will throttle us in our sleep if we ruin the flowerbeds," Drake said. "Shit. Wanda, can you...?"

"No!" Wanda threw handfuls of frost magic at the fire, but the snow melted into a trickle that further fed into the rising flames. "It's out of control!"

A sudden torrent of water descended, drenching us all. I spat out hair that had come loose from my ponytail, looking for the source of the unexpected downpour and zeroing in on Lady Harper. She'd risen from her chair, glowering at us. "I called the Mage Lord. He won't be happy when he comes back."

"What did he do, displace half the canal over here?" By the taste of the water, I'd say so, though he'd been too late to save the grass.

I spat out another mouthful, while Drake lay in a bedraggled pile of red hair and singed clothes. "That was uncalled for, Vance."

"He isn't here," said Wanda, shaking water out of her shoes. "I haven't seen you start a fire that intense in years."

"Vance is the one who told me to practise." Drake picked up his own shoes and looked ruefully at the ruined soles. "Anyone would think the Sidhe were on the brink of another invasion, the way he's driving us."

I stiffened. His comment was unintentionally close to the truth. Vance had only told a handful of people that Fionn had been partially—if not entirely—responsible for the invasion, and that he far outmatched any other Sidhe I'd met. We hadn't wanted to cause a widespread panic, and it'd been months since our last encounter with the leader of the Wild Hunt, but I didn't blame Vance for insisting that all his fellow mages should pursue an intense training regime.

"What's the deal with the Sidhe, then?" Drake trudged to the patio and perched on a deck chair. "What makes them so special?"

I joined him, my sodden clothes leaving a trail of water on the paving stones. "Sidhe lords are the most powerful beings in Faerie. They're overpowered, pretentious egotists who think they're the centre of the universe."

"Pretty sure you just described Vance."

A current of air thwacked Drake in the back of the head. "Ow. Also uncalled for, Vance."

The Mage Lord had quietly reappeared behind us, cloak rippling in the breeze stirred by his arrival.

I tilted my head back to grin at him. "How are the necromancers?"

"It's a wonder they're still alive," said Vance. "Half of them wouldn't know an obvious fake spell until it blew their eyebrows off. Drake, what did I tell you about exercising control?"

Drake pulled a face. "Bloody grass is too flammable."

"I nearly set him on fire with his own flames," I told Vance. "Might be a gap in your strategy there."

Drake snorted. "It's like being apprentices all over again."

"Well, you are acting like children." Lady Harper beckoned with a crooked finger. "Mage Lord, a word, please."

She'd used his title, which must mean serious business. Why had she come to the manor in the first place? I'd been under the impression she was mostly retired these days. She'd already given up her title as head mage when the faerie invasion had forced her to step in as leader as well as raising and training Vance after his parents had died in the invasion, but she still kept a watchful eye on the mages from afar.

As the pair of them went back into the manor, Drake groaned softly. "I'm on her shit list for life now."

"Thought you already were." Lady Harper made no secret of her disdain towards Drake's lax approach to his role as council member. "Along with the rest of us. Did you know she was coming?"

"Nope." Wanda grimaced. "If I had, I'd have warned you."

"Figures." I peered through the conservatory's glass door at her and Vance, but I couldn't hear a word either of them said to one another. "I know absence supposedly makes the heart grow fonder, but she still hates me as much as ever."

"She doesn't hate you," Wanda said. "She thinks Drake's irresponsible—which is true—and, well… she doesn't know you, Ivy."

"It's okay." Who cared if Lady Harper didn't like me? She was one bad-tempered eighty-five-year-old retired mage who had no influence aside from being the world's worst house guest. Her last visit in January had ended without fanfare, or at least not as much as the departure of Lady Granville following her unsuccessful attempt to oust Vance from his position as head mage. The last I'd heard, Vance's former rival had gone to impose her reign of terror over Gloucester instead, while her close friend Lady Penrose had also resigned from her position. Lord Carlisle, too, though he'd been in the tricker position of having committed a crime while possessed by a ghost. In the end, Vance had the go-ahead to replace all the council members except for himself and Drake and start afresh. While I was sceptical that the mages would ever entirely be rid of their deep-rooted biases, nobody on the new council had put me on trial for murder yet, which was a win in my book.

"Want to try again?" I asked. "This time, Drake, throw the fire at *me*, not the garden."

"Got it." He grinned. "Wouldn't want to piss off your boyfriend."

"Were you flirting with Ivy?" Vance enquired, having left the conservatory without my noticing. Lady Harper, mercifully, had not followed him.

Drake covered his head with his hands. "No!"

"You know Drake flirts with everyone except Wanda and me," I said.

"That's because Wanda's like Vance's little sister, and he's been taken with *you* ever since you decapitated a hellhound in front of him. And they say I have questionable taste."

"Would one of you please stop that ungodly noise?" yelled Lady Harper from the conservatory doorway.

"What noise?" Vance disappeared, and a second later, he pressed my phone into my hand. "Someone's been calling you for the last twenty minutes."

"Oh, crap." I skimmed the touch screen of my new phone —Vance had replaced my old one after it'd taken an unplanned swim during a fight with a territorial bridge troll —and saw Isabel's name. "Hey. Something up?"

"Oh my god, Ivy," Isabel gasped into the phone.

Every nerve in my body stood at instant alert. "Isabel, are you okay?"

"The leader of the Laurel Coven." She gulped. "She's— she's dead."

3

"What?" I gripped the phone tight. "Isabel… what happened?"

"Francine…" Isabel's tone steadied a little, but I heard the tremor beneath. "We found her body outside the warehouse."

The place the thieves had struck. "You don't think—"

"I don't know, but it wasn't an accident." She took in a shuddering breath. "Shana and I are on our way to the warehouse now, to check for more clues."

"Got it." I turned to Vance and quickly explained. "I know you have clients coming in later, but—"

"I'll come with you," said Vance. "The death of a coven leader is something I'm required to report to the rest of the council. How did she die?"

"Isabel didn't say, but it was no accident." Witches might not demonstrate the sort of overt displays of power that the mages and the half-faeries did, but anyone who laid a hand on Isabel was either flung ten feet into the air, burned with invisible tongs or hit in the face with itching powder or glitter, depending on her mood. The head of the coven would have had the best defences available, which made her death a glaring anomaly. And a warning, both to the other witches and to every other supernatural in the city.

Vance gave some quick instructions to Drake and Wanda and then checked in on Lady Harper before rejoining me on the patio. "Whereabouts is Isabel now?"

"On her way to the warehouse where they found her body," I told him. "It's also the same place that was robbed yesterday."

The thieves had disabled the wards, indicating that they knew their way around magic, but there was a world of difference between committing a robbery and murdering one of the most powerful witches in the city in broad daylight.

Vance took my arm, and we landed outside the warehouse. Isabel was already there, tighter with a plump blond woman of around thirty or so. Shana exclaimed and shielded herself from the gust of wind that accompanied our arrival, while I belatedly remembered my clothes were still sodden with canal water.

"Mage Lord." Shana recovered, eyes widening. "I didn't know you were coming."

Isabel stepped in. "This is Ivy—you've met, right?"

"A while ago, yes." Shana's voice shook a little, but she nodded and she clasped her hands together. "Nobody outside of the coven knows yet."

"Vance won't tell anyone else," Isabel said, with a meaningful look at me. "Not until our say-so. Right?"

Vance frowned. "The council will need to be informed."

"Can't it wait?" Shana's voice cracked. "Her body's barely cold."

"Of course," said Vance. "I'm here to offer my help. Whereabouts did you find her?"

"There." Isabel pointed at the warehouse entrance with a shaking hand. "I think she was resetting the wards, and someone—well, *shot* her."

"As in.. shot her with a gun?" What kind of weapon choice was that? The faeries' magic rendered gunpowder useless, more or less, and witches had no need of conventional weapons besides.

Isabel blinked, tears leaking from her eyes. "It makes no sense, but I don't know what else could have caused that injury."

"Have you scanned the area using tracking spells?" Vance asked, somehow sounding both soothing and authoritative at the same time. "I assume an event of that magnitude will have left an imprint."

"We've tried everything," said Shana. "Tracking spells of all strengths, from both inside and outside the warehouse. The whole area was wiped clean."

"Cleansing spells." My heart gave an unpleasant jolt. "The thieves stole some, didn't they? But they didn't use them during the robbery." Evidently they'd saved them to commit a far more serious crime. An impossible one for a regular person to commit, or so I'd thought.

"There wasn't even any blood on the ground." Isabel's face crumpled, and I moved over and hugged her.

"I'm sorry." I didn't have any other words of reassurance to offer. I'd have offered to kill the bastard responsible if I'd had the faintest idea who it was, but faeries were my area of expertise. Not humans.

Assuming the killer *was* human.

Isabel wiped her eyes on the back of her hand and stepped back from me. "Do you want to see her? The coven will probably let you in, but… ah. I'm not sure if they want to hire the mages."

"You don't have to hire us," said Vance. "Francine was a

friend to the mages, and I'd be more than willing to contribute any resources you need in order to catch the killer."

"Oh," said Shana, visibly taken aback. "If that's the case, you can come and see her, but I can't promise the others will be as keen on letting outsiders in."

"I'll risk it." Without seeing the body, I had no hope of figuring out who was behind this, and the glamoured writing on the warehouse remained as a glaring reminder that someone out there had been willing to go to any lengths to snag our attention. Didn't explain why they'd gone after Francine, since two of us hadn't even met, but our shared connection via Isabel was enough to make me regret not redoubling my efforts to find the dickheads responsible for the burglaries. Though I'd never have guessed anyone could best the head of the Laurel Coven, least of all a group of petty thieves.

The coven's headquarters lay on the other side of the local shopping district. Exhaust fumes from the few cars on the road mingled with the scents of the local bakery, and the rumble of traffic drowned out the chattering commuters passing through to catch buses to work. Here, witch-run shops stood alongside convenience stores, grocers and banks, bathed in lights designed to keep the monsters that roamed at night at bay. That someone had violated this safe haven made me itch to bury my sword in the person responsible. Several times.

"Did anyone know Francine was at the warehouse this morning?" Vance asked Isabel.

"Me," Isabel said quietly. "I didn't know she planned to go alone. She said she wanted to check the wards, and… I just don't understand. Whatever weapon the attacker used was small enough to slip through her defences, yet powerful enough to kill her instantly. I've never seen anything like it."

"And we've seen a *lot* of weird shit." My mind, inevitably, went straight to the faeries, but I couldn't imagine any kind of fae hauling a manmade gun around. Not least because the iron would melt the skin from their fingers. "Yeah, we need to find this fucker."

The local witches met in a converted town hall in dire need of renovation. The red brick walls were scorched from backfiring spells, the door was chipped wood, and the inside smelled vaguely of damp from rain getting through cracks in the roof. Next door was Francine's house, which was more of an unofficial coven headquarters as well as a much more pleasant place for the local witches to spend the night than a draughty hall. She'd been a widower with no children and had often let new witches stay at her house when they first joined the coven, if they had nowhere else to go. Her death would leave a void in the coven in more ways than one.

The town hall was packed with brightly dressed people, an image that somewhat went against the conventional stereotype of witches, though according to Isabel, they'd originally adopted their colourful attire so that non-supernaturals would stop mistaking them for necromancers. 'Witch' wasn't an exclusively female term either; Isabel had told me that the male witches had kicked up a fuss about the term 'warlock', while 'wizard' sounded too stagey, so everyone opted to use 'witch' regardless of gender.

Unlike the mages, who'd once prided themselves on their all-magical bloodlines a few centuries ago, witches had spread out amongst the general population and some had even hid their abilities from their own families. As a result, it was entirely possible for someone in an otherwise non-magical family to be born with witch magic and the coven was cobbled together from a mixture of social classes and backgrounds. Isabel's coven alone had more than two hundred registered members. Not all of them regularly showed up to meetings, but there must be at least fifty people gathered in the hall, most of whom I'd never met. I wouldn't have a hope of figuring out if any of these people had a reason to bump off their leader, but the witches were egalitarian for the most part and their highest-ranked member was the one tasked with ensuring the coven's protection, not simply someone who sat back and watched everyone else do the work like a certain head necromancer I could mention.

Must have been personal, then, whispered a cynical voice in the back of my mind. *Or a shot at the witches as a collective.*

Shana led us to a long table lay covered in a sheet that didn't quite mask the body that lay beneath. A pale thirty-something woman with a shock of bright-blue hair stood in front, talking to a shorter, younger Asian woman with a pretty enough face to make me suspect she had faerie ancestry somewhere.

"We already used a tracking spell to replay the incident," said the blue-haired woman, who I belatedly recognised as Chloe, Shana's wife. "We didn't see who was responsible."

"But you said they *shot* her," said the Asian woman. "Shouldn't have her protective wards kicked in?"

"They should have." The blue-haired woman's mouth turned down at the corners. "We're certain she was killed by a bullet, though it's difficult to tell with the body in this state. We need a professional healer to look at her to see how—"

"Hey, it's Isabel." The Asian woman let out a small gasp. "And—the Mage Lord."

"He has my permission to be here," Isabel said quickly. "So does Ivy. They both have experience investigating crimes of this nature."

Vance inclined his head. "I can also send mages to assist you if you find yourself in need of security."

I winced inwardly. Vance didn't mean to sound condescending, but his attempts to express concern often came out sounding like orders.

"We have our own security wards," said the blue-haired woman, narrowing her eyes at him.

"Someone broke through them to steal from the warehouse," I reminded her. "I was there with Isabel yesterday. Might the same thieves have killed Francine?"

"Whoever they are, they fucked with the wrong coven." The witch gave Vance a distrustful look, then at a prompting nod from her wife, she whipped the sheet off the table.

I gagged, both at the coppery smell of blood and at the horrifying state of Francine's face. Her wrinkled skin had turned the greyish colour of old stone; blood trickled from the corners of her mouth and ran in rivulets through the cracks spiderwebbing across her skin. I closed my eyes, trying to regain some composure.

"What the hell did that?" Not a spell. A potion, perhaps, but most traditional witches were pacifists and potions were generally used for health or cosmetic purposes.

"Poison," Isabel said quietly. "It entered her body when she was shot, I assume."

"Are you quite sure she was shot?" Vance held up a thin black object I recognised as the dispeller that he must have bought custom-made from the coven. "If the effect was caused by a spell, this ought to react."

"We've already used one," Chloe snapped. "Don't touch her, Mage Lord."

Vance's posture stiffened, but the lack of response from the dispeller spoke for itself. No spell had caused Francine's death. At Isabel's prompting, Shana and Chloe carefully turned Francine's body onto her side and indicated a dent in the back of her neck.

"There," said Shana softly. "See what I mean? Looks like a bullet hole."

Isabel shuddered a little. "Yes. I assume the poison entered her body that way, but I haven't had time to use detection spells to narrow down what, exactly, was used on her."

"That was the plan." The blue-haired witch gestured to a low table stacked with various bottles and boxes. "You brought more trackers from the warehouse?"

"Everything I could find." Isabel reached into her shoulder bag. "Ah, we might need another table. Ivy?"

"Sure." I beckoned to Vance, as there wasn't a great deal either of us could do except carry the equipment and try not to get underfoot. Our abilities had little effect on an unseen foe with no physical presence and moreover, no traces of faerie magic were on the body. That made Francine's murder pretty much none of my business at all, but I refused point-blank to turn my back when my best friend had a potential target on her head. Usually, the witches were the stark opposite of the mages, who were prone to back-stabbing and trying to wrangle positions on the council by deposing their predecessors, but the murderer was no witch, and their next target might well be the coven leader's successor. And while Isabel herself had yet to publicly acknowledge her title, she'd undeniably been been Francine's second-in-command, and the rest of the coven would expect her to take on the leadership position next.

Given the horrific turn of events, I didn't blame Isabel for not giving voice to her upcoming promotion. Shit, I wouldn't have either, in her position. Even with Francine's body lying in front of us, it was hard to process that the coven leader was really gone.

While Isabel muttered incantations and drew chalk symbols, I watched the interplay of coloured lights within the detection spell and wished Chloe would stop giving Vance the evil eye. I didn't blame the blue-haired witch for being a little snippy after her leader had been brutally murdered and the Mage Lord had come striding into the coven's hall giving orders, but Vance's extensive contacts coupled with his unforgiving approach to any strikes against the supernatural community was exactly the combination they needed to enact brutal revenge on the killer.

"She wasn't drugged." Isabel lifted her head from the detection spell. "It's no normal poison either. The effects weren't gradual but immediate."

"That's what it looked like." Chloe released a breath. "I don't know if the bullet is still inside her, but her body's in too delicate a state to remove it without causing damage."

"I can still identify the ingredients," Isabel said tremulously. "They make a concentrated poison designed to cause instant death, but I've never seen it administered by bullet before. Let alone against a coven leader.

The room chilled. Vance's fists had clenched at his sides, and his magic had lowered the temperature at least ten degrees. I glanced at him. His expression was impassive, but his reaction alone proved he'd had an idea. "Vance?" I whispered.

His gaze slid to Francine's body. "Are you sure it isn't possible to remove the bullet? I can try."

"Absolutely not," Chloe said sharply.

"It might have—disintegrated on impact." Isabel choked on the words. "Like a witch spell."

Was the killer another witch after all? I didn't quite dare to mention my theory in front of the coven; all around us, the witches had gathered in whispering huddles, and I caught a few hostile stares in the direction of the Mage Lord and me.

"We need to confer with all the senior coven members," Chloe said. "Ask everyone with expertise in magical poisons. Otherwise, I think the two of you have done enough here."

I blinked at her abrupt tone, catching Isabel's eye. "All right. Let me know if you need me."

"Of course," she said. "Ivy, you can come back at any time. Chloe, don't look at me like that. She's a registered coven member, technically."

That was true, but while I might have 'witch' on my official licence, that was for the lack of another word that adequately described my weird brand of magic.

"And bodyguard," I added, lifting my sword. "I won't step on any toes, though. I just want to help you find the scum who did this."

"We're more than happy to help out." Vance accepted the dismissal without argument. "Like I said, the mages are a phone call away."

"And me," I added, lifting a hand in farewell.

Isabel accompanied us to the door. Whispers trailed us, but Vance's gaze was fixed ahead, his brow furrowed as though he was thinking hard.

When we were outside, I asked, "Vance, you haven't seen a poison like that before, have you?"

He shook his head slowly. "We should wait until the results come back before jumping to conclusions."

"She was *shot*. That's worth jumping to conclusions for." I studied him. "Got any theories? Because I'm in the dark here, to be honest."

"Someone wished to eliminate the leader of the witches," said Vance. "They employed poison delivered in a way that would break through the coven leader's defences."

"Which is impossible," Isabel added. "That's what I don't get. The coven leader has protective wards built into her *skin*. A bullet should have bounced clean off her."

"She does?" I looked at her own chalk-stained arms. "When does that kick in?"

Her gaze turned downward. "I—I need to look it up."

"Sorry," I said quickly. "Forget I said anything. We need to figure out the link with those thieves, though. Was that writing they left at the scene some kind of warning?"

"Writing?" Vance asked.

"I found a message at the scene of the robbery," I explained. "It wasn't written in a language I could read, but it was also glamoured, so I don't know that it was aimed at the witches."

Vance swore softly and lifted his phone. "The necromancers want my attention again."

"Speaking of necromancers." There was one obvious way to get Francine's account of her own death. "Might the coven want to call back Francine's spirit?"

"Shit, I don't know." Isabel glanced at the hall, biting her lip. "It won't work this soon after her death, I don't think."

"When her ghost shows up, the necromancers will be the first to know." Another possibility slammed into me. "Shit, might it have been a ritual killing?"

The death of a coven leader would certainly have created a stir in the spirit realm if she'd been sacrificed similarly to Lord Evander.

Isabel blanched but shook her head. "No, the warehouse isn't on a spirit line. We didn't find any necromantic equipment at the scene either."

Calder didn't need any. Though if the location of Francine's death didn't overlap with a spirit line, harnessing the energy stirred up by her death would have been a tall order. Unless the killers had cleaned up the equipment along with scrubbing all traces of blood from the scene.

"I know what you're going to say, Ivy." Isabel sighed. "There's no way I can go behind the coven's back at this point. We'll have to come to an agreement to speak to Francine's ghost."

"At least it's an option." The shifters wouldn't even entertain the possibility, and the same went for the half-faeries. "Though I'm not sure how the necromancers would react if you all showed up at the guild."

"We can't tell them how she died," she said. "Not until we have a new leader anyway. And we can't have the whole supernatural community finding out someone bested the most powerful witch in the city. No way."

"Don't forget the necromancers don't even *have* a living leader," I reminded her. "When will you pick yours?"

Being Second, I assumed Isabel herself would be the obvious contender, but she'd never expected her mentor to meet her end in such a gruesome and abrupt manner.

"It'll have to be tonight." She spoke quietly. "There's no other way to ensure the title passes on smoothly and without Francine's death being discovered before we're ready for the news to go public."

"The mages won't intervene," Vance reassured her. "We stepped in at the necromancers' guild because of the lack of a suitable candidate, but the witches have a long history of stability, at least within this coven. Unless there are likely to be problems?"

"The leadership contest isn't the issue." Isabel's voice grew stronger, though emotions warred within her eyes. "Our coven is small, compared to the mages at least. The real problem is how she died, and whether her killer will come after..."

"Her successor." A shiver travelled down my spine. "Is it out of the question to hold off on picking someone new until you catch the person responsible?"

"Definitely not an option." Her mouth turned down at the corners. "It's complicated, but tradition dictates the transfer has to take place as close as possible to the former leader's demise. Otherwise the protections might not kick in."

Shit. Yeah, we don't want that. "Then we need to identify

what she was shot with, where it came from, and who needs to be introduced to my sword."

"Yeah." She nodded. "I'll have to run some more tests, as best I can without access to the bullet. Chloe shouldn't have blown up at you for suggesting using your abilities to remove it, Vance."

"It's fine," he said. "You might have been correct in that the bullet dissolved on impact. Testing her blood would likely have the same results."

She nibbled on her lower lip. "True, but it'd be easier if we had access to the actual weapon. I'm convinced there was something in there designed to have a particularly deadly effect on anyone with magic."

Again, a chill dampened the warm air, and Vance's shoulders stiffened. "Are you certain?"

"No, but short of testing the poison on a regular human without magic, we don't have a lot of options to know for sure."

"Anyone know a willing volunteer? Maybe I'll give Larsen a call." My attempt to defuse the tension deflated like a balloon. "Actually, it wouldn't hurt to snoop around the mercenary guild. They hear things we don't, and most of them are regular old humans too."

One of few disadvantages to no longer working for the mercenaries was that I'd become oblivious to any new developments around my old haunts. Vance had contacts almost everywhere, but the mercs were more inclined to get their hands dirty and go to areas of the city no person without a death wish would dare walk into. I didn't think any of them had committed the murder—mercs were often loners, but some were friendly with the local covens and worked together on cases like Isabel and I had—but I could pretty much guarantee any dodgy new weapon in the city had crossed paths with a merc at least once.

Vance scowled at his phone. "Colby requires my assistance again. He seems to be under the impression that *I'm* his boss."

"You did buy the guild a bunch of shiny new equipment," I reminded him. "He probably hero-worships you now."

"He doesn't know about Francine's murder, does he?" asked Isabel, looking alarmed.

"No," said Vance. "That information remains confidential."

"Good," said Isabel. "I know we can't keep it under wraps forever, but I'd rather get through this leadership change first before we think of spreading word beyond the coven."

"Yeah, and then we won't have two groups of supernaturals without a leader." Though the necromancers had been leaderless for going on six months now. "Lord Evander and Frank will probably see Francine on the other side of the veil right away, since the Guardian are first in line to greet the newly dead. Someone might need to warn them not to blab."

"Right, of course." Her expression turned downcast. "I guess it's probably inevitable that people who can see ghosts will figure it out."

"I can give them an incentive to keep their mouths shut. It's no big deal." I made at least one round-trip over the veil per week to check in with Frank, regardless, and it wouldn't hurt to ensure that this latest development wasn't part of another dickhead's world-destroying scheme to unleash the horrors of the veil upon the mortal world.

Vance took my arm. "We'll go to see the necromancers now. Isabel, let me know if the coven needs anything."

"Keep safe," I said to Isabel. "Best to carry a few more tripwire spells in the meantime."

"Oh, I plan to." A sharp edge entered her voice. "They won't get *me* next."

But they already broke through the defences of the strongest witch in the region. I pushed the thought aside. The killer might set their sights on Isabel next, but she had yet to hold the title of leader, and we had hours yet until the ceremony. Time enough to get some answers from the other side of the grave.

If the living held no answers, perhaps the dead would oblige.

4

The necromancers' headquarters wasn't anyone's favourite place to spend their time, including the necromancers themselves. The gloomy building bordered the final resting place of the people who'd lost their lives in the invasion and was run by individuals who dressed like a cross between cosplayers and adults who'd never outgrown their teenage emo phase.

The cemetery gate opened with a click, courtesy of Vance using his abilities to manipulate the lock. Lord Evander had granted me permission to use the necromancers' mausoleum, back when he was still alive, but he made no secret of his annoyance at my habit of walking into the guild without knocking.

Tough shit. Time was of the essence, and while no ghosts were overtly present, I made a point of not lingering near the gravestones for too long on my way to the small wooden building. The mausoleum resembled a garden shed and contained nothing more than twelve white-flamed candles that formed a perfect circle of light against the bare floorboards when lit.

I didn't particularly enjoy being shut in a dark shed, but it was that or risk being eavesdropped on by the living as well as the dead, so I closed the door before addressing the column of grey smoke rising from the blazing circle. "Hey, Frank."

The smoke took on a vaguely human form. Frank always had a slightly blurred look, a common malady of spirits who'd stuck around long after their time on Earth had expired, though necromancer Guardians had an uncommon level of longevity compared to most spirits.

"Ivy." He surveyed me with his usual expression of mild disapproval. "I'd hoped your recent absence meant you'd broken your habit of disturbing my living counterparts. I notice you didn't knock on the front door before you walked in here."

"Sorry to disappoint you." I took in a breath. "I'm gonna have to ask you to promise not to tell anyone else—and that includes the dead as well as the living—but the leader of the Laurel Coven was murdered this morning. If you haven't already seen her ghost, you will soon."

Frank's blurry form distorted even further. "Francine? She was one of the most accomplished witches I've ever known."

"Yeah, tell me about it, but it's true. She's dead."

"And does Francine's Second know you're here?"

"She's my best friend, so yes. Have you seen any disturbances with the veil?"

"No. It's been quiet. I should have guessed you'd make up for lost time, Ivy."

"Hey, this has nothing to do with me," I protested. "Not this time, anyway. Listen, the coven's going to vote on whether to contact Francine's ghost when she does show up, but the way she was killed is just plain weird. I don't suppose you've ever seen bullets that cause someone's body to like… fall apart?"

"Bullets?" he asked blankly. "No. You forget I haven't walked on the earth for over thirty years, Ivy, and I was a necromancer in life, not a witch. In any case, I will endeavour to assist if you need me to find Francine's spirit before she passes through the gates."

"That'd be great," I said. "Not sure if she saw her killer, but we need to track them down."

Before they kill again.

"The death of a coven leader is a bad sign," Frank muttered. "I rather hope that the cause lies among the living rather than the alternative."

"Me too." Isabel and I had dealt with enough trouble from Death, and from the dark side of Faerie to which the afterlife was inexorably linked. I was fairly sure a magical bullet wasn't the Sidhe's style, but I wouldn't rule anything out at this point.

With Frank's departure, I left the mausoleum and found Vance waiting outside the cemetery gates. "Is Colby okay?"

"Yes," he said irritably. "The foolish apprentice accidentally tripped into his own summoning circle and got stuck. Three other novices got trapped trying to rescue him."

I snorted. "They *really* need a new leader."

"Yes, they do," Vance said. "But I gather the witches will get there first. Is Isabel most likely to take Francine's title?"

"Yeah, and she has a pretty good chance," I said. "She's younger than most of the other contenders and has also only been Second for a couple of years, but she's proven herself a hundred times over."

"And did Lord Sydney have anything to say?"

"Not about the killer, but he said he'll let me know if he runs into Francine's ghost," I said. "Otherwise, there's not much we can do until we speak to her and get her account of her death."

"Even if she didn't see her killer, she might be able to identify them by process of elimination," said Vance. "I don't see the witches as having a lot of possible enemies."

"Because they don't walk around pissing people off like you and I do." That someone had targeted the most mild-mannered of all the local supernatural groups made it unlikely that they were trying to start a cross-supernatural war. What, then, was their motive?

Vance inclined his head. "That was my thinking. I'll ask my people to keep an eye on the coven's hall from a distance, and I'll also check in with my contacts to see whether anyone's seen any unusual bullets on the market lately. This seemed like a coordinated attack, and there must be a trail of evidence somewhere. Even magic can't hide everything."

"Good plan. I'll go see the mercs and ask if they've seen anything, too. Drop me off at home first so I can grab more weapons?"

"Of course."

In a blink, we landed inside the flat's living room. The usual chalked circles covered the faded carpet and ceiling, and Isabel's array of colour-coordinated spells made it look like she'd raided a stationery shop. I picked up a few daggers but left the spells behind, as Isabel needed the protection more than I did. Worry for her gnawed at me, though I told myself that checking in on the mercs was a more productive use of my time than playing bodyguard outside a hall packed out with fifty-odd witches. Our killer ought to have more sense than to attack the whole coven at once.

I went to my room to change and redo my hair. Even when I didn't go into the necromancers' headquarters directly, I always seemed to come back from the place smelling of grave dirt. After sheathing my daggers and picking up my sword again, I rejoined Vance in the living room. "Want to come?"

"I think the mercenaries will be less inclined to talk to you if I'm there," Vance said. "I need to check in with Drake and the others at the manor, anyway."

"I'll come and see you after I'm done with the mercs," I said. "Oh, and I'll drop in on the Chief of the half-faeries and see if he can read that glamoured writing I found at the murder site last night. I wish I'd done that sooner."

"You couldn't have known this would happen." Vance's reassuring tone lifted some of the pressure from my shoulders. "I can't remember the last time anyone's made an attack on the witches."

"Nor me." The robberies had been their opening act, but none of us could have guessed the situation would escalate this rapidly. "See you in a couple of hours?"

"Of course." He gave me a quick kiss and disappeared, while I made for the door.

The day was unseasonably hot—unseasonable for the middle of England, anyway—and the sudden rise in temperature made me wonder if the local Summer faeries had got fed up with the rain and had decided to extend their magic to cover the whole city. The summer solstice would be soon, marking the time of year when the Seelie faeries' magic was at its peak, and they usually celebrated with an all-out party. The longest day of the year was important for the witches, too, though for different reasons. Isabel had a busy first week as coven leader ahead of her.

At midday, the most popular mercenary hangout was the shopping centre nearest to Larsen's place. I picked up a cheap sandwich from the food court and walked casually through the crowd, blending in with my fellow mercs in my leather jacket and boots with Helena strapped to my waist. Admittedly, I looked less ragged than my mercenary days, since I could apply a repair spell whenever I wrecked my clothes and they'd come out good as new. Given that Quentin the manor's housekeeper also had a habit of dousing my clothes in cleansing spells when I wasn't paying attention, I'd long since given up complaining about the sheer number of spells the mages burned through on a daily basis. At least Isabel and the coven got paid for the expense.

Guilt twinged at me when I spied a group of homeless mercenaries in threadbare clothes hovering near the food court, casting hopeful looks at passersby. Of course, I could never tell if they were genuinely in need of assistance or scammers trying to wrangle money out of people who didn't have much to spare in the first place. The guild let pretty much anyone sign up, and a large proportion of people who joined were slightly lacking in the morals department. Or, like me, had discovered that stabbing monsters was their only viable skill.

My gaze snagged on a brutish-looking man with twin swords strapped to his back. Spotting me, Gregor stalked in my direction, elbowing a fellow mercenary in the spine as he did so. Last time I'd seen him, I'd threatened to blow his testicles off with a tripwire spell, so I assumed he wasn't coming to offer me a free coupon for the local weapon shop.

"Nice to see you," I said through a mouthful of sandwich. "Does Larsen still have you cleaning up hellhound entrails or have you progressed to fishing corpses out of the canal?"

"Lane," he growled. "I didn't think you came here anymore, now you're the Mage Lord's—"

"Tripwire spells, Gregor," I said, pointing to my sleeve with my free hand. "Please go ahead and finish that sentence."

He wisely closed his mouth.

I tossed my sandwich wrapper into the nearest bin and

rested a hand on my sword hilt. "While we're here, have you seen any weird creepy guys in black lately?"

He grunted. "Thought you were with the mages, not the necromancers."

"I didn't mean the necromancers. They don't wear masks. That ring any bells?"

"No," he said. "Why, are you looking for a side job? I thought you got paid millions for doing nothing all day."

"That's what you think the mages do?" I snorted. "Tell Larsen to remind his mercenaries to check for trolls before running around a bridge waving their swords."

Larsen, naturally, had been indirectly responsible for the debacle that had resulted in my old phone taking a swim. And the mercenaries, too, come to that.

I turned my back and went looking for more familiar faces, but unfortunately, trying to get a straight answer from a merc without threatening them was like squeezing water from a rock. I didn't see Larsen either. Knowing him, he was probably at the casino spending every spare penny he could find on the slot machines. In addition to him being a persistent annoyance in my life, his failure to offer hazard pay and avoidance of any responsibility were the reason the local mercs were in such a sorry state compared to the efficient organisation of the mages.

Then again, the Chief of the local half-faeries, my next stop of the day, was hardly a shining example of leadership either.

Someone had turned up the heating while I'd been indoors. As soon as I left the shopping centre, the sun torched the skin on the back of my neck and turned my leather jacket into a furnace. By the time I arrived at the gates to half-blood territory, I was drenched in so much sweat that I felt like I'd taken a bath in the canal. Wiping my forehead, I approached the armoured guards at the gate.

"Hi, Bob," I said to each sour-faced half-Sidhe. "You might want to ask the Chief turn the heating down."

Outside the territory might be unseasonably warm, but entering the half-bloods' part of the city was like walking into a jungle. Thick plants towered over my head, bright flowers bloomed from every corner, and a series of chirps, growls and other unidentifiable sounds filled the background. The the air was thick with perfumed scents that made my eyes water. I'd long since discarded my jacket, but even draped over my arm, it was like carrying a warm, heavy furred animal. No wonder the half-faeries had ditched their clothing. Most were running around naked, swimming in the rivers or lounging beneath wide-leafed trees.

At least the Chief's meeting spot was in a shaded clearing, but a number of would-be visitors already queued up in front of his throne. Two ogres waved their clubs at me until I shuffled in line between a group of bat-eared teenage boys who seemed to have superglued their feet to human skateboards. I suppressed a snort as they shuffled along and waited for the Chief to save them from their predicament. The half-faeries' leader had at least bothered to wear clothes, unlike most of his subjects, and his ceremonial staff gleamed brighter than I'd ever seen. Though the staff might not be the genuine article, the Summer half-Sidhe was at the height of his power at this time of year.

When I reached the front of the line, his jaw tightened in irritation. "Ivy Lane. Is there something you need?"

"Chief. I'm here to ask you to decipher something for me," I said. "I believe it's written in the faerie language."

I held out the notebook to show him the text I'd copied. The Chief squinted, presumably unable to read my scribbled handwriting, and then he shook his head. "This isn't the faerie script."

My arms fell to my sides. "Isn't it?"

"I can read both our modern and ancient languages, and this isn't either."

"By ancient, do you mean these?" I unsheathed my sword, revealing the glyphs carved up the hilt.

The Chief nearly fell off the stump he called a throne, panic flickering across his face, but caught his balance at the last second. With a muttered curse, he pushed the notebook back into my hands. "Look for yourself. It's not the same."

I peered closer at the page, then at my sword. "I see your point."

The glyphs on Helena's hilt were smooth curling lines, carved with expert precision. The text I'd copied from the wall was harsh and jagged, hardly what I'd call elegant.

"Then it's a human language?" I pushed the blade back into its sheath and closed the notepad.

"Obviously."

"There's no need to be rude, Chief." I tucked the small notebook back into my pocket. "The writing was glamoured, so I assumed it was written in the faerie language. Or the ancient language Invocations are written in. I can't always read those."

A muscle ticked in his face at the reminder of my insight into a branch of magic that was supposed to be reserved for the Sidhe alone. "Nobody would have been foolish enough to leave an Invocation lying around where anyone might stumble across it. Nobody except you, perhaps."

"Hey. I've never done that." I'd *stopped* someone else stealing the Invocations from the storeroom a few months ago, as well he knew. "Why can *you* read Invocations if you've never been to Faerie, anyway?"

Probably an unwise question to ask, but it'd been a while since we'd had the chance to talk, and the Chief's mood today was positively mellow, at least by his usual standards.

"Because," he growled, "for the Sidhe, the ability to read the ancient language is in our very blood. It's not a learned skill."

I raised a brow. "And me? I'm a hundred percent human."

"Evidently, that magic of yours allows you the same ability." He all but shot the words at me. "To the Sidhe, magic and blood are one and the same."

Ah. That made sense, and certainly fit with the way I experienced my magic as though it was both part of myself and a separate entity. It said volumes for how fucked-up my life was that I'd readily accepted that a foreign substance ran through my blood and altered my perception of the world, but we humans were nothing if not good at adapting. The first time I'd spoken an Invocation, my spirit had nearly been severed from my body and sent into Death. Claiming a talisman of my own had lessened the side effects, but I seemed to be able to access the language only while in circumstances that required its use. Which was fine by me, because suddenly being able to speak a language I'd never learned was a tad disorientating to say the least.

"Is that it?" he asked, no longer hiding his impatience. "I have other visitors to see to."

"Guess so." I turned away. "Thank you for your assistance."

Honestly. He didn't have to be such a prick. It was hardly my fault that I'd concluded the text I'd found at the warehouse must be in a faerie language. Who else would use glamour to hide their secret message? What game were they playing at?

When I escaped the jungle-like maze of half-blood territory, I called Vance.

"The writing's a no-go," I told him. "The Chief says it's not a faerie language."

"Let me have a look at it," he said. "I take it you and the Chief didn't come to blows?"

"We were positively civil. Pity he wasn't any help."

"Did he elaborate? Is the text a language he doesn't read, or is it not related to the faeries at all?"

"Could be either. He thinks it's a human language. It doesn't match the writing on my sword anyway, and that's ancient."

"It might have been a made-up code instead," he suggested. "You know, the sort that only a handful of people know, designed to communicate a message."

"Why would they leave it on the door to the witches' storeroom, though?" I checked for oncoming traffic—or wandering piskies—before crossing the road. "It doesn't seem the kind of place for a romantic tryst. Or a dodgy business deal, either."

There was still a chance the writing had nothing to do with the murder, but the coincidental timing of its appearance nagged at me like one of the mosquito-like insects that had hounded me in half-blood territory. I shook one of them off my clothing, wincing at the itchy rash spreading up my exposed wrist.

"I'll look at the text myself," Vance said. "I can check it against our resources at the manor. Though I should warn you, Lady Harper is still here and she's incredibly displeased about Francine's murder, to say the least. She knows the witches well."

"Can she help us find the killer?"

"Not if the other witches don't want the mages involved."

"They might make an exception for someone who knows them." Then I remembered who he was referring to. "I wouldn't blame them for not wanting *her* involved, mind."

"Don't talk about me as though I'm not here!" growled Lady Harper's voice from somewhere behind Vance.

"I'll be there in five," I told Vance, though I didn't relish the idea of another run-in with Lady Harper. She wasn't a witch herself, but Isabel had mentioned she'd had close ties to the coven for years. Maybe because her son had married one. Wanda's mother, who'd died in the invasion.

Vance met me outside the manor. Neat hedges encircled the large house and its extensive gardens, and the glyphs painted onto the walls shimmered even brighter in the glaring sunlight. Through an open window came the sound of a piano playing, and an instinctive shiver rose to my arms.

Vance gave me an apologetic look. "I'm afraid the only way I could think of to distract Lady Harper from the murder was to let her have full run of the house."

"She's an eighty-five-year-old mage, not a dog." Though I really did hate that noise. After my narrow escape from Faerie, piano music invariably brought my worst memories rushing to the surface. I pushed down images of Avalin's fondness for cursing humans to dance until they died and followed Vance down the wide, carpeted corridor into his office. There, I pulled the notebook from my pocket and passed it to him.

Vance studied the page, resting his other hand on the cherrywood desk. I closed the door, willing to suffer the stifling temperature if it shut out that bloody noise. The piano's melody crept in regardless, and I gritted my teeth. Vance sometimes played the piano—generally when I wasn't around—but he at least gave me warning. Lady Harper, though, was either unaware of its effect on me or had pulled the fear from my head when she'd broken into my mind and decided she didn't care enough to stop.

"I did ask her not to do that," Vance said, as though *he'd* read my mind. His attention was on the notebook, and a breeze rose up, a welcome balm to my sunburned neck.

"Do you recognise the text?" I asked. "I copied the words

the best I could, but since I couldn't read it, I don't know if there were any mistakes in there."

He lowered the notebook. "Are you certain the writing was glamoured?"

"Isabel couldn't see anything. Why?"

"I might be jumping to conclusions," Vance said, "but the last people who used a text similar to this definitely weren't faeries. Not to mention they're dead."

I blinked. "Who?"

"It's just a theory," he said. "I'll run it past Lady Harper first."

Great. So much for avoiding an encounter with Vance's old mentor. I was curious as hell as to what had him so rattled, though.

Inside the conservatory, the music ceased, and the old mage glowered at me from the wickerwork chair behind the piano. "What?"

"This might be of interest to you." Vance handed her the notebook. "This text was found at the site of Francine's death, concealed by glamour."

She gave the page a cursory glance. "I can't read it."

"Does it not look familiar to you?" he pressed. "It resembles the League's code."

"The League died out a long time ago." She all but shoved the notebook back into his hand. "Have the witches chosen a new leader yet?"

"No, the coven meeting will be this evening. Sorry, who are the League?"

She scoffed. "If I were you, I'd be busy identifying any enemies known to have enough persistence and knowledge to bypass Francine's defences, not speculating on long-dead entities."

"Who, me?" Did she think *I* was in charge of finding the

killer? "The text appeared less than twelve hours before the murder took place, near the spot where Francine's body was found. Which also happens to be the same storeroom that was robbed yesterday for the third time in a week."

"And?" She fixed me with a dark stare. It was impressive how a frail old woman wearing several layers of shawls on the hottest day of the year could look so much like a Bond villain.

"And I don't know who the League is," I added. "So it'd be great if you could fill me in."

Vance shifted on his feet. "Francine was shot with a bullet designed specifically to kill supernaturals."

Lady Harper's brows lifted. "Why didn't you lead with that?"

I'd assumed he'd already told her. Or she'd swiped the information from someone's head, though she rarely used that side of her mage powers. I'd been particularly unlucky to find myself on the receiving end.

"The bullet killed her instantly and no others were found at the scene," he said to her. "I wasn't allowed to remove it and check if the design was the same."

"The same as what?" I had the distinct sense I'd missed some unspoken conversation between the two of them.

"Those bullets are laced with lethal poison," Lady Harper said. "Deadly to mages, torture to humans. Terribly unpleasant way to die."

My heart missed a beat. "You know them?"

"I know of them." She fixed her stare on Vance.

"They were thought to have disappeared after the invasion," he said, for my benefit. "Right now, our priority is confirming the details of Francine's death. I believe the witches intend to contact her spirit on the other side of the veil once they've chosen a new leader."

"Waste of time," growled the old mage.

"What makes you say that?" It wouldn't hurt for her to fix her attitude. I'd thought she and the witches were allies, if not friends. "Wouldn't her ghost be able to tell us about any enemies who might have been in a position to take her life?"

"A coven leader has no shortage of enemies." She gave me a dismissive stare. "As you should know, considering you live with Laurel Coven's Second."

"Care to elaborate?" I mimicked Vance's most condescending tone so exactly that the corner of his mouth twitched. "She was shot with a magic bullet. Pretty sure that rules out the faeries as the culprits and probably the shifters, too. And I don't see the mages or necromancers shooting anyone either. Nor the other witches."

Which left… well, normal, mundane humans. People who would have no chance against a trained witch, much less a coven leader.

"Your imagination is limited."

"Then what?" I challenged. "Go on, give me a clue here. As you just pointed out, my best friend is the coven's Second. I have a personal interest in introducing anyone who threatens her life to the sharp end of my sword."

"I can't help you." Lady Harper shifted her chair away from me and her fingers returned to the piano keys.

I knew a losing battle when I saw one. Breathing hard, I followed Vance out of the conservatory. Then I turned on my heel and fired the middle finger in Lady Harper's general direction.

"What the fuck?" I fumed, stalking into Vance's office. "If she knows something that might stop the killer from getting at Isabel next, I'll shove this notebook up her—"

"She doesn't." He shut the office door. "She also doesn't like admitting when she's in the wrong."

"Sure." I glowered at the closed door. "Now, will you tell me who the bloody hell the League is?"

"The Orion League," he said. "If the person responsible for this is connected to *them*, I'm afraid I'll have to involve the other mages. Ivy, those bullets—and that code—once belonged to a cult who tried to destroy the Mage Lords."

5

I stared open-mouthed at Vance. "Tried to destroy the *mages?*"

"I thought I recognised the bullets' effects on magic users," Vance said. "I might be wrong, but if not…"

"Then what?"

"Then everyone in the magical community may be in danger."

"Dramatic, much?" I hurried after him down the corridor. "Where are you going?"

"To find Drake. He can confirm my suspicions."

"What *are* those bullets?" I asked. "What did she say— deadly to mages, torture to humans?"

"The bullets were designed to instantly kill any supernatural," Vance said. "A human might survive a day after being shot. A supernatural would die immediately."

"Damn." I didn't know if I fit into the category of 'human' or 'supernatural', as a regular old human with a Sidhe's magic, but Isabel and Vance both shared the same vulnerability.

We found Drake outside the manor's front gate in the

position that had once been occupied by Ralph, the quarter-faerie guard, before Calder's minion had killed him a few months ago.

"Come to let me off guard duty?" The fire mage groaned and rubbed his ankle in an exaggerated manner. "Nobody else wanted to stand outside in this heat, but it's a bit much even for me."

"I have another job for you," said Vance. "The leader of the Laurel Coven was murdered this morning. She was shot with a bullet which had similar effects to the ones the League used."

Drake's mouth dropped open. "What? Someone killed Francine—"

"Keep it down," Vance cut in. "We're under orders not to let the news go public until the coven has a new leader in place, but Ivy also found a message at the murder scene written in the League's code and hidden by faerie glamour."

Drake's eyes flickered towards me. "Shit."

"It might not be them," he added. "Given the glamour. But those bullets aren't the sort typically found on the market."

"No kidding." Drake shuddered. "Bastards. I thought we killed them all."

"I'll ask another mage to take over your shift. Is Bailey around?"

"Yeah, the arsehole's been lounging around reading a book for the past hour."

"Who exactly are this Orion League?" I asked Drake as the three of us entered the manor again. "Vance said they were a cult."

"A fucking efficient one." Drake gave a shudder. "Seven mages were killed by their hunters during our first week as Mage Lords."

"By those bullets?"

"Amongst other things."

Vance disappeared—presumably to find Bailey—while Drake went into the informal meeting room where mages who didn't live at the manor spent most of their time. Mahogany bookshelves lined the walls, some filled with paperbacks and others with boxes of spells. The heavy wooden table was currently covered with a hand-drawn map of the city, onto which someone had drawn a cartoon dragon near the spot where the shifters' ancient god had awakened on the Ley Line.

"Like my embellishment?" Drake asked. "I was going to draw a piskie on top of half-blood territory, but they won't keep still long enough for me to use one as a model."

Vance reappeared and closed the door behind him. "That map was supposed to be displayed in the council meeting room."

"It's much more interesting like this." Drake pulled out a chair. "All right. What do you want to know?"

"Who are these would-be assassins?" I didn't sit down. I was too wired, my nerves buzzing from the revelation that someone had tried to exterminate the Mage Lords as recently as Vance's appointment as head mage.

"Very much dead," said Drake. "Vance killed their original leader."

"I did," said Vance. "The original League was once an organised collective that lived underground as supernaturals did. Their prime belief was that one day there would be a large war between humans and supernaturals in which they intended to ensure that humans would be the victors. They initially believed the invasion was that war, but needless to say, that didn't work out in their favour."

"I should bloody well hope not." Supernaturals had undeniably come out on top after the invasion, but it seemed absurd to imagine a collective of regular humans organising any kind of strike force against them. "What were they, like a private army?"

"Close," he said. "They called themselves the hunters, at least as individuals. They split after the invasion into local factions that we assumed were mostly stamped out, but their beliefs lingered in some circles. The particular cult we encountered held the position that the mages should be exterminated and control given back over to the people."

"They wanted to exterminate you?" Cults weren't unheard of, but nobody in their right mind would issue a challenge to the mages. "I get that some humans don't like supernaturals, but it's pretty obvious who has the upper hand." Any weapon humans could devise paled in comparison to the power of the average mage, and even untrained witches could run circles around regular people.

Except... someone killed their leader. Might these hunters have been involved?

"I know," said Drake. "It's a hell of a lot harder to kill off supernaturals when they're in charge, but some people live in their own little worlds."

"It seemed a more plausible goal when all supernaturals lived in hiding." Vance's mouth twisted. "And before the Sidhe exposed their power for the world to see. Regardless, the hunters made a decent attempt to bring the mages down in the aftermath of the invasion, due in no small part to those bullets. Six months after the peace agreements were drawn up, all such weapons were confiscated and destroyed. However, as we found a year or two ago, a small number survived."

With a bullet that could kill any supernatural, I understood why a group like that might have been around before the invasion, but after? No human invention, save for cold iron, could leave a scratch on a Sidhe or even a half-blood. No, those bullets were designed to kill *humans*.

A sour taste filled my mouth. "Did they ever work with the faeries?"

"Faeries?" said Drake. "Didn't you hear the part where I said the hunters hated all supernaturals?"

"The message at the murder scene was glamoured."

Drake shook his head. "Why would a faerie use bullets when they have magic?"

"Who can say?" said Vance. "Those bullets were manufactured abroad, I believe, before the invasion, but they shouldn't be around any longer. I was a little too thorough in taking care of the problem. After I killed their leader, the survivors shot one another rather than surrender themselves to the angels. None were left alive."

"Whoa." I'd known Vance had been the target of assassination attempts early in his career as one of the Mage Lords, but not that the situation had been that dire.

"I wouldn't call it the highlight of my career."

"Understatement of the bloody century," said Drake. "We managed to keep it quiet, just to stop other people getting the same idea."

"But apparently someone has."

The question was, when had this started? And why had they chosen to target the witches first?

"Yes," said Vance. "Drake, I'll call a council meeting to inform the others. In the meantime, I want you to organise more patrols near the witches' storeroom. That's where Francine was killed."

"And it was also robbed three times in the last week," I added. "Isabel said the thieves didn't take anything valuable, but I don't believe in coincidences."

"No," Vance said softly. "This can't be a movement on the scale of the League—not as it existed before the invasion, anyway—but all the supernaturals need to be on guard. The witches may have been singled out as the first target, but it wouldn't surprise me if the hunters went after a different supernatural community next."

"Or their leaders." My gaze slid to Vance.

"They're welcome to try." Drake conjured a flame to his hand. "We'll take them down like the last fuckers who tried."

"What's the endgame?" I asked. "I mean, do they plan to take power themselves, or what?"

"Maybe," Vance said. "I'm more inclined to believe these are anarchists who want to destabilise the magical community."

"Except they used faerie glamour to hide their message," I reminded him. "That means either one is half-blood or they have other fae working on their side."

"Perhaps," said Vance. "If we decipher the text's meaning, we might be able to work out their plan."

My phone vibrated. I pulled it from my pocket, my heart racing. "Isabel? Did something else happen?"

"No." She exhaled. "I thought you should know I got in. I'm the new coven leader."

"What—already?" I asked, disarmed. "I thought you weren't doing that until tonight."

"The official ceremony is tonight, but I'm in."

"Oh." I didn't want to say *congratulations*, not when the price had been so high. "You should know Vance and I came up with a theory. Have you ever heard of the Orion League?"

"No." She sounded bewildered. "Should I have?"

"Probably not." I gave her a brief summary of what we'd found out, including the mages' history with the same group.

"No, I haven't heard of them before." Isabel sucked in a breath. "You think they might go after the other supernaturals' leaders next? I have fifteen witches offering to guard our house tonight, so if Vance wanted to send some of his people in, he can deploy them to guard the other supernaturals instead."

"Oh, no, I'm not taking any chances." The shifters didn't even *have* a leader, not a formal one, and the necromancers were a lost cause. As for the half-bloods, the Chief would turn away any protection the mages offered. "We don't know if our theory is right. I mean, if this is an offshoot of a group who hated supernaturals, it makes no sense for them to use glamour to disguise their secret messages. But if Vance thinks it's the same people, it probably is. He's usually not wrong." Much to my annoyance sometimes.

"We can talk theories later, when the ceremony is over," she said. "The others have decided to honour Francine's wishes and cremate her right away. I know there haven't been any undead incidents lately, but it's a precaution. The actual funeral will be tomorrow."

"Do you want me to come?"

"It's witches only," she said apologetically. "Same with the ceremony this evening. We have to reorganise our ranks now that Francine is gone. And... well, some of the witches are saying you attract trouble."

"Oh." I squashed my instinctive hurt feelings. I understood why the other witches would be wary of me, given my reputation, but whoever had committed the murder had switched off those powerful wards like snuffing out a candle. All my instincts told me to take my sword and plant myself between Isabel and whoever wanted to hurt her, but it wasn't fair to hover around like an overprotective parent either. Not when she wanted to prove herself worthy of following in Francine's footsteps. "I get it. Tell me if you need me and I'll be right there."

"Of course. I'll let you know when I'm home, okay?"

"Yeah. Bye."

I hung up. Tears stung my eyes, not so much from hurt at the witches' rejection, but because Isabel didn't deserve to get dragged into this level of turmoil. I was the one who went around poking monsters and paying the consequences when they poked back.

"What is it?" Vance rested a hand gently on my back.

"Isabel's officially the new leader. The ceremony will be tonight, but we aren't invited. Nor to Francine's cremation this afternoon."

"I expected so."

"I just…" I swallowed. "Someone tried to kill the last leader. What if they go after her next?"

"Relax," said Drake, walking back into the room. "Nobody'll screw with us again. Or the witches. I just asked Bailey to put together teams to patrol the whole area near the witches' headquarters. Didn't tell him why, don't worry, but I did mention we might have another issue like when we first took leadership."

"Good." Vance nodded. "Bailey will remember those bullets. He'll know what to look for."

Why the witches, though?

To distract myself from my growing list of questions, I pulled out the notebook and offered it to Vance. "You said you might be able to figure out the meaning of this text?"

"I might," he said. "The League never had official documents and each branch used a slightly different version of the code. I'll have to look through our old notes."

"All right." Sweat gathered on the back of my neck. "Call me paranoid, but every time something like this happens, I think it's him. Fionn."

"No." Vance's steady gaze grounded me. "I wouldn't dismiss the possibility, but the Sidhe's arrival all but destroyed the original League. If these new hunters bear the slightest resemblance to their previous incarnation, they'd never ally themselves with the faeries."

Unlike me, Vance didn't bear an open grudge against the Sidhe, but they'd killed almost his whole family, and I strongly suspected Fionn had been directly involved if not the perpetrator. When I'd told Vance my suspicions, he'd replied that he'd come to the same conclusion.

"Fionn is an enemy to our realm, but I wouldn't be foolish enough to seek him out on my own," he'd said. "If he comes here, however, I will show him no mercy."

Neither would I. That Fionn had since disappeared for six months and counting meant that he was long overdue to strike again, especially given that he'd made me an open offer to join the Wild Hunt and was less than thrilled that I'd turned him down. Then again, time passed differently in the Grey Vale, as I'd learned myself when three years of imprisonment had turned into a decade in the human world. Maybe I'd luck out and he'd never return in my own lifetime… though it wouldn't look good for the rest of humanity if he did.

I dragged my thoughts back to the present. The odds of an immortal with a god complex targeting a local coven were next to zero, and as Lady Harper had condescendingly pointed out, the witches already had plenty of enemies. "Assuming it is them, do either of you know why the League chose to target the witches first?"

"If I might hazard a guess, it's because working out a witch's weakness is marginally easier," said Vance. "All witches use the same spells and the same protections, for the most part. Each mage has a different ability, so it would take more effort to figure out how to approach them without being taken off guard. I can displace the bullets, for instance."

"Good point. Faeries are unpredictable, too." Though someone had helped the burglars use glamour to hide their messages, and the idea of supernatural-hating zealots allying with even the most minor of faeries pointed to a match made in hell.

"The enemy is in the minority," said Vance. "What little

power the hunters have is immaterial. The majority of us want peace, and we're willing to use all the abilities we have to defend the people of the city. The mages haven't forgotten the last time we faced the League. We'll defeat them again."

I let myself believe him, at least for now. "All right. Because if they want the top spot on my list of enemies, they'll have to get in line."

6

———————

A beeping noise woke me from sleep. I jumped and fumbled around in the dark for my phone. I'd gone to bed fully clothed despite the heat, for precisely this reason.

I pressed the phone to my ear. "Isabel?"

"Ivy!" Isabel whispered. "There's someone in the house."

Shit. "Don't move."

I flung the covers aside and shoved my feet into the shoes that I'd left beside the bed. Scooping up my blade with one hand, I moved to Vance's side.

His hand closed around my wrist, and we reappeared inside the darkened living room of the flat. He'd tugged on jogging trousers and a loose shirt, and his own sword appeared in his hand as we landed. My feet caught on a spell circle—one of Isabel's—and I stiffened at the flutter of movement, but it was just Erwin. He hovered inside a cage on the windowsill, tiny fists beating at the sides. Isabel probably put him there to stop him making too much noise and alerting the trespassers.

As I tip-toed across the room, Isabel's wide-eyed face

peered around her bedroom door. "They're upstairs. They got past our security spells, but I don't know what they're doing up there. Unless they're looking for something in the office."

"Give Vance a trapping spell," I whispered. "He can displace it directly on top of our unwanted guests. Did you see them?"

She nodded. "I saw someone through the spyhole. Masked. He had a gun."

My heart lurched. "We'll glitter-bomb him to death and see how stealth works out for him then."

She gave me a faint smile and handed a spell over to Vance. I picked out a shadow spell for myself, assuming the trespassers didn't have the Sight and that they wouldn't be able to see my magic. Though if they'd shut down the wards... *how did they do that?* Our security was matched only by the mages', and they used witch wards, too.

Vance activated a trapping spell and it vanished from his hands. Two more followed, and a distinct thud came from overhead.

I hope he got them. When he disappeared, I turned on the shadow spell and ran out into the corridor. More noise came from upstairs and I climbed to the upper floor as swiftly as I dared. Vance crouched at the top, near the closed door to the office. Judging by the muffled thuds and grunts from inside, the trapping spells had found their mark. *Gotcha.*

The trespassers had left the door slightly ajar. I nudged it inward and peered in. Darkness shrouded the room, but faintly glowing red lights encircled three human-shaped figures.

A loud crack sounded, followed by the unmistakable thud of something small but very fast hitting the door at speed. I recoiled, releasing the handle. *What the fuck?*

Louder thumps sounded. I went for my blade and Vance

rested a hand on my arm, pulling me away from the door. Through the gap, I glimpsed three figures running in the opposite direction. "What—they're running away?"

Too late, I remembered the fire escape at the back of the office. I drew Helena in a wave of glittering blue light and ran into the room in time to see the last black-clad hunter disappear through the door.

"They're heading for the roof!" I called over my shoulder to Vance.

Not a trace remained of the trapping spells. Their residue clung to my bare feet as I crossed the room, and my blood chilled when I caught sight of the bullet embedded in the back of the door. It'd missed my hand by inches.

At a gesture from Vance, a gust of wind swept in and the bullet disappeared outright, presumably back to the manor. I flung open the fire escape door and ran upstairs after the retreating figure. Magic sprang to my palm, but the hunter vanished onto the roof before my attack made contact. I swore and ran in pursuit.

The stairs trembled beneath my feet as a tremor ran through the entire house, so sudden and intense that for a moment I wondered if a troll had landed on the roof. I staggered to the side, holding onto the rail for balance, and let go when a thick stem burst through the step below me, blocking the entire stairway. As I stared in bafflement, the plant continued to grow at an unnatural speed, its sharp stem piercing the ceiling. *Fucking faeries.*

"What—?" A quick-growing faerie plant inside the house was as incongruous as a bunch of humans escaping Isabel's trapping spells, but no mere plant was a match for my sword.

Blue light ignited along my blade as I thrust it forward, straight through the thick stem. *The wards are down.* The house was unprotected, and any faerie this side of the veil had free run of the property.

Laughter sounded, followed by the slither of tentacles. An Unseelie fae crept into view, mouth agape to expose pointed teeth. Tentacles lashed at me, and I dodged, leaping to a higher stair. Magic pulsed from my blade, piercing the shadows with puncture-like wounds that spilled shadows like blood. The beast crumpled, its tentacles receding as it died. *Dammit.* If every fae in the region skipped past the house's wards, the odds were low that I'd corner those intruders before they made a quick getaway.

I started to run upstairs, more laughter pursuing me.

"Tasty human," growled a voice from somewhere above. "I will feast on you."

Oh, for crying out loud. I lifted my blade, blue light shining on a creature that clung to the wall with limpet-like tenacity. Its limbs, I knew from painful experience, were covered in octopus-like suction cups designed to latch onto their prey, while their heads were ninety percent mouth. They usually survived exile by sucking the skin from humans and then devouring their innards, and they smelled like rancid meat to boot. Needless to say, this brand of fae did not get many party invitations.

I formed my magic into a shield as I continued to climb. A sudden rush of weakness made me sway on the spot, and I steadied myself against the wall. Ah, shit. I'd forgotten the little bastards had an energy-draining ability on top of all their other charming traits.

"I can taste your magic, human," the creature crooned. "Come closer."

"Taste this, then." I turned my shield into a wave of magic. Blue light surged towards the ceiling, but the beast let go, hitting the stairs with a horrible sucking noise like a plunger being pulled out of a blocked drain. Greying skin scattered everywhere, and its proximity sent a wave of weakness over me. My knees buckled, my talisman sudden unbearably heavy.

Screw this. I lifted my sword, fighting the draining effect. I focused on the rage of my home being violated by the faeries, of the threat to Isabel's life. Fury burned in my blood, and my magic responded.

Blue light rippled out, and the monster burst apart into shadows and dead skin.

"Good riddance." I took off at a run for the open fire escape. As I'd expected, the roof was markedly free of any human presence, as though the hunters had simply vanished into thin air. "You've gotta be kidding me."

My gaze dropped to the wards circling the garden. Or rather, the haze of darkness in place of the usually vibrant glyphs painted onto the garden walls. Snarls and growls issued from the flowerbeds, something with tentacles poked its head of out the recycling bin, and the entire front of the house was covered in some kind of creeping plant.

Isabel ran outside, brandishing a dagger in one hand and an explosive spell in the other. A fae with a long, scorpion-like tail ran in pursuit, and the tentacled beast in the recycling spell rose upright, too. My heart plunged. I couldn't do much to help from the roof, and if Vance was fighting more monstrosities back in the house, he might be tied up, too. Hopefully not in a literal sense.

Nothing for it. I called my magic, forming a shimmering shield that I hoped would break my fall. Then I jumped.

Magic caught me like a parachute, slowing my body as I plummeted towards the ground. The snaking vines covering the house attempted to grab me on the way down, but they slid off my shield, and I continued to fall in graceful slow-motion.

A crack shattered the night, and something whizzed past

my shoulder. The bullet—it could only be a bullet—hit the plant instead of me, and the effect was instantaneous. The vine's colouring turned to murky grey, and its tentacles withered like someone had upended a canister of weedkiller over them.

Another shot bounced off the brick above my head. *Shit, what if my magic can't deflect those things?*

As a third bullet came at me, I let go of my shield, bracing myself for a rough landing. My shoulder took the impact as I slammed down on the lawn, landing on my arm with an ominous *crack*. Ow. Blinking tears from my eyes, I rolled sideways and straight into the tentacled monster bearing down on Isabel.

"Get *out!*" She flung an explosive spell that blasted the creature off me and sent it flying halfway across the garden. "Ivy!"

"The iron wards," I slurred. "Turn... back on."

"You need a healing spell." She dodged the jabbing tail of the scorpion-like fae and threw a second explosive. As the monster flew into the fence, she ran to the house and crouched down beneath the window.

Grey-green light shone as the iron ward activated, its effect spreading up the walls. Both fae fled in a slither of tentacles, while Vance materialised on the lawn. "The attackers have gone. Ivy—did you jump off the roof?"

"Bastards tried to shoot me on the way down." I groaned. "I don't suppose you have a healing spell?"

———

"Broken arm and concussion," said Vance. "What did I say about not taking risks?"

"How was I supposed to know they were still lurking

outside?" Every word I spoke drove a hammer into my skull. Healing spells had mixed results on head injuries. "What were they even looking for upstairs?"

"No clue." Isabel leaned over me, anxious. Vance had convinced her to come to the manor, not just for safety's sake, but because the damage the faeries had inflicted on the flat had been too severe to fix with a simple charm. The trespassers hadn't just disabled the wards on the front gate, they'd killed the defences around the whole flat, and I hadn't the faintest idea how they'd single-handedly neutralised every one of Isabel's tripwire spells without batting an eyelid. "Ivy, why didn't you use the stairs?"

"Because you were being attacked by two monsters." I rubbed the back of my head. "And I didn't know our delightful intruders would try to knock me out of the air."

Vance had searched the street—extensively—but the hunters had made themselves scarce after their failed attempt to knock me out of the sky. Luck alone had spared me from being hit by one of those bullets; for all I knew, even my magical shield wouldn't have been able to deflect a projectile that had cut straight through a coven leader's protective spells like paper.

One thing was clear. Seeing those bullets up close had disputed any doubts I might have had that they'd been responsible for Francine's death. That fae plant had shrivelled up on the spot like a slug doused in salt.

"The good news is that they left evidence behind this time." A clatter sounded as Vance dropped a handful of bullets on the table. His shirt was torn in places, stained with the blood of whatever faerie creature had attacked him while I'd been doing battle with the skin-sucking leech upstairs, but he'd mercifully escaped unscathed.

"Are you sure it's a good idea to bring those in here?" I

lifted my head. A mistake. Pretty lights danced before my eyes. I groaned and put my head down again.

"The bullets won't harm anyone if we're careful," he said. "We need to know what we're up against."

"Agreed." Isabel slumped in the armchair next to me. "Shit. The landlord's going to murder us."

"I'll fix the damage," Vance said. "I'll make sure there aren't any more hunters lurking around, too."

"You already checked." I rubbed my forehead. "Four times, last I counted."

"I know." Vance leaned down and kissed me on the forehead before disappearing.

I half sat up, groaning when pain bit through my skull. "Damn breakable human body."

"Ivy, did you forget you aren't in Faerie?" Isabel attempted a light tone that didn't quite land. "There are limits to your healing powers, you know."

"Think I've learned that lesson by now." I propped my head against a cushion and looked her in the eyes. "Our house isn't safe anymore."

"Don't forget this place has the same wards as our house does."

"Yes, but there aren't dead fae all over the manor," I pointed out. "You can stay here until we've fixed the place up. Vance won't mind. There are a dozen spare rooms and the only current guest is Lady Harper."

"He already used that argument." She sighed. "But there's the chance the killers might be after *all* the witches, not just me."

"It wasn't you they wanted." I thought back to the intruders' bizarre behaviour. "They went into the office, didn't they?"

"They might have thought we lived upstairs." Isabel

released another sigh. "I'll stay here tonight, but I have to meet the coven first thing tomorrow morning. They need to know about the attack, too."

"Yeah, including how they switched off all our wards." The hunters had wriggled out of Isabel's trapping spell, too. "How'd they do that? Is there some kind of… I don't know, a counter-spell that works against both wards and trapping spells? Like Vance's dispeller, but more powerful? It can't have just been the bullets. You didn't hear any gunshots when you woke up, did you?"

"No." Isabel frowned. "Good point. I don't know how they did it, but we need to find out."

Vance reappeared. So did a shrieking winged figure who immediately broke into shrieks of "Bad faerie!"

Oh, crap. "Sorry I forgot about you, Erwin."

"You didn't see how the intruders took out the wards, did you?" Isabel asked him.

Erwin flew shrieking into the TV screen. "Bad faeries everywhere. All bad!"

"Yeah, they are."

Vance's baffled expression made me laugh, which I regretted when my head throbbed. "I'd keep him away from the antique china."

Needless say, it was not a restful night. I lay on the sofa while Isabel insisted on sleeping in an armchair rather than a guest room. Not that either of us slept a wink. Vance didn't even try. He kept vanishing from the room each time Erwin attempted fly upstairs, and eventually, he trapped the piskie in a small cage he'd found somewhere in the manor. What kind of pet it had originally contained, even Vance didn't know.

"If you're wondering how we put up with him living in our flat, I've no idea." My throbbing headache had subsided, though sleeplessness did not help my general mood. "Have I told you the story of how Isabel and I met him?"

"No." Vance left the cage on a shelf and crossed the room to my side. "Are you okay?"

"Sure." I rubbed my tired eyes. "Aside from the sleep deprivation, but that's pretty usual when you live with a piskie. He was part of a colony living in the attic when we moved in."

"And he stuck around after that incident with the goblins." Isabel gave me a smile, which I returned. Recalling our first case together was a welcome diversion from the current shit show, but the dawn light spilling through the window told me that it wouldn't be long before she had to meet with the coven.

Seeing, Isabel checked the clock on the wall. "It's nearly five thirty in the morning. I'm meeting the coven at seven."

"And the necromancers?" Vance asked. "Did you discuss contacting Francine's ghost?"

"Oh—shit, you're right." Isabel swore to herself. "Sorry, I forgot to mention that last night, Ivy. The coven agreed— grudgingly—that we need to visit the necromancers."

"They're okay with calling up Francine's ghost?"

"No, but they'll be even less thrilled we got attacked in the night." She stifled a yawn behind her hand. "It'll probably be easier if we visit them before the meeting, since I don't know how long it'll go on, but I'm not sure if they're early risers."

"They'll have to deal with it." I winced at another shriek from the piskie. "I'd suggest using a soundproofing spell, but I don't know that you'll be able to keep him in one room long enough for that to be effective."

"I'll take him elsewhere." Vance picked up the cage and left the room.

Isabel slumped in an armchair. "I still can't believe they took out *all* my wards. I spent weeks making some of those."

"I know." My hands fisted. "I'd be more than happy to play bodyguard in case they try the same at the coven meeting."

"No way," she objected. "You nearly got *shot*."

"Yeah, but the bullet might not have killed me. I don't know that I'm the same as a regular supernatural." Pity there wasn't a way to do a test run that didn't potentially involve a permanent trip over the veil. "Also, I'd happily take a bullet for you."

"Ivy." She shook her head at me. "You can come along when we speak to Francine's ghost, since I'm pretty sure we need your expertise. But no more."

"All right." I'd revisit the subject later. *Nobody else is going to hurt Isabel. Not on my watch.*

I walked to the kitchen in search of sustenance and found a tired-looking Vance buttering toast.

"What did you do with Erwin?" I asked.

"Left him in the spare room with strict instructions to Quentin to keep an eye on him and make sure nobody else goes in there."

"You know Drake will do it anyway, right?"

"Yes," he said irritably, refilling the coffee maker. "I'd prefer it if he didn't disturb Lady Harper."

"Ah, shit. Yeah, we don't want that."

Isabel walked in as we were laying plates on the small table. "Where's…?"

"Erwin? In a spare room."

"How do you tolerate him being in your flat?" Vance conjured a third chair to join the two that we usually sat in to eat.

"He keeps out spiders, if nothing else." Isabel nibbled half-heartedly at a piece of toast before running off to answer a call from Shana.

I wished I could take some of the hassle off her hands. Vance and I were used to dealing with wrangling unreliable supernaturals into order, but I didn't even know where to begin with witch politics.

The necromancers, though? I hoped Frank had kept his word and prevented Francine's spirit from moving on. I had a stack of questions to ask her, starting with whether *she* had any experience with this notorious Orion League.

7

Six of the witches came with us to the necromancers' headquarters, including Shana and Chloe. They both seemed to have mellowed towards Vance and me after hearing about Isabel's narrow escape last night.

"It's lucky you were both awake," Shana said to Isabel as we gathered on the doorstep. "Do you need help with the damage? Chloe can help you out. She pretty much built our house from the ground up."

The blue-haired witch almost smiled. "Sure, I can fix whatever you need doing. Sounds like the faeries really trashed the place."

"We're good." I nodded to Vance. "Thanks for the offer, though."

"Right, the Mage Lord can probably pay for it." The brief friendliness vanished from Chloe's demeanour. "Are you sure this, ah, *summoning* is going to work? I don't want to disturb Francine's rest."

"If she's still around, she isn't at peace yet anyway," Isabel said. "And... and I hoped she might have advice."

A pang hit me. Isabel hadn't expected to take Francine's place for at least another decade or two, and while she was more than equal to the challenge, I'd caught a few whispers at the coven headquarters the previous day that suggested some of the senior members were sceptical that she had the capacity to handle the job. Luckily, none of those people were present today. Shana was Isabel's chosen Second and the others had been Francine's close friends, too. They wouldn't take any shit from anyone, including the necromancers.

The guild member who answered the door was a six-foot-tall guy with shaggy blond hair and glasses who looked entirely too perky for someone who spent his free time re-burying the dead. "Hey, Isabel. And this must be Ivy."

"That's me." I gave her a quizzical look, wondering how he knew her name. "You're…"

"This is Rick." Isabel introduced the other coven members while I puzzled over how she'd had time to befriend a necromancer. He knew Vance, too, but that was to be expected, given Colby's recent habit of calling the mages over the slightest issue. "Did you ask the other necromancers if we can use the main room?"

"Yes, but I didn't say why," Rick said. "I also told them to leave you alone during the summoning."

Isabel's face relaxed. "Thank you. We're still searching for the killer, so we're keeping the details of her death under wraps."

In the corridor, I hung back to whisper to Isabel, "I didn't know the necromancers were friendly with the coven."

"They aren't," she said. "I mean, I delivered some spells, and Rick and I have talked, but the others are… well."

I raised a brow. She wasn't usually so tongue-tied. "Talked?"

Isabel flushed, to my surprise, but we entered the main room before I could ask her what I'd missed.

A large summoning circle dominated the floor, its twelve candles already lit. Colby stood nearby, holding the copy of the necromancer handbook that I'd returned to him after borrowing it for research purposes. The blond necromancer offered Isabel a final smile before disappearing through a side door. Rick, huh. I felt a weird sense of protectiveness towards Isabel, though I knew she was more than capable of handling herself. This was a vulnerable time for her, after all, and if some guy came in and took advantage, he'd find himself on the receiving end of my sword as soon as I was done with the killer.

The witches clustered around the circle. Their bright attire formed a stark contrast with the gloomy walls, but somehow the candles made even their vibrant clothes and spells look grey and washed-out. Between them, me, Vance and the necromancers, the room was more crowded than I'd ever seen it.

"You'll have to speak the name of the spirit you want to contact," Colby told the witches. "I can do the rest."

"Francine Blackwood." Isabel's voice trembled a little, but she held her head high and faced the circle.

Colby repeated her words and read several incantations from the handbook. Twelve candle lights surged up and smoke coalesced between. A kindly-faced woman in her early sixties flickered into view, eliciting a gasp from the coven members.

"Isabel," said the witch. "Oh, Isabel."

"Oh—Francine." Isabel choked on a sob. "I'm—I'm sorry. I didn't know what else to do."

"It's okay, dear. I expected you'd want to talk to me."

Isabel wiped her eyes furiously with her sleeve.

Seeing that she wasn't in a fit state to speak, I stepped in.

"Sorry. I'm Ivy. Isabel probably told you about me. I know you won't have long, so we need you to tell us the last thing you remember."

Some ghosts didn't know they were dead, though I didn't think that was the case for Francine. A coven leader was bound to have the strength of will necessary to hold onto her personality beyond death.

"No." Her voice was soft. "I wish I remembered, but to tell you the truth, all I recall is reaching the warehouse. Then… nothing."

"You didn't see anyone at all?" Shana asked, and the former coven leader shook her head.

"You don't have anyone you suspect, either?" Isabel asked. "Any who'd have a reason to target the coven?"

"No," said Francine. "There are certainly some individuals and groups who would want to cause the witches harm, but none who presented an immediate danger."

"Whoever they are, they attacked Isabel last night, too," I said. "They disabled the wards on our house. *All* of them. The whole house went out like a light."

"I don't know how they did it, but they broke out of my trapping spell, too," Isabel added. "Do you know how that might have been possible?"

Francine's brow furrowed. "Were they witches?"

"No. Human, I think."

The other witches were all watching me, perhaps irritated at me for monopolising their time with their deceased leader, but someone had to ask the questions before Francine's time ran out. Already her ghostly form was flickering around the edges, fighting the pull of the veil.

"What about bullets?" I asked. "Have you ever heard of magical bullets that cause harm specifically to supernaturals?"

"Bullets?" she echoed. "No… not that I recall."

My shoulders slumped. "You don't?"

"I'm sorry." Her voice sounded fainter than before, gaining a static quality like a phone signal fading out. "I'm sorry to put this burden on you, Isabel."

"Wait." Isabel took a step forward.

Francine smiled and vanished, her ghostly form dissipating into the fog. Everyone except for me jumped when Lord Evander appeared in her place. Including Colby, who gave such a violent double-take that he nearly kicked over one of the candles.

Lord Evander shooed him away with an impatient hand. "Her time was up," he told the assembled witches. "She went through the gate."

"Couldn't you have stopped her?" *Or Frank?* The old necromancer must be around, but he was unlikely to show his face in front of the coven.

"No." His tone was devoid of any level of sympathy.

"She shouldn't be dead at all," Isabel whispered.

"I'm sorry, Isabel." I glared at Lord Evander. "You might have tried a little. I assume you know how she died."

Typically, the one supernatural leader who most deserved a visit from the Orion League was the one who was already deceased.

Lord Evander vanished without a word. My hands curled into fists and I swivelled to face the grief-stricken witches. "Sorry. That dude has even less empathy as a ghost than he did as a living person."

"What a wanker," Chloe muttered under her breath.

Colby shot her an alarmed look, probably worried his boss would hear her. I didn't much care if he did. We'd lost our chance to ask Francine any more questions and I hadn't even got to mention the glamoured message I'd found at the warehouse. Granted, she'd displayed no recognition at my mention of those bullets, which suggested she hadn't been aware of the Orion League's existence either.

Outside the guild, the other witches departed as a group, conversing in low voices. Isabel made to follow, and I fell into step with her, lowering my voice.

"So," I said. "You and *Rick*. How long has *that* been going on?"

She didn't meet my eyes. "How long has what been going on?"

"You're not going to pretend to be dense, are you?"

Isabel gave a soft snort. "When I was on at you about Vance, you didn't need to pretend."

"Touché." I sneaked a look at Vance, who was contemplating the cemetery gate as if to make it clear he wasn't listening to our conversation. "All right, have it your way. Are you going back to the coven headquarters now?"

"The meeting's in less than an hour." Her expression turned downcast again. "Then the funeral's at noon. After… I guess we'll work on finding Francine's killer. I really hoped her ghost would be able to give us more direction."

"Lord Evander didn't help by being an utter prick. Though from what she said, it sounds like she never met the Orion League."

"No." Vance rejoined us. "It's not overly surprising, given that the mages were the primary targets last time. How much do the other coven members know?"

"None of them have heard of the League," Isabel said quietly. "I did ask."

Then why would the League pick Francine as a target? Or had they been banking on the coven not having the benefit of experience to identify her killer?

"The one departure from the League's old methods is how they managed to shut down your wards," Vance said. "I don't recall the League ever doing that the last time. They certainly never got near the manor."

"And the message they left hidden by glamour. I'm guessing they didn't do that last time either." Which, again, suggested someone was using the League's name but none of the methods. But Vance was the expert, not me. "Need me to do anything, Isabel? We should probably put a sign over at the house, so clients know not to come into the office while it's full of bits of dead fae."

"I think the disintegrated faerie plant all over the walls would give them a clue," Isabel said dryly. "I did set up a voicemail message for clients, but I'll turn it off after the funeral."

"You don't have to go back to client work this soon," I reassured her. "We can take a few days off while you make the adjustment to being coven leader."

She made a noise of protest. "No, that wouldn't be fair on you."

"I'm fine. I have the mages, remember?" I had actual savings, for the first time in my adult life. "Anyway, finding our elusive supernatural killer is our current case, technically speaking."

"Are you coming back to the manor?" Vance asked me. "We might be able to translate that code you found at the warehouse. Bailey found his old notes from the last time."

"Oh, good." I was glad to have something useful to do. "I'll let you know if we find anything, Isabel."

"I'll call you after the funeral." As she ran to catch up to the other witches, Vance transported us back to the manor.

The sound of a piano playing at high volume wafted down the hallway from the conservatory. I groaned. "Didn't we scare her off last night when we brought a piskie crashing into the house?"

"No, she sleeps in a soundproof guest room," Vance said. "We might need her help, anyway."

"I doubt it." I was sorely tempted to set Erwin loose in the conservatory to shut that bloody piano up. "Where to now?"

"In here." He beckoned me into the small room where the mages kept their computers. It was the only room in the manor that looked like it belonged to this century. "Bailey should be on his way back from patrol soon. While we wait, I'm going to retrieve the documents on the last incident with the League."

"Didn't know you had a digital record." Most technology hadn't fared well after the invasion, between the magical surges affecting the power grid and the collapse in overseas manufacturing and shipping. It made sense that the mages had hoarded everything they could, and they seemed to have stashed it all in this room. Laptops and desktop computers were stacked on high shelves, ranging from old nineties models to newer, flashier ones that hadn't even been removed from their original packaging.

"Of course we do." Vance took a seat at one of the desks and turned on the desktop computer in front of him. "We learned the hard way that information is too easily lost."

True enough. I'd had easy access to a computer for the first thirteen years of my life, but after three years living in a medieval-style castle that didn't even have electricity, I'd never quite fit into the world I'd come back to. It'd taken weeks for me to even acquire a phone.

I pulled up a chair next to him. "Isabel's going to run herself ragged. She's trying to hold her coven together while finding a killer, and there's bugger all I can do to help her."

"You've done all you can," he said. "We'll figure out the code. I'm sure the text is a variation on the one the League used last time."

"And that information is in those files?" I gestured at the

computer. "What did they typically do, send each other coded messages?"

"That's right. They were often daubed in public places so that members would know where to meet."

Why glamour? That was the part I kept tripping over. Nobody aside from the fae had access to that kind of magic. Even *I* didn't, despite having the Sight.

Vance printed a few documents and stacked them on the desk. "These are a starting point. I'd also like to track where those bullets came from, but it's possible they were left in one of the League's old hideouts. We were never certain we found all of them."

"You did say you wiped them all out."

"Evidently they're harder to kill than I thought."

"Like cockroaches." I fidgeted in my seat, thinking of Francine's confusion in the face of my questions. "I guess they didn't go after the witches, at least not during Francine's time as leader."

"No, the mages were the primary targets," he said. "And before that, the shifters. I believe the bullets were originally designed to be used on them. Generally, witches and mages were adept at hiding their true nature before the invasion. Shifters were more likely to expose themselves to the public, but they're also considerably more resilient than regular people."

My hands curled into fists. "Bastards."

"Mage Lord." Bailey appeared in the doorway with his boyfriend, Rod, close behind him. "You asked for me? Sorry we're late. We had to take a detour after a troll caused a pile-up on the main road."

"Oh, fun." A reminder of what I was *not* missing out on by temporarily closing to clients for a couple of days.

"Yeah, the mess looked nearly as bad as the aftermath of Drake's driving," Rod said. "Ah, he's not in here, is he?"

"No, he's patrolling," Vance said. "Can you take these into my office?"

"Sure." Rod took the stack of documents from him, while Bailey joined Vance at the desk.

"Something you need?" he asked.

"Yes, we need your help with this code." Vance showed him the notebook I'd placed on the desk. "I understand that it's similar to the League's last one. Do you still have your notes?"

"I might." He took the notebook from Vance, his gaze roving over the symbols. "Yes… this is the same. It's a variation on the witches' glyphs."

"The witches?" The hunters had used *their* script? "Are you sure?"

"It's been altered, but the basis is the same." He peered closer at the page. "Let me see if I can figure this out. I might not need my notes."

"I didn't know anyone could actually read the witches' language," I murmured to Vance as we watched Bailey pace the room, staring at the page and muttering under his breath. "Isabel only knows the glyphs that are necessary to use in her spells."

"That's pretty common, I think," he replied. "It slipped my mind that the hunters used it as the basis for their code. It's not an obvious choice."

"Probably because, you know, it belongs to the same supernaturals they wanted to exterminate," I said. "Didn't they have enough of an imagination to create their own secret code?"

Apparently not. Within minutes, Bailey had scribbled several words alongside the symbols on the notebook page and handed it to Vance. "I hope one of you knows what that means, because I have no idea."

I peered over his shoulder, and read the words, *"Beware the solstice, faerie killer."*

"Why...?" My throat went dry. "That was written in the *witches'* glyphs?"

Why would the hunters have used their text to leave me a message? Of course it was aimed at me. The glamour alone proved that, if the term 'faerie killer' didn't, but I hadn't the faintest idea how they'd expected me to read the code without a translator. If not for Bailey, I'd be clueless.

"It's not an exact match, and most witches wouldn't be able to read it," said Bailey. "I only know the entire syllabary because I had to learn it backwards to pass my Masters degree."

"I didn't know they offered Masters degrees in witch magic." I hadn't even finished school. Being kidnapped by faeries had ended any brief ambitions I might have entertained for academic achievement. When the modern world fell, most universities had shut down, but I did recall that the mages had claimed a college as their own and turned it into an institute of magical research. It went without saying that I'd never set foot there myself.

He flushed. "Well... they don't, usually. I asked for an exemption."

"He's being overly modest." Rod entered the room behind us. "He's the one who *created* the course. They've made it a regular thing now. Also, Mage Lord, you should probably know Lady Harper is in your office."

I groaned inwardly. "What's she doing in there?"

"I'll talk to her," Vance said. "Thank you both. You can go."

I reread the scrawled text. Looked at Vance. "Faerie killer. There aren't a whole lot of those around."

"A number of people know you by that title."

"Yeah... the whole mercenary guild, the half-bloods, and most of the local faeries, too." Probably every supernatural in the city had some idea of me by now, even if I'd never met them in person. "And what did they mean by telling me to beware the solstice?"

"The solstice is a significant date for the witches," he said. "The faeries, too, but the message is too vague. We should start by narrowing down who might have left it."

"We still have too many options," I said. "Or none, because the only people who have an issue with me *and* who can use those bullets without risking harm to their own allies are the mercenaries, and they're too divided to form a vigilante group. Also, half of them are practically illiterate. I don't see them screwing around with complex codes based on witch glyphs. Oh, and they can't see through glamour."

"True," said Vance. "What of the necromancers? Who was Isabel's friend?"

"Rick?" I blinked. "I doubt she'd give anyone the time of day who might be a villain. You've seen how many wards we have on our flat. Besides, she's even pickier than I am when it comes to romantic prospects, and that's saying a lot."

He half-smiled at that. "I was just throwing out ideas. The necromancers are the sole group of supernaturals who, to my knowledge, were never targeted by the League."

"Maybe they didn't want to piss off people who could raise the dead." Most likely the necromancers had been better at blending in, at least before the invasion. "Or they'd run up against dead ends if they went after every single person who claimed to have seen a ghost. Pun intended."

"True," he said. "I did hear there were some disagreements in the guild over leadership, according to Colby. Nothing to imply any defectors, however—and none who have an obvious personal problem with you."

"As opposed to the faeries." I gave an eye-roll. "The glamour alone proves their involvement. And the *faerie killer* part proves that they're fucking with me specifically, but why? Are you positive the League never allied with the fae?"

"Not to my knowledge," said Vance, "but the League as we knew it is gone, and anybody might have taken their name."

"Fools," growled a voice, making me jump. Lady Harper had crept into the room behind us with surprising stealth.

I lifted my head. "Who, us or the League?"

"The fools who left that message, of course."

"In what way?" I put down the notebook. "If you've been eavesdropping, I'd appreciate it if you'd offer us some help rather than standing there growling cryptically at us. I damn near died this morning, and so did Vance." If nothing else, she'd practically raised Vance after his family had been killed in the invasion. While I hadn't seen a great deal of affection between the two of them—more respect on Vance's part, and tolerance on the old woman's part—she surely had a vested interest in his well-being.

Vance looked at her, too. "Lady Harper, if you know anything that might help us prevent the League from striking again, I'd invite you to share it with us."

She grunted. "I don't. However, any scheme that involves the League's old methods is bound to backfire upon the perpetrators."

"Leaving threatening messages hidden under faerie glamour doesn't sound like one of their methods." I caught Vance's eye, and he nodded.

"No, it isn't," he said. "The message says, *beware the solstice.* Do you have any idea what they might be referring to?"

"Many things, some likelier than others."

"That's no answer." I rubbed my forehead, utterly perplexed. "I mean, is there another faerie killer that I don't know of? Someone who'll know what the message means?"

Lady Harper scoffed. "I suspect whoever was responsible intended to use the message as a distraction. It'd work out in their favour for you to tie yourself in knots trying to work out their meaning while they picked out their next target."

"There is that." I turned back to Vance. "I'm honoured that they singled me out. I should call and tell Isabel the bad news. Or good news, depending on how you look at it. Seems I'm just as much a target as she is."

"Ivy, only you would be glad to find yourself in the crosshairs of anti-supernatural zealots."

I snorted. "Whether it's the League or not, I can guarantee I'm *not* like any supernatural they've ever met before."

8

I decided to wait to tell Isabel what we'd discovered until after the funeral. Vance and I went to meet her outside the town hall and ducked under shade from a sun that seemed to be doing its best to make up for being absent ninety percent of the year. Given the heat, the hunters would draw attention in their thick black clothes and masks, though they'd mostly operated in the early hours or the middle of the night so far.

"Hey." Isabel walked out of the hall, her eyes red and puffy. I hugged her, because she probably needed it. "It's warm out here. Have you been standing there all day?"

"Nah, just a few minutes."

"I got your message," she said. "You mentioned you figured out the code?"

"Apparently, it's an adapted version of the glyphs you use in spells." I showed her the notebook again. "Can you read it?"

Her forehead scrunched up. "No, but I can't read most of the glyphs either. You can make spells work without actually knowing all the meanings. What does it say?"

"Yeah, that's the issue." I took in a breath. "The message said *beware the solstice, faerie killer*."

"Faerie killer." Panic flitted across her face. "It was for you?"

"Yep. It's my lucky day." I pocketed the notebook again. "Since I don't know what's important about the solstice, they need to work on their threats. We're officially out of ideas."

Isabel produced a handkerchief from her pocket and blew her nose, her eyes watery. "So are we. Francine didn't remember anything, and everyone we've contacted about those bullets has never seen them before."

"The bullets are likely holdovers from the League's previous efforts," Vance said. "Manufactured before the invasion. Finding out if they're being sold on the market might have merit. If they're circulating among regular humans, it'll cause more problems later down the line."

"I hope not." We didn't need the mercenaries screwing around with those bullets. "We need to find out where the enemy is hiding. And if they're working with the faeries."

Those fire imps didn't count. Or did they? For all I knew, they were the ones who'd put a glamour on that text, and the fae weren't otherwise involved. Except for the obvious: the message had been aimed at me.

"Yeah." Isabel heaved a sigh. "We also need to clean up the mess they made of our house."

"Shit, I forgot." I hoped no clients had shown up and found the place vandalised by faeries. Or the landlord, come to that.

"Easily taken care of," said Vance. "I've already cleaned up most of the obvious damage. There's just the matter of removing the debris."

"Meaning the bits of dead fae all over the stairs." I pulled a face. "Actually, I should probably check nothing else has moved in. I know the iron barrier's back up, but we don't need anyone else to get ideas. Want to head there now?"

With Vance's help, I convinced Isabel to stay at the manor. Nobody needed to be saddled with cleaning up dead fae after speaking to the ghost of their dead mentor and then attending her funeral, and I was less than convinced the renewed wards had dissuaded any local rogue fae from moving in. Fortunately, all Vance and I found in the garden were the shrivelled remnants of the creeping vine that had crawled all over the house. I studied the withered husk, wondering if it would be worth trying a tracking spell. Probably not. The hunters might have fled in any direction after they'd climbed off the roof—how they'd done *that* was a mystery as well—and tried to shoot me out of the air.

"I guess they might've used the faerie plant as leverage to climb down." I tilted my head back, squinting at the roof. "Or else they had some kind of protective spell to cushion their fall. I can't think how else they did it."

"Before they shot the plant." Vance moved closer to the house, where the remnants of the vine formed a shrivelled heap. "The bullet caused that effect. Looks like iron."

"Along with whatever they use to kill other supernaturals." It seemed impossible that plain old humans had come up with such an invention. "Guess I should be glad the Sidhe wiped the League out when they screwed over the rest of us."

"No." He displaced the plant's shrivelled remains and moved to the front door next. "Even when we fix this place up, I think Isabel should stay at the manor for the time being. It's easier if you're both in the same place."

"That's what I thought," I said. "She'll understand why. Since so many of our cases come from the mages, it won't make all that much difference to clients either."

"Will she need to take on fewer clients now, being coven leader?"

"Huh?" I blinked. "No. The coven's pay is notoriously shit. It's effectively volunteer-run."

"I expected the position of coven leader to come with more benefits, though."

"It's not like being on the mage council," I said. "Most of the coven's budget goes on ordering in spell ingredients." Unfair if you asked me, but witches rarely inherited huge fortunes like the mages did, and many of the local covens had been built from the ground up, following the invasion.

Vance frowned. "Doesn't Isabel get paid whenever someone buys her spells?"

"The coven does," I replied, "but there are two hundred or more members, so the money doesn't stretch that far when you factor in the cost of ingredients. Digging up mandrake leaves isn't cheap."

"Perhaps you and I should discuss with the mage council the ways in which we can better compensate the local witch covens."

"Yeah, Lady Granville shot that idea down in my first meeting." I scowled. "I haven't tried it with the new council, though." Mostly because I hadn't *been* to any meetings in a while. Another perk of the recent lack of world-ending events: fewer tedious council meetings to attend.

"I'll put it on the list," he said. "Some of the coven members might perceive the offer as an attempt to make them indebted to the mages, so we'd have to frame it right."

"Good call." I had to admit I was pretty impressed with him for coming to that conclusion so rapidly. When we'd first met, it'd taken a long time for me to make him understand my reluctance to stop working for Larsen and join up with the mages instead, and I'd had to spell out why I wanted to maintain our freelance business on the side a dozen times before he got it. "Say you want to pay a higher rate for exclusive first access to new spells they make.

Isabel and I can bring spells to you as soon as they're ready, even."

"Then you'd have to spend even more time with me." He drew his arm around me, and I leaned against his warm shoulder, taking comfort from his closeness.

"Maybe I want to spend every day with you."

He nuzzled the back of my neck, his lips brushing the delicate skin. "Don't jump off any more roofs, Ivy."

"Believe me, it's not an experience I'm keen to repeat." I shivered, leaning into him. "Honestly, I want a holiday from all this crap."

"As a matter of fact, I do have a coastal house near the sea."

I drew back to look him in the eyes. "I was being figurative, but seriously?"

"Yes, of course."

"That as well as your house up in the countryside in Scotland, and the place you moved your uncle's family to?" Sometimes it still felt like Vance and I lived in separate worlds. The days where I'd barely scraped together rent payment were long behind me, but there was a distinct difference between living in a flat with holes in the ceiling and owning multiple houses.

"If you'd like to, we can spend some time there later this summer." His hands rested on my waist, thumbs circling my hips through the fabric of my jeans. "What do you say?"

"Sounds good." More than good. He'd improved my mood thoroughly. "Better make sure I have a house to return to first."

Within an hour, the flat was as good as new. Which is to say, as good as the landlord allowed, so the holes in the upstairs ceiling remained intact and so did the broken heating system. Not that we needed it at this time of year. I was dripping with sweat by the time we left the house and starving, too. On the upside, Isabel's potion cabinet had survived the carnage, and I retrieved some of the essential custom-made concoctions to take back to the manor, including her potion for high-strength sun protection and the potent long-term contraceptive brew that I'd repeatedly told her could be a lucrative business all by itself.

Vance and I returned to the manor to the heavenly smell of baking drifting down the corridor.

"Your witch friend insisted on taking over the kitchen," said Lady Harper, with a disapproving sniff.

"That's what Isabel does in a crisis," I said. "Bakes cookies and makes tea. Excellent."

In the kitchen, plates had been stacked on every surface. I stole a cookie and took a bite of cinnamon-flavoured divineness. "I assume these are for the coven?"

"For tonight's meeting." She tipped cookies from a baking tray onto another plate. "There's not much else I can do except make spells, and I left all my ingredients back at the flat."

"Sorry, I should have brought some," I said through a mouthful of cookie. "I didn't know which you needed. Have you been baking the whole time we've been gone?"

Vance shot me an amused look. "What do you know. I told her to stay here, and she did. If it'd been you, you'd have climbed out the window and come back covered in blood by now."

"Don't get used to it," I said. "Besides, she's scheming. Not just baking. Right, Isabel?"

"You make me sound like a supervillain," she said. "I'm *thinking*, not scheming."

"About our elusive nighttime visitors?"

"Among other things." She arranged more plates on the table. "Actually, clients keep trying to call me. They automatically go to voicemail, but there have been at least five."

"Seriously?" I checked my own phone. "Should I be insulted that they haven't tried calling me?"

"Maybe they know you're the new coven leader," Vance suggested, stealing a cookie for himself.

"Might be a selling point," I agreed. "You really don't have to rush to go back to work, though, Isabel. I can get rid of these clients if they're persistent."

"No, there's no need," she said. "Like I said, I need the distraction. If the office is usable again, there's no reason we can't go back."

"Except the hunters," I pointed out. "And that we now know there are skin-sucking death faeries waiting to get through the wards."

"Lovely." Isabel gave me a look. "Honestly, after living with you for so many years, Ivy, I'm not surprised in the slightest."

"Ha." I picked up another cookie. "Vance said we can run our business from the manor instead, though. It's no big deal."

Before I could bite into the cookie, my phone began buzzing. "Oh, good. I was starting to feel left out."

"Another one?" Isabel asked. "This is the most calls we've had in weeks."

"You might know it." I reluctantly put the cookie down and moved into the corridor to answer. "Hello?"

"Malfunctioning spell," said a nasally male voice on the other end.

"I'm sorry, what?"

"Malfunctioning spell," the voice repeated. "That's what I'm calling about."

"Right." Obviously. "Let me get back to you. Our office is currently closed, but… listen, can you make it to the mages' headquarters at 15 Oak Drive?"

"You want me to hire a mage?"

"No, we're working from there until our office is open again. Our fees are the same."

I ended the call and ducked back into the kitchen. "Is it okay if we use your spare office, Vance? I mean, one of the spare offices."

"Of course. Pick whichever is easier."

"Cheers." I retreated from the kitchen and spied Lady Harper hovering at the corridor's end like a particularly malevolent ghost. "Is there a problem? Surely you don't want to be stuck in the house on a nice day like this."

"You're bringing clients here," she said. "Why not ask them to come to the mages in the first place?"

"Not everyone can afford their fees. My business is independent for a reason."

"And what, pray tell, is that?" Her cutting stare put me on the defensive. It was a little too close to our first meeting, in which she'd pinned me like a moth and broke into my memories.

"For one, if I gave it up to work entirely for the mages, Vance and I wouldn't be equals," I informed her. "For another, there aren't a whole lot of alternatives for people who can't afford the mages, aside from the mercs, and they're of no help whatsoever when it comes to the fae. Does that satisfy you?"

"It's important to you to be the Mage Lord's equal?"

"Yes."

She grunted. "Just don't let any of your clients disturb my nap."

"God forbid," I muttered under my breath.

As she vanished into the conservatory Wanda slipped out of a nearby door and gave me an apologetic look. "She'll be gone soon."

"Not soon enough. Is the spare office open?"

"Yes, it is. Fourth door on the right," she added, rightly remembering that I always got all the doors confused.

Time to go back to work.

————

"This spell is defective," said the short old man, resting his grubby fingernails on the desk. His greying, straggly hair looked as though it hadn't been washed for weeks, and his smell of sour sweat was all the worse in the heat.

"The spell isn't defective," Isabel said patiently from beside me. "It should work for anyone with a hint of magical talent. I haven't seen you around our coven meetings. Do you belong to one of the others?"

"Other what?"

"Covens. Which?"

"None," he gritted out. "Are you going to make my spell work or not?"

"I can't use it for you," said Isabel. "That's not how it works."

"What a waste of my time." He turned and stormed out of the office, muttering obscenities under his breath.

"He wasn't a witch," Isabel said in an undertone. "I can usually tell."

I bit back a laugh. "This is the first time a client's asked us to *use* a spell for them. Maybe we should charge for the service."

Isabel didn't smile. I'd protested that she didn't have to help me deal with clients, but she'd rightly pointed out that she knew more about malfunctioning spells than I did, and Vance was busy filling in the council members on the recent developments. I'd figured that since the mages were the ones with the history with the Orion League's hunters, they could discuss the subject without me needing to be present.

Mostly, I hadn't wanted to leave Isabel alone. If she wanted a distraction, I'd oblige, and I'd be more than happy to shake some sense into any client who insulted her.

"How can you tell if people are part witch?" I asked Isabel. "I mean, there's no physical signs, like with faeries or shifters."

"Intuition and a lot of practise," she answered. "One of my first memories is sitting on a park bench with my mum while she pointed out witches among the passersby. I was… four or five, maybe. Obviously, back then, we had to hide what we were."

"That's so bizarre to think about now." Isabel rarely talked about her life before the invasion, and I didn't like to pry, given that I'd spent so long hiding my own history. Pre-invasion, I hadn't known the supernatural world existed, but I'd had three years in Faerie to prepare me for the magical chaos that awaited me upon my return. "That you had to hide. Did you know *I* wasn't a witch? When we first met?"

I'd told her I was, needing a cover story that explained some of the inexplicable effects of my faerie magic, but it hadn't taken long to expose the non-conventional nature of my powers. Luckily, Isabel had respected my desire for privacy.

"You didn't register to me as a regular human," she replied. "I wondered why the coven didn't take you in after the invasion, but I assumed you didn't find out you were a witch until later in life."

That fit, kind of. I'd had to find a rational way to explain the time I'd spent in Faerie, where three years had turned into ten and had left me scrambling to come up with a decent cover story. Some witches—and necromancers— went through life without any awareness of their talents, but it was much less common in the post-invasion world. It was hard to stick your head in the sand with undead wandering out on the streets and covens meeting in the local town hall.

"I felt bad for lying to you," I said to Isabel. "You know that, right?"

"I get it, believe me." She offered me a tentative smile. "Look at that guy. People have all sorts of reasons for living a lie."

"Hmm." I thought. "Like those hunters are pretending to be normal humans? Do you think they're out there on the streets right now without anyone being any the wiser? They can't be wearing those masks all the time. They'd roast in this weather."

"I don't know that they're normal humans," she said. "Don't forget they took out our wards."

"Right." Even Francine hadn't known how they'd managed to bypass our security as easily as switching off a lamp. "But what *are* they? Vance said the only group of supernaturals who weren't previously targeted by the League were necromancers."

"Oh." A flush spread across her cheekbones. "No, it definitely isn't them. I've been keeping tabs on them."

"Meaning your friend, Rick?" I grinned.

She ducked her head. "Yes. I haven't had a chance to properly talk to him since—you know."

"Ah. Sorry."

"Don't worry. Things are way too complicated anyway—" Isabel's phone rang. "I'll get that."

"Did Larsen go bust overnight?" I remarked. "Maybe he finally has the reputation he deserves."

Isabel answered the phone. "Sure… come to the manor. Yes, that's 15 Oak Drive. Thank you."

She ended the call. "Another faulty spell, this time from a coven member. And I have three voicemails from people who called us earlier. What're the odds that they have similar complaints?"

"What, you think there's… like, an epidemic of fake spells or something?"

Just what we needed. Isabel had enough on her plate as a new coven leader without adding dodgy spell manufacturers on top of everything.

"I don't know, but…" She trailed off. "Remember our wards? They were completely negated, like they switched off of their own accord."

"Right." I thought back to our conversation with Francine. "They might have used some kind of dispeller. One that worked on your trapping spell, too."

"Yeah." She skimmed down her phone screen. "I'll check the other messages and see if I'm right."

I watched her, my mind ticking over the possibilities. Dispellers were pretty limited in their reach. They negated some tripwires, but not iron wards, and not alarms either. No handmade contraption could negate over a dozen wards at once.

Isabel finished listening to the messages and put her phone down on the desk. "That's bizarre."

"All of them mentioned spells malfunctioning?" I guessed.

"Not only that, but they all seem to be within the same part of town," she said. "I know a lot of witches live close to one another, but this seems sketchy to me."

"Weird." Was someone selling defective spells? Hardly unheard of, but it was usually naïve humans who bought those spells. Not coven members. "Might it be worth paying one of them a house visit?"

"Might be," she agreed. "The area is close to the Ley Line. Spells should be strong there."

My phone buzzed. Another client. "I'll tell this one to wait. We need to focus on one at a time."

"Good plan."

"Hey." I answered the call. "We're out of office. Or we will be. Can you wait an hour?"

"Oh." The female voice on the other end sounded somewhat deflated. "I just… I don't know what to do. Every single one of my spells has stopped working."

"All of them? Seems to be happening a lot." I weighed the odds, and then pushed ahead. "Have you seen anyone dressed oddly in the area? Any people wearing dark clothing and, er, masks? They'd catch attention in this heat, I imagine."

She sucked in a breath. "You know… yes. When I went up to the corner shop earlier. I saw a group of them walking down the street. I did think it was strange that they were dressed like that."

My blood ran cold. I gripped the phone and did my level best to keep my tone free of emotion. "I'll call you back in a minute. Don't leave the house until then."

Isabel stifled a laugh behind her hand. "Sorry. You sounded exactly like Vance then."

"Shit, I did." I needed to tell him. Needed to tell her, too. "The witch on the phone just then said she saw the hunters out in public earlier."

Isabel's smile melted to horror. "What, they're wandering around right now? Near the coven? I have to go—"

"You're their target."

"So are you!" She gripped the desk with both hands. "I can't let you jump in front of a bullet again, Ivy."

"They weren't using the bullets." No, they were shutting down everyone's spells instead. But to what end? And how was it even possible?

Vance nudged open the door and stepped in. "What's going on?"

"A spate of malfunctioning spells that might mean something worse." I gave him a rundown of the conclusions Isabel and I had reached. "I think we should go check it out. If the hunters aren't overtly attacking anyone, we might be able to get the jump on them."

"I agree," he said. "I'll get a team together."

"I don't want anyone else to get hurt on my account," Isabel protested.

"The mages know the risks," Vance said. "I pay compensation for running into hazard zones, if they choose to do so."

True. The mages' policies were a welcome change from working as a mercenary for Larsen, who didn't care if I came back in one piece or not. But compensation didn't change the fact that when you were dead, you were dead. Those bullets didn't come with second chances, and no magic could defend against them.

Except mine? I hadn't put my faerie magic directly against the hunters yet, but my magic had repelled even the Lady of the Tree when she'd been wielding a talisman. I'd almost been a match for Fionn... well, for about five seconds. Human and faerie magic were in different classes. Maybe mine *could* stop the effects of those bullets.

Or maybe I'd end up the same way as Francine had.

9

Within half an hour, the backup crew had assembled in the main room. I'd wanted to leave right away, but we'd had to wait for Vance to brief the other mages first and answer their various questions. Some had prior experience with the hunters, some didn't, though none except for Bailey and Drake knew about the message I'd received. There seemed little point in causing unnecessary confusion, and I'd been the intended target, not the mages.

"Are you sure you want to come?" I asked Isabel for the tenth time.

"I think we've pretty much established that this is a trap for one or both of us," she said. "And you know what? Bring it on. I'm not going to be ambushed in the night again."

"We've never gone up against anything that can negate witch spells before." I knew better than to argue, though. This was personal—for both of us. Over my dead body would I let those hunters run amok around a witches' neighbourhood terrorising everyone. "All right. If trapping spells are out, I think Vance's ability is probably the best way to corner them."

"Oh, don't say that in front of him," said Drake, coming into the room. "He'll never let you forget it. Anyway, fire's just as strong."

"How do you know they can't turn off *your* magic?" Bailey sounded as if he was already having regrets about volunteering to come, but he'd stepped in as soon as Rod had signed up and his knowledge of how to read those glyphs might come in handy if the hunters had left any more threatening messages lying around.

Drake conjured a flame to his palm. "They're welcome to try. Lead the way, Isabel."

Some of the mages took cars, but it wasn't a long walk and the notion of sitting in a stuffy car in this heat was unappealing. There was also the obvious attention the mages' cars would draw, though approaching on foot wasn't exactly inconspicuous either. I groaned when Rod and one of the other air mages conjured a breeze to make the heat more bearable. Isabel's earlier comments about supernaturals once living in hiding came to mind and made me wonder how in the world they'd got away with it.

"Can you ask them to tone it down?" I hissed at Drake, who was in charge of the backup crew. "And put that fire out."

Drake extinguished the small flame he was tossing between his hands. "We need to let the bastards see what they're up against."

"If they shoot at you, you'll be dead before that flame goes out."

"Morbid, much?"

"Your funeral." Hopefully not literally.

I'd given Isabel the witch's address and she knew that part of the city like the back of her hand, but she still had to ask for directions a couple of times. The address the witch had given was at the far end of witch district, near a set of shops.

At our request, the mages pulled back to let Isabel take the lead. I walked closely behind her and we came to an abrupt halt at a street's corner.

"Ivy…" Isabel trailed off. "Does that sign say what I think it does?"

I followed her gaze to an old pub that looked as though it'd been closed for a while. The windows were boarded up and the crooked sign hung above the closed door read, *The Huntsman.*

Alarm bells rang in my skull. "Where's this address?"

Isabel looked at her phone and back at the pub again. "Ivy… that's the address the witch gave you. It's not a house."

The alarm bells amplified. "Someone is fucking with us."

Either this was a not-subtle-at-all joke, or the name was a genuine coincidence, but my suspicions of Fionn's involvement came roaring back with a vengeance. Heart racing, I pulled out my phone, intending to call the witch's number again.

"Don't." Vance placed a hand over mine. "If this is a setup, we don't want to give our location away."

"Right." No shit, Ivy. The thought of facing *him* again had scrambled my thoughts. *He can't be here. He can't be in this realm.* If Fionn wanted another bout, he'd have shown his face in person. Right?

The pub might look abandoned, but an odd rippling over its doors that made it resemble a reflection in water suggested someone had thrown a ward in front. Stolen from the coven, no doubt.

"That pub's been there forever," Isabel murmured. "It's been closed since before the invasion, I think."

Vance disappeared, then reappeared a second later. "I

peered in through the back window. There are at least ten people inside."

"Or hunters." I rested a hand on my blade's hilt. "I hope that so-called witch *is* in there. I'll rip out her teeth."

"I'll ask the team to surround the house." Vance disappeared again, while I fought the urge to sprint at the building and unleash my faerie magic to its full extent. If a single bullet could end me, I'd have move with more caution, but damn, it was tempting to blow the place to smithereens. Whatever ward was on the door was surely no match for my talisman.

Vance returned to my side. "The mages have the place surrounded. Let me know when you want us to go in."

I gave Isabel a questioning look. "Your call."

With mages circling the pub, the hunters would be hard-pressed to flee, and we had more or less equal numbers. Their main advantage was those bullets... but we had the element of surprise on our hands.

Isabel held up a shadow spell. "I'll see if I can get close enough to take out that ward."

"Okay, but don't let them hit you with that dispeller." Or whatever it was. Worry fluttered in my chest. I grabbed a shadow spell of my own, resigning myself to using the stealthy approach.

The mages had other ideas. Thumps sounded from near the pub, followed by a flash of fire. *I bet that was Drake.*

Even his fire hadn't broken through the wards, but the burst of fire set off a chain effect of elemental attacks, and a hail of frost, water, earth and lightning stuck the pub from all angles. I waved farewell to subtlety. My talisman came free of its sheath in a shower of glittering blue and I sprinted over the road.

I ducked as a bullet whizzed overhead. I lifted my gaze, seeing a masked figure take aim from an upper window.

I deflected the next bullet with my blade, feeling a rush of satisfaction when it bounced off the edge and was crushed beneath the heel of my boot. Bursts of elemental magic came from all sides, but none made contact with the building until the rippling lines of the witch ward vanished with a sharp *crack.*

"Nice going, Isabel," I whispered. "Let's smoke the fuckers out."

"Damn right," Isabel's voice whispered back from where she was hidden beneath her shadow spell. "Let's see if their dispeller works on my explosives."

"Make sure you don't hit the mages, too."

Fire and lightning streamed overhead and collided above the roof, while several windows shattered under a gust of wind. Baring my teeth, I called magic to my own hand and flung a blast of vibrant blue at the upper window where I'd been shot at. The glass burst inward, but I didn't hear the satisfying thud that suggested I'd hit my target.

Vance reappeared at my side. "There isn't anyone in the upper rooms. I checked."

"What?" I tilted my head and spied a flicker of black up on the pub roof. "Damn. They used the fire escape trick again."

Vance vanished in a whirl of air that shook the roof like a hurricane. Tiles flew in all directions and I ducked to avoid being hit in the face. Several black figures came sliding down, and I grinned. *There they are.*

I ran down the side of the building where I'd seen one of the figures fall and skidded to a halt when a bullet bounced off the wall, perilously close. *Whoa.* That'd teach me to get cocky. Above, a masked figure ducked out of sight on the neighbouring roof. Ah, shit.

When my eyes locked onto him, he fired again. I lifted my blade to block and leapt, using the wall for leverage as I put on a boost of magic-enhanced speed. I landed on the roof of the shop next door to the pub and slammed into the black-clad figure, pinning them down with my knees.

The hunter's mask slipped, revealing a woman with dark hair and a clearly broken nose. Long hair flew free as she snarled and tried to lift the gun she held in her hand. I shifted my knees to pin down her weapon hand and pointed the tip of my blade at her throat.

"I prefer old-school weapons myself," I said. "Got a name? I figure it's more polite to know who I'm killing beforehand."

"You're Ivy, right?" She put on a high-pitched voice, not at all fazed by the blade pressing to her throat. "Oh, help me, Ivy! My spells aren't working!"

What the fuck? She was the one who'd made the fake call? "I'm flattered that you chose to hire my business and not someone else's, but I haven't the faintest idea who you are."

"You will." She hissed between her teeth. "Everyone will know our name soon enough."

"The Orion League, right?" I ducked, and another bullet clipped at my sleeve from somewhere behind. *This isn't the place for an interrogation.* "You wait here. I'll be right back."

The hunter snarled and tried to buck me off. I kicked her in the kneecap, hearing an audible crack. She screamed, her eyes screwed up in pain. Trusting she wouldn't be making a quick getaway, I reached for her gun hand and twisted until her fingers released the weapon.

"Get the witch!" the woman yelled at whoever had shot at me from behind.

Isabel.

"No, you fucking don't." I kicked her again and ran in the direction of the gunshot. Another sniper crouched behind a chimney, taking aim at the alley below.

Vance appeared behind him. The man fell from the roof like a stone, and a heartbeat later, the gun I'd taken from the female hunter disappeared from my hand.

"Please tell me you displaced that somewhere safe." I turned to Vance, who'd materialised at my back. "Want to help me talk to this delightful woman? She's the one who made the call."

The hunter spat at both of us. "You're already too late."

"For what?" A deafening bang cut through my words, somewhere below. I peered over the edge and saw two masked figures closing in on the front of the building. Was Isabel hiding somewhere out there?

Dammit. The interrogation would have to wait.

I leapt off the roof, using magic to boost my speed and hold my balance, and slammed down in front of the hunters. One ran to each side to avoid the sweep of my blade. Vance reappeared, cutting off one escape route, and the hunter changed course to join their buddy, aiming a gun over their shoulder. The bullet bounced off the road as Vance disappeared again. I picked up speed, adrenaline surging in my blood. *Don't you dare.*

I tackled the hunter and sent them sprawling, pummelling their face beneath the mask. A blazing flash lit the air—a spell?—and the hunter squirmed out from underneath me.

"You have some nerve using my own spells against me," Isabel's voice yelled. "Get back here!"

The other hunter had slipped away, but the flash from that direction told me they'd used a light charm. *Why are they using magic now?* In fact—

"Isabel." I ran over to the spot where I'd heard her voice. "They aren't blocking our magic. Change of tactics?"

"Makes our lives easier." An explosive spell flew out of the air towards the fleeing hunters. "Take that, you thieving bastards."

The blast hit a nearby fence, sending bits of wood flying

in all directions. The hunters dodged, narrowly, and ran down a side street.

Straight into Vance. A billowing current of air caught them in midair and sent them flying several feet into the air. One hit the wall with a bone-jarring thud, while the other was sent soaring out of sight. Vance ran in pursuit, while I tracked down Isabel next to the pub door.

"Ivy… look in there."

"Huh?" I peered through the door, and the answer as to how the other hunters had escaped greeted me in the form of a half-open trapdoor next to the long-abandoned bar. "They have a basement? Is that where they're hiding?"

"I don't know, but Ivy—don't go in there alone."

"I want to see what they've been hiding." The hunter I'd left on the roof wasn't going anywhere, while the mages would chase down the others. The open trapdoor drew me closer, and I readied my blade.

A gun poked out of the trapdoor. I leapt aside as a bullet skimmed the floor, narrowly missing my ankle. My foot slammed down on the hand that held the gun as I kicked the trapdoor the rest of the way open. Then I fired a blast of magic into the room below and was rewarded by a scream.

"Nice try." I kicked off from the bare floorboards and leapt into the hole, crashing into the hunter on the ladder. We fell, and I landed on top of him with a crack and a yelp, blinking in the sudden darkness.

My shoulder burned with sharp pain. Had I landed harder than I'd thought? My magic should have broken my fall, but a strange fuzziness took hold of my mind, and my fingers struggled to maintain their grip on my sword hilt.

"Ivy!" Isabel's voice came from above.

"I'm fine." My voice slurred. "Shit. Maybe I'm not."

I reached up for the ladder, but the left side of my body

didn't cooperate. I heard Isabel yelling, but the sound became a meaningless buzz.

Then I was in Vance's arms. "Ivy, I'll get you out of here."

A heartbeat later, I lay on hard ground, Vance standing over me. or rather, two Vances, both saying, "Ivy, they shot you."

"Oh." That would explain a lot. Through my hazy thoughts, panic filtered in, together with the memory of Francine's skin turning grey and cracking open.

Oh, god. Am I actually dying?

Air rushed over my burning skin, and the manor's main room replaced the street. Isabel appeared next to Vance in the flicker of a dying shadow spell. "What are you doing?"

"Getting the bullet out," Vance said. "Can you grab a healing spell?"

"That won't work—Ivy!"

I groaned as Vance tugged off my jacket and pushed up my sleeve. My shoulder throbbed, alternating between numbness and pain. The next instant, he held a knife in his hand.

"Wait a moment," I slurred. "Are you going to stab me with that?"

"The bullet is poison." Vance's voice was steady, but even through my pain-drugged haze, I heard a hint of panic beneath. "I have to get it out. I'm sorry."

His hand touched my shoulder. I screamed, my vision flickering to whitish blue.

Isabel sucked in a breath. "You're hurting her."

"There's no other way to do it. The bullet's impervious to healing spells."

"Arseholes." My back arched, my whole body aflame. "Get it out!"

"Ivy, keep still." Vance's concerned face swam in and out of focus. "Sorry, but this is going to hurt."

He leaned over. I yelped as something sharp dug into my shoulder, then I passed out.

Seconds later, I blinked awake to the unmistakeable flash of a healing spell. Vance stood over me with Isabel at his side. Both regarded me with a mixture of profound relief and absolute shock.

"What?" I flexed my fingers and then lifted my arm. From what I could see, the skin looked normal, not grey and cracked, but from their expressions, I might as well have sprouted horns. "Shit, I'm not turning into a piskie, am I?"

"No," said Vance. "You aren't showing any side effects from the poison at all."

I looked down at my shoulder. Blood soaked into the fabric of my shirt, but beneath lay nothing. Not so much as a scratch. "Huh."

"How do you feel?" Isabel's voice was taut with anxiety.

"Tired." I shrugged. "Glad I'm not dead."

Isabel's eyes nearly popped out. "So am I, but—Ivy, even humans who get shot by those bullets suffer from most of the side effects."

"Your magic must have numbed the damage." Vance carefully ran a fingertip over my upper arm. "I'm sorry I hurt you. I didn't want to risk leaving the bullet in for too long."

"You probably saved my life." Even my enhanced faerie magic might not have held off the effects forever. "Damn. Just when I thought I'd figured out all the weird side effects of stealing from the faeries."

"I'd rather you'd found out in less dire circumstances," Isabel said tremulously. "And didn't you learn anything from jumping off the roof?"

"To look before I leap?" Right. The basement. My mind went back to the confused moments before I'd been shot. "Were there any others hiding in that hole?"

"No," Vance said. "I didn't get a good look, because I was

getting you out of there at the time, but I'm positive I saw some kind of door in the basement."

"Hidden escape tunnel?" I guessed. "Are the hunters where I left them? That fucker on the roof deserves a chat with my sword."

"Ivy." Vance gave me an exasperated look. "Do I need to remind you that you jumped into the path of a bullet a few minutes ago?"

"Technically, I fell on it."

"Ivy." He sighed. "Your knack for getting yourself injured in absurd ways is unmatched."

"You know you love me for it."

"Yes," he said quietly. "I do. I wish you'd be more careful."

Oh, Vance. "I'll try. Really, I appreciate you getting the bullet out of me."

He brushed my hair from my shoulder with one hand. "Let's not make it a recurring habit. I'll find the others."

"Hey!" I half-rose from my seat as he disappeared. "Dammit. I hope one of them stayed conscious enough to interrogate. I want to know why they changed tactics."

"They didn't block any of my spells this time," Isabel said. "Something was… off. It was almost too easy."

"Maybe they thought the instant-kill bullets would be enough." I rubbed my bloodied shoulder. "The one on the roof… she's the witch who called. She lured us over there on purpose."

"Why?" Isabel watched me climb off the sofa, her face ashen. "Dammit, Ivy. I thought you were dead, and it was my fault."

"How is any of this *your* fault?"

"I was being overly cautious," she said. "Because of those bullets."

"And I was being overly reckless. It's what we do. You

took out their wards, remember?" My gaze snagged on the low table where a bloodied bullet lay. "Is that…?"

"Yes." Isabel's shoulders tensed. "It's definitely the same as the others."

Damn. I'm actually immune to anti-supernatural bullets. Or as immune as possible for a human, anyway. "I can mount it on the wall as a trophy."

"Definitely not." She shuddered. "That was too close."

Vance reappeared. "They've gone."

"Who's gone?" I lifted my head, startled. "Not the hunters?"

"The survivors, yes. Five of the ten were killed."

"And the others… ran off?" No way. I'd broken that woman's kneecap, for a start. "How?"

"I don't know." His jaw tightened. "They must have had an escape route planned and intended to take any survivors with them to ensure nobody could be questioned."

"Weren't your people watching them?"

"They acted fast, while the mages were gathering the dead. Drake insisted on going into the basement to check out that tunnel."

"He didn't, did he?" I grabbed my sword. "I want to go back. That hunter I left on the roof… there's no way she got down from there without help."

"They were using spells this time," Isabel reminded me. "*My* spells."

I swore. "Yeah, they switched tactics on us. This despite how they lured us in by pretending their magic wasn't working."

Except not all of those calls had been faked. Some witches had been affected, and the calls had seemed genuine. What were the hunters playing at?

"I need to warn the coven," Isabel said. "If this is something they're making a habit of, the others need to know, but

I'm honestly not sure what they're playing at. There doesn't seem to be a coherent strategy at work."

"No," Vance said. "My fellow mages are searching the surrounding area, but if the hunters are running around underground, they'll be harder to find."

"That place wasn't their hideout," I said. "It can't have been. They abandoned it too easily."

"The last time we fought the League, they used a number of abandoned houses as temporary shelters and travelled via underground tunnels. That part of their strategy hasn't changed."

"And there I was hoping they had a top-secret lair we could storm. I'm joking," I added, seeing the warning flash in his eyes. "Seriously, though, they're on the run and a fair few of them are injured, too. Including the one who made that fake call asking for my help."

"Scumbags," Vance said. "I'll make them pay for that."

"Oh, no, that bitch is mine."

A shriek came from the hallway, followed by a thud. "Bad faerie!"

"Shit," I said. "I think Erwin got out of his cage."

The piskie's shrieks rang past, interspersed with thumps and Lady Harper's irate voice. "What *is* this creature doing in the house? Get it out."

Oh boy. I darted out of the room, fighting a laugh. Erwin flew in dizzying circles around her head while she tried to poke him out of the air with her cane.

"That's Erwin," I called to her. "He's our resident piskie. He's staying here for a bit until our flat's safe."

"He's certainly *not.*"

"The house belongs to me, Lady Harper," Vance reminded her. "Did you let him out of his cage?"

Lady Harper swung her cane. Erwin screeched and flew into the ceiling, yowling. "Bad humans!"

Vance took a sudden step back, his phone in his hand. "Drake said the mages are being attacked again."

"What?" Isabel ran up behind him. "The hunters came back?"

"No, fire imps. Someone sent a swarm."

"You're shitting me." I caught Isabel's eye. "Can you stop Erwin from destroying the house?"

"You aren't coming…" Vance trailed off when I gave him a look. "Fine, but if any more of those bullets show up, I'm bringing you back here."

"Deal."

Seconds later, we landed on the road opposite the Huntsman.

And the pub was on fire.

10

Flames blazed from the pub's shattered windows while a number of four-foot-tall creatures ran amok, throwing handfuls of whirling flame into the air and laughing gleefully.

"Hey!" I yelled at them. "Cut that shit out."

Fire imps were almost as diminutive as piskies but with considerably more potential for damage. At the sight of my sword, they scattered, emitting shrill yells when Vance sent a blast of displaced air at them. My blade cut three down and Vance's knife took care of another.

"Need a hand?" said Drake, running over to join us. "Want to fight fire with fire?"

"We have enough fire." I grabbed an imp by the scruff of its neck. "Hey. Tell me who sent you here and I might reconsider blasting you into tiny pieces."

"Nobody," screeched the imp.

I gave the creature a shake. "Are you working with the hunters?"

"Huntsman, yes!"

My instinctive recoil caused me to accidentally drop the imp. "Oh, shit."

A blast of displaced air hit the remaining imps. Vance stalked towards them, his coat billowing behind him, and the imps were flung, shrieking, into their own fire.

"Vance—" I broke off. "Don't kill them all. One of them just said *Huntsman*."

"It spoke to you?" Drake threw another fireball and dissolved several imps on the spot.

"Drake, I told you *not* to start any more fires," said Vance. "Huntsman?"

"That's the name of that place." Drake gestured to the pub.

"I asked if they were working with the *hunters*, and that was the imp's response." I looked for more to question and saw nothing but twitching bodies and dismembered body parts.

At the pub, the other mages had got the blaze under control. Three water mages ran back and forth, dousing the various fires that had spread to the neighbouring buildings.

"Nobody lives in there." Vance indicated the building whose roof I'd left the injured hunter on. "I bet that's how she escaped. Someone came in through the house and helped her down."

"Shit." My thoughts spun. *Huntsman.* "What was the point in setting the place on fire?"

"To hide the evidence?" Vance trod towards the door, which now resembled a singed piece of wood hanging from its hinges.

"Er… about that," said Drake. "I saw those little bastards and panicked. It was me who set the pub on fire."

"But the hunters did send them." I wished one had been left alive, but fire imps had zero concept of loyalty and would obey anyone who gave them free rein to cause havoc. Yet the hunters supposedly hated all supernaturals… and the word 'huntsman' had shown up twice now.

I trod through puddles of water to the pub's door, screwing up my eyes against the sting of smoke. A faint blue light caught my eye from within.

"Is that…?" I peered in and coughed, the smoke burning my nose and throat. The fire was out, but I wouldn't do my lungs any good by walking in there.

An idea occurred to me. I called my magic into a shield around my body, like I'd done when I'd waded into the canal to fight an undead hydra. My magic formed a cocoon, preventing anything outside from touching me. I didn't know how long I'd be able to keep it up, but the shield would prevent me from suffocating when I stepped into the smoke.

I pushed past the door and into the ruined bar. Greyness fogged my view, but the blue glow of my magic drew me to a door on the right into an unfurnished room with bare floorboards.

My heart lurched. Symbols were scrawled onto the wooden floor, and though the smoke obscured my vision, I knew without a doubt that they were identical to the glyphs I'd seen at the warehouse. With a few alterations.

I whipped my notebook from my pocket—thanks to the fire imps, the edges were slightly singed—and scrawled the new symbols onto the page. My magical shield held, but some alarming creaking noises overhead suggested the whole building was at risk of collapsing on top of me. I finished scrawling the symbols and legged it out of there.

Vance appeared at the door so suddenly I ran into him. Catching my balance, I released my shield, taking in a gulp of clean air. "Vance—they left me another message. Wait, were you inside?"

"To see what they wanted to burn. There were a lot of

destroyed papers in the upstairs room." He held up a charred fragment. "None are readable. We'd better go."

His hand closed over my upper arm, and we reappeared in the manor's hallway. The notebook fluttered in my hand, and I coughed, traces of smoke tickling at my throat. "The message was glamoured like last time. There's a faerie involved in this. Has to be."

"Oh, good, nobody got shot this time." Isabel came out of the living room with Erwin sitting on her shoulder. "I told Lady Harper I knew how to control him. She's in the garden with Wanda."

"Finally some good news." I held up the notebook. "Someone left me another present before they sent fire imps to burn down the pub."

"What—the hunters did?" Horror flickered over her face. "Wait. Weren't you attacked by fire imps outside the store-room, too?"

"I don't know if it was the same ones, but we can shelve all our doubts that the hunters are working with the fae. At least in some capacity."

Damn. Maybe if I'd tracked where the first batch of fire imps came from, the trail would have taken me right to the hunters before they'd killed Francine.

I shook off the thought. None of us could possibly have known. My magic might give me some level of immunity to anti-supernatural bullets, but it didn't give me clairvoyance.

"Fire imps aren't intelligent," Vance said.

"Neither are the hunters," I said. "The only reason they shot me was because I landed on top of one of them. Did Drake mention whether he found anything when he went into that hidden tunnel?"

"He didn't," Vance said. "According to him, the passage came out in a nearby side street. I would assume anyone who escaped via that route is long gone."

I swore. "Back to square one."

"Except for that message they left," Vance said. "Was it the same as the last one?"

"Partly." I passed him the notebook. "Run that past Bailey and see what he says. We'd better get something useful out of this clusterfuck."

Vance's phone began buzzing on the table. He picked it up. "Hello?"

"Mage Lord!" I jumped when Chief's voice came out of the phone, so loud that he might have been standing next to us.

"Chief," said Vance. "What is it?"

"There you are!" he yelled, at such a volume that you'd think he was trying to catch the attention of someone at the opposite end of a busy shopping centre. "Two of my people are dead!"

My heart plummeted. "What? How?"

"I knew *you'd* be there, Ivy Lane. Get here at once."

"Who, me?" The call cut out in a buzz of static. I met Vance's eyes, bewildered. "What—you don't think it's the hunters?"

"I'd be surprised if it isn't," Vance said darkly.

"Are you sure it wasn't another prank call?" I said dubiously. "The last I checked, the Chief didn't have a mobile phone."

"I believe it's a recent acquisition." Vance's mouth thinned. "This isn't a good time. You're—"

"Not injured, as well you know." My clothes were in a state, but being covered in blood was nothing new for me. "We should go and see what he wants."

I said goodbye to Isabel and Vance took my arm, transporting both of us to half-blood territory.

Blazing sun greeted us, coupled with the shouts of angry half-bloods. A crowd had gathered at the edge of the Chief's clearing, and armoured guards attempted to hold them back from reaching him.

"I didn't mean appear right in the middle of my territory!" The Chief stood in his usual spot, flanked by two hulking ogres and circled by more armoured guards. Evidently, his fellow half-bloods were displeased at the recent deaths.

"Sorry, I'll wait outside the gates the next time you tell me you're under attack." The ungrateful arse. "Since when did you have a mobile phone?"

"The Mage Lord insisted it was the best means of communication, but I've been trying to get through to him for an hour!" he said indignantly.

I raised a brow at Vance, who said, "I left my phone at the manor while we were dealing with another urgent situation."

"Forgive us for failing to realise you've finally time-travelled into the right era." My annoyance faded when I spied the two bodies lying at the clearing's edge. "What happened to them?"

"They were attacked while patrolling," he said through gritted teeth. "Ambushed from the other side of the hedge. It's outrageous."

"Ambushed?" I echoed. "With what kind of weapons?"

"With magic, I assume, given their wounds."

"Let me see." I took a step closer and the ogres closed in, barring my path. "Come on, the Chief *demanded* I come and help. I can't do that without looking at the bodies."

The Chief made an impatient noise. "Fine."

The guards parted to either side, revealing a trail of crimson droplets leading up to the bodies of two half-faeries. One male, one female. Both were from Summer, judging by their leaf-patterned armour, and their faces were twisted into grimaces of pain. Blood seeped from between their cracked lips. Similar cracks webbed across their skin.

It's those bullets.

One had suffered a wound to the arm and the other had been hit in the neck, with similar results. I reeled, thinking of my own wound. The bullet hadn't affected me in the same manner. These two were both half-Sidhe, descended from nobility, but possessing the power of the highest-ranked fae hadn't protected them. Why had I been an exception?

"Well?" said the Chief. "Any conclusions?"

I exchanged concerned looks with Vance. "The person responsible might have been associated with the same hunters who tried to kill us today. They use bullets specifically designed to target supernaturals."

"Hunters?" exploded the Chief. "How did I guess this would lead back to you?"

"Don't shoot the messenger." I wrenched my gaze from the bodies. "I don't know why your people were targeted, but the first victim was the leader of the Laurel Coven."

The Chief's eyes bulged. "You didn't think to inform me of this?"

"The coven wanted to keep it under wraps," I said. "It's only been a couple of days, and we assumed the witches were the intended targets."

"Evidently not." He glared at me. "If you got my people killed, Ivy Lane—"

"That's right, blame me again." I didn't need to deal with his crap after the day I'd had already. "For the record, I just got shot myself. I barely survived. So I'd appreciate it if you shut the fuck up."

The Chief's mouth hung open. "You—*dare*—"

Vance came to my rescue. "I can give you all the information I have on who I believe is behind this, but many of our conclusions are based on guesswork. We encountered the hunters less than an hour ago, but we were unable to secure any survivors to question."

"Hunters," he rasped. "What hunters?"

"They're known as the Orion League," Vance said. "You might have heard the name, or not, but they're following in the steps of anti-supernatural zealots who attacked the mages several years ago."

"With one major difference," I added. "They're also working with the faeries this time. Remember the coded message I showed you? That was them. They left glamoured messages at the site of Francine's murder, written in their own secret code."

"Glamoured?" he echoed. "That's preposterous. Nobody here on my territory would ally with humans of any kind."

"You're allying with a human right now," I pointed out. "I'm not accusing anyone, but someone involved in this is trying to fuck with me personally." I left out the mention of the *Huntsman*. It'd take too long to explain, and the Chief hadn't directly encountered the terrifying Sidhe who Calder had woken up. Nor had he seen the Wild Hunt ride, as I'd brought them to a halt before they'd reached the city.

"With your permission, I can use a tracking spell to identify the individual who killed your fellow half-faeries," Vance offered.

"No spells here," growled one of the ogres.

Big surprise. "There's no other way to find out who did this. Those hunters are sneaky bastards. They broke into my flat last night and switched off all the wards. I think they have some kind of dispeller." Which they hadn't had with them at the pub. While it wouldn't have worked on faerie magic, the Chief had said his people had been shot from the other side of the fence. Weren't there supposed to be defences around his entire territory?

The Chief exhaled in a sigh. "If there is no other way to find the people responsible, do as you will, Mage Lord."

"You'll allow witchcraft on our territory?" said an armoured Unseelie guard with jet-black hair whose spiked armour looked incredibly uncomfortable in the heat.

"Yes," the Chief said shortly. "This is out of our hands now."

Grumbles ensued, but nobody moved to stop us from walking over to the bodies. It wasn't hard to find blood to use in a tracking spell, given the trail the bodies had left on the cracked soil. I knelt and fished a spell out of my pocket, setting it on the ground.

The protests from the half-bloods vanished in a flare of green light. The forest didn't, though the vision showed a slightly different view. The guard I followed must have been walking through this part of the territory. Trees covered one side while the hedge bordering the half-bloods' home was on my right. A narrow path led alongside the boundary, heading northward alongside the hedges that encircled the entire territory.

A sudden jolt brought my steps to an end. My vision blurred, and as I fell, I glimpsed a slender figure slip away into the trees.

Shouts filled my ears as I blinked back into my own body again. Vance crouched beside me. "Are you all right?"

"Yeah… that was weird." I rubbed my forehead, disorientated. "I saw the attack, but the guard must have died too quickly to see his attacker. Except I did see… movement. In the forest."

"On this side of the hedge?" Vance frowned at me. "If the perpetrators were inside the territory…"

"They might still be here." I looked for the Chief, but he and the guards were engaged in a heated argument over the merits of allowing witch spells to be used on their territory and were no longer paying us any attention.

"Chief." Vance raised his voice. "We saw a possible witness inside the forest. Would you like us to search for them?"

"Witness?" The Chief broke away from the guards. "What witness?"

"I didn't see, but they were definitely on *this* side of the hedges." I wasn't sure the shot had come from that direction, but that wasn't a chance I'd want to take, in the Chief's position.

The Chief uttered a curse in the faerie tongue and turned back to his fellow guards. "Gather a patrol. We need to search the forest."

The Unseelie knight gave him a withering look. "You believe the word of a mage over your own people?"

"I called the Mage Lord here myself." The Chief looked to his fellow guards for backup, but nobody stepped in.

"I think that's our cue to leave," I murmured to Vance. "Someone's having trouble maintaining order."

"Agreed." He gestured eastward, and we left. Nobody stopped us, and while I wasn't certain on the precise location the vision had shown, the trail of blood was enough of a clue. The crimson streaks led us north, with the forest on our left and the hedge on our right.

"This place is bigger than I remember," I remarked after we'd walked for several minutes. "Where does the forest end?"

On our left was a thick barrier of trees, dense enough that I couldn't see what lay on the other side. The blood splatter continued, indicating we were on the right track, and came to an end at a dip in the ground.

"The first body was found... here." I scanned the area, but the dense trees made it impossible to see if anyone might be hiding inside.

"And the shots were fired from over there." Vance held his hand-and-a-half sword as he peered over the hedge. "I'd suggest using another tracking spell, but I'm not sure if the killer would have been visible through the hedge."

"True." I tensed at a rustle from amidst the trees. I'd never been this deep into half-blood territory before, and frankly, I was more likely to be in danger from whatever was lurking within the forest than from hunters wandering past. This was the domain of those who found it harder to blend in amongst humans or just plain didn't want to. The forest itself had the appearance of a stretch of ancient woodland from a time before humans had ever existed.

"You said you saw someone?" Vance asked. "Where?"

I pointed into the trees. Vance followed my gaze, a deceptively unconcerned expression on his face, but I could tell he was thinking of our last, disastrous trip into the Vale. Though this place wasn't Faerie, it sure as hell looked like it.

"Let's see who's hiding in here." I lifted my sword and ducked underneath a tree branch. "At least we know your magic can get us out if we end up lost."

Unlike the Vale, though here, too, faerie magic held sway. Trees grew in improbable contortions, forming gnarled barriers, while the air smelled of rot and decay, suggesting that this was where Winter's magic retreated to when Summer was in control. The trees rang with a chorus of shrieks and yowls that sounded like a bag of cats falling off a cliff.

I held my sword ahead of me to deter potential attackers, but I didn't see anyone until the sharp smell of burning stung my nostrils.

Tensing, I followed the smell and saw a group of shrieking imps flinging fireballs into the trees.

"Does the Chief want you setting his territory on fire?" I called to them.

A pair of talons lashed out from the shadows, spearing one imp on each. I raised Helena, ready to face the new threat.

The banshee sprang onto the path and tore the imps to pieces.

11

It's her. The banshee. Certainty hit me that she was the person I'd seen in the vision, too, watching the guard's murder.

I approached the banshee, keeping a wary eye on her sharp talons. "I have some questions."

"You waste your time, humans." She wore no shoes, her bare feet splayed on the forest's earthen floor. A black silken dress draped her body from head to toe, resembling a funeral shroud. Her black hair floated around her alabaster-pale face in a dark halo.

"Why are you skulking around the forest?" I lifted my blade. "Are you working with the hunters who killed those two half-blood guards?"

"My power draws me to death, Ivy. That is the only reason I am here." She flashed me a smile. "Why, have I not already proven I am no enemy of yours?"

"Debateable."

In Faerie, death clothed itself in beauty, and the banshees were notorious even amongst the Unseelie. Mostly because of their appalling singing, which heralded someone's upcoming demise.

"Have you seen a group of humans wearing black masks outside the territory?" Vance asked her. "Did you see them shoot the Chief's guards?"

"I did not see them, human. I sensed the half-blood's death and was drawn to its presence."

Hmm. The banshee had acted in an unintentionally incriminating way before and had turned out not to be involved with the enemy, and I couldn't think of a reason she'd turn on her fellow half-bloods or ally with anti-supernatural hunters. Still, death fae owed nobody their allegiance.

"Then why are you here?" I asked. "Don't you live outside of the Chief's territory?"

"Yes." An enigmatic smile flitted across her face. "I am here because I felt the winds of change blowing, and it is my desire to bear witness to that change."

"What does that mean?" I didn't need an interlude with a cryptic faerie, but she *had* been of assistance, kind of, when I'd been trying to stop Calder. We'd never made a direct bargain, and since it'd been so many months since I'd last seen her, I'd all but forgotten her role in that debacle.

"Some of us grow tired of the manner in which the Chief runs his territory."

"You don't even live on the Chief's territory," I pointed out. "You can leave any time you like."

"The Chief is nevertheless responsible for setting the rules governing my kind," she said. "Many disagree with his stance that our only options are to work with humans or exile ourselves."

"You *are* mortal," I said. "Also, most half-bloods are perfectly capable of working with humans, if you can swallow your pride a little. I can't say I like the Chief much, but what's the alternative? I mean, the Grey Vale is probably open to members, but I can't say much for your survival chances there."

Maybe my suspicions were unfounded. She'd been the one to warn me against the Wild Hunt, after all, in a roundabout way.

"We're looking for someone who killed your fellow half-bloods," Vance told her. "Are you quite sure you saw nothing?"

"I am in the forest because I sensed death, nothing more."

Right. I'd spent enough time close to Death not to trust anyone who had her talons buried in it as deeply as she did. "If you sensed someone die, does that mean you can see into the afterlife?"

"No," she said. "I can only sense when death has touched a person. *You* have touched death many times, Ivy Lane."

If she was trying to creep me out, she'd have to try harder. "Tell me something I don't know."

"I can tell you many things," she said. "But my duty calls to me."

She was gone in a flash of talons. Vance watched her with narrowed eyes. Then he took my arm, and we vanished.

"She knows something," I said as we landed in the manor's hallway. "If I were more of a diplomat, I'd try to gain her trust, but I don't have time to play head games with half-bloods."

Vance's weapons disappeared, as did his coat. "You're more than a match for her. I believe she's untrustworthy, but I also don't think any of the half-bloods are linked to the hunters."

"The fire imps are." Though she'd killed the ones we'd found in the forest. "Maybe it's not her, but if she's allowed to sneak in and out of his territory without being challenged, I'd bet she's not the only one. It's no surprise his guards are angry with him." Not just the guards, judging by those angry half-bloods who'd been trying to get close to the bodies.

"No," he said. "I suspect the Chief might find himself faced with a leadership challenge soon."

"I hope he doesn't expect us to vouch for him." I kicked off my muddy boots. "I probably shouldn't have lost my temper, but today's been a shit show."

We found Isabel sitting at the meeting room table with Bailey of all people. Someone had moved the city map that Drake had doodled on and replaced it with half the contents of the mages' spell supplies. Boxes filled one end of the table and the other was occupied with neat piles of colour-coordinated spells.

"Ivy." Isabel rose from her seat. "Why am I not surprised you're covered in blood?"

My gaze dropped to my knees. Sure enough, I'd picked up traces of the half-faerie guard's blood as well as mud and general debris from the forest. "It's not mine."

"I should hope not, since it's blue." Bailey gave Vance a sheepish look. "Isabel offered to help reorganise our spells more logically. Rod was helping, too, but he got bored and wandered off somewhere."

"Where's Drake?"

"Outside," he replied. "Claimed he needs to work on his tan."

I snorted. "Did he forget he's a fire mage?"

"I'll fetch him," added Bailey, scooting towards the door. "I know he's supposed to be organising the evening patrols."

"Yes, he is." Vance eyed the boxes. "We've needed to sort those for a while."

"Tripwire spells shouldn't be in the same box as explosives." Isabel sounded so much like her old self that I snorted. "It's a fire hazard waiting to happen. I assume the Chief's okay, since you aren't panicking?"

"Two of his guards aren't." I sheathed my sword and leaned it against the table. "The hunters shot them from the other side of the hedge. Oh, and we met the banshee again."

"Her?" Isabel wrinkled her nose. "Doesn't she live outside of half-blood territory?"

"I asked the same question. She said she came because she sensed the guard's death." I flopped into a seat. Man, it'd been a long day. "I know she tipped me off about the Wild Hunt, but she's also a screaming death fae with a habit of showing up in incriminating places."

"What exactly is this?" Lady Harper came into the room, waving my notebook in the air.

"Mine." I lifted my head. "Must've dropped it earlier."

"And why, exactly, is someone trying to conduct the Rite of the Devourer?"

"The what?" I got up and took the notebook from her. "That's what someone wrote in glamoured writing on the floor in the hunters' old hideout. You can read it?"

"It's an adaptation of a set of glyphs originally created by the Hemlock Coven. Clearly, they don't teach young witch-lings anything these days."

"You knew what the text was all along?" I sat back down and flipped open the notebook. "What do you mean by the Rite of the Devourer? What in hell is that?"

"I can't be expected to know everything that goes on in here," she said. "Don't tell me you have no idea who the Hemlock Coven is."

"I do," Isabel said. "They haven't been heard of in decades. Francine said they'd exiled themselves."

The old mage snorted. "In a manner of speaking. I'd have thought the future leader of the Laurel Coven would have more knowledge than that."

Anger flashed through Isabel's features. *Oh boy.* Messing with her was *not* a good idea, even for a retired Mage Lord. "I was under the impression the message was aimed at Ivy. And I can't read the glyphs. What does it say?"

"*The Rite of the Devourer begins on the solstice.* Fairly self-explanatory."

"To some people, maybe. What *is* the Rite of the Devourer?"

"Rite... like ritual?" Vance asked. "Some rituals are stronger when performed on the solstice, I've heard."

"Not like summoning a spirit?" Oh, *shit.* Summoning anything other than a ghost was a one-way ticket to disaster.

"Precisely," said Lady Harper, "and that ritual is not one that any self-respecting witch would be wise to invoke."

"They aren't witches," I said. "Or wise either, come to that. What do the Hemlock Coven have to do with this? You mentioned they *created* the glyphs?"

Vance's gaze snapped to her. "Is that the coven you used to be part of?"

"Fifty years ago, yes," said Lady Harper.

I gawped at her. So did Isabel. "You worked with them? Do you know... do you know why they disappeared?"

"I wouldn't seek out the Hemlock Coven unless you have a good reason," said Lady Harper. "They aren't known for taking kindly to trespassers."

Says the person making a nuisance of herself in Vance's house.

"But you think they can help us?" Isabel asked. "Will they... will they know what this Rite of the Devourer is?"

Lady Harper's eyes flickered to Isabel. "Now you're asking the right questions."

"Do *you* know?" I asked. "What does this ritual summon?"

Whatever it was, I was willing to bet that I wouldn't find the details in the necromancers' handbook.

"That," she said, "is something you should hear directly from the Hemlock Coven, if you're able to find them."

"Which is... where?" I asked.

"In the forest." In response to my raised eyebrow, she added, "You were there today, weren't you?"

"On half-blood territory?" I looked at Vance. "That's the faeries' forest, isn't it?"

Lady Harper gave a humourless laugh that frankly gave me the creeps. "The witches were here long before the faeries, and the Sidhe would do well to remember that."

Okay... "That whole area used to be a park, pre-invasion. I'm fairly sure the humans would have noticed a coven of witches squatting in the middle of the city."

She tutted. "You above all know how the faeries' arrival altered our realm down to its very foundations. Spirit lines shifted. Liminal spaces expanded. Those places that once solely existed in between the realms became accessible even to humans, if they knew where to look and were willing to risk their lives."

"You're as cryptic as a bloody Sidhe yourself." I tensed when she gave me a sharp look that made me abruptly recall the sensation of being lifted off the ground against my will and the air squeezed from my lungs.

Then my thoughts landed on Fionn, and the tomb we'd found inside a hidden space between the spirit lines that nobody knew existed. Who was to say there wasn't a secret forest between worlds hidden inside a local park, too? Fionn had been imprisoned in a cage imprinted with an Invocation to make everyone outside forget he'd ever existed. Perhaps the witches had employed similar trickery.

"You mean to say that forest on half-blood territory also leads somewhere else," Vance said. "To the place in which the Hemlock witches dwell."

"I knew I didn't raise a fool."

"Then how has nobody else found them?" Isabel asked. "The covens have been wondering for decades."

"Also, you know, the half-bloods live on their doorstep," I said. "Didn't they notice they have a coven as neighbours?"

"Faeries are not the only beings capable of concealing their true nature," said Lady Harper. "The half-bloods might think they own the forest, but those who wander off the paths rarely return."

That's ominous. And concerning. "I thought the fae were the dangerous monsters lurking in the forest."

Lady Harper gave me a contemptuous look. "The Sidhe might be ancient, but the witches have had their roots planted deep in that forest for centuries, and they will not be so easily ousted."

"You make them sound like—like they're immortal." Isabel clamped her mouth shut as though worried she sounded foolish. "Which is absurd."

Lady Harper uttered another dry chuckle. "The Hemlock witches have magic that no other supernatural can comprehend. If you *do* visit them, you're likely to be tested to your limits."

"Sounds like the faeries all over again," I muttered. "Isabel, what do you think?"

"I'd like to meet them," she said. "Francine never did, and I'd like to know why they never revealed themselves. I didn't know anyone alive had ever made contact with them."

I looked warily at Lady Harper, but she merely sniffed at the accusation embedded in Isabel's words.

"And why the hunters stole their glyphs," I added. "Wait, how many days is it until the solstice?"

"Two days." Isabel bit her lip. "If whoever wrote that note was telling the truth…"

"They plan to act on the solstice." Two days. We'd have to act sooner rather than later, but despite the sun setting late, wandering into the forest in the evening was a great way to end up on an Unseelie faerie's dinner plate. "We'll go tomorrow."

Vance cleared his throat. "And is there any advice you would give, Lady Harper?"

"Take every precaution," she said. "The Hemlock witches' magic is nothing like the cheaply produced spells that most witches use these days."

"Cheap?" Isabel's eyes narrowed. "I custom make my own spells. Even the ones used on this manor are from my coven."

I hastened to intervene. "What of the invasion? Did the Hemlock witches fight the Sidhe alongside the mages? If they're that powerful, they must have."

Lady Harper grunted. "They made the greatest of sacrifices in the invasion. More even than the mages did."

"Care to specify?" asked Vance. "I have a hard time believing they gave up more, if they're still alive."

The strain in his voice betrayed his annoyance. I didn't blame him. His parents had both given their lives in battle against the Sidhe. Who was Lady Harper to imply their sacrifice had held less meaning than a coven that seemed to have abandoned the human race outright?

Lady Harper offered a grim smile. "That's for the Hemlock witches themselves to tell you, if they so desire. I will say this, though… some decades ago, they gave up their mortality and their magic in defence of this realm and became tethered to their forest, unable to leave."

"Their mortality?" Isabel's eyes rounded. "What, they physically *can't* leave the forest? Is that why nobody has ever found them?"

"Have they heard of using a phone?" I suppressed a flinch at the cutting stare Lady Harper offered me. "Or, I don't know, a messenger? They can't be completely cut off from the outside world."

"That's their choice," she growled. "You shall see for your-selves, and you may pay a severe price for your mockery."

I folded my arms. "It's how I deal with messed-up shit like nearly getting killed by overpowered immortals. I make fun. Not my problem if you don't like it."

"I am not the one whose approval you need to win, Ivy," she said. "If you *do* manage to find the Hemlock witches, however, there are a few choice words I'd like to say to them."

"Such as…" I prompted.

"They were fools to sacrifice as much as they did, and bigger fools if they thought the past would lie buried."

"I'll pass it on, assuming we get there in one piece." I gave her an eye-roll. "And I'll tell the other mages to direct the blame at you if their head Mage Lord dies in this cursed forest in the middle of a crisis."

"I've given you all the direction I can, but there are some things that you must witness with your own eyes alone," she said. "The forest *changes,* depending on who sets foot inside. There's no warning I can offer that will prepare you for that."

So, just like Faerie, then. Wonderful. "This better be worth it. We have less than two days until the solstice."

"Yeah." Isabel's mouth pinched. "If we're going into the forest tomorrow, I'll have to call the coven and let them know first."

"Hang on," I said. "There are Unseelie faeries living in the forest and hunters outside. It's dangerous, and with you being coven leader now…"

"I have to speak to the Hemlock Coven," she said. "You know I do."

I did. She was coven leader. This was a hundred percent her business. More even than mine.

"Bad faerie!" Erwin flew into the room and crashed headlong into the table, scattering Isabel's carefully stacked spells all over the floor.

Isabel blew out a breath. "We need our flat back. Now."

I couldn't have agreed more.

12

L ady Harper didn't show up at breakfast the next morning. Vance insisted on an early start, and I agreed that the quicker we got this excursion into the woods over with, the better. Isabel, too. I wasn't sure she'd actually slept; I'd walked into the meeting room at dawn to find her making a new batch of spells, her hands stained with chalk and her eyes underscored with shadows.

"Are you sure we'll need all these?" I slotted more explosive spells into my inside pocket. Isabel's point-and-shoot spells were shaped like pencils and were fairly compact, but I didn't want to accidentally blow up the Hemlock witches' forest just by stepping inside. Though if they'd endured this long without a faerie leaving so much as a scratch on them, their trees must be made of solid iron. I also grabbed as many healing spells as possible, hoping I wouldn't need them.

"You never know." Isabel put away her phone, yawning. "I've let the coven members know where we're going."

"I just heard from the night patrols." Vance walked into the meeting room to join us. "Three mages reported seeing several figures in black and followed them for half a mile before realising they were necromancers."

"Figures." I snorted. "You'd think they'd have noticed sooner. The necromancers aren't coordinated enough to climb off a roof."

Vance had selected three swords of his own, which he sheathed in a weapons belt securely fastened underneath his coat. Lady Harper hadn't outright said his mage powers would be ineffective inside the Hemlock Coven's forest, but after our experiences in Faerie, I didn't blame him for not taking chances.

Isabel, meanwhile, wore dark colours rather than her usual bright attire. Though her baggy coat seemed unremarkable, she'd sewn extra pockets inside to conceal an array of spells and a few iron daggers for good measure.

"I put Drake in charge of security at the manor," Vance said. "If anyone tries to get in, they'll have a dozen of our most powerful mages to contend with."

A worried undercurrent to his words betrayed his knowledge that magical prowess didn't matter in the face of those bullets. Nobody, if struck, would walk away alive.

Vance transported us to the back of half-blood territory, bypassing the gate altogether. We landed near a sprawling tree near the spot where the guard's body had been found. Not a droplet of blood remained, though with the number of predatory fae living in the forest, that wasn't exactly a reassurance.

"The Hemlock Coven have lived in the forest all along without anyone knowing except Lady Harper?" I spoke to distract myself from the grisly mental image. "And the faeries are cool with that?"

"The coven withdrew entirely from public life a long time ago," said Vance. "After the invasion, I inferred from Lady

Harper that they wanted no part in the new world order, and when the mages took power, they refused to join in the partnership and allowed themselves to be forgotten entirely. It seems she omitted to tell any of us that they appear to be under some kind of curse which prevents them leaving their forest."

"I didn't even know that," said Isabel. "You'd think someone would have passed on word to the other coven leaders."

"Yeah." I gave her a worried glance. "Sure about this? Last chance to turn back."

"I'm sure," said Isabel. "If you have any tips for surviving a faerie forest, though, I'm all ears."

"Firstly, don't step off the path."

Isabel's gaze drifted across the thick trees. "Slight problem. I don't think there *is* a path."

"Oh." She seemed to be right. "All right. Secondly, don't get split up. If it's anything like Faerie, the forest will do everything it can to trick us into going our separate ways. Don't go wandering off, no matter whether you see a shiny light, or the spectre of a dead loved one, or anything."

"Spectre?" she echoed. "An actual ghost or just an illusion?"

"Probably the latter," I amended. "The Grey Vale's teeming with spirits, but that's because they have nowhere to go. It's mind-trickery that's the biggest threat. I got lured into a dozen traps in my first week alone because I kept running into illusions of my parents." I clamped my mouth shut as a thousand worries came cascading down on me. I'd sworn never to bring my loved ones near Faerie, but at least the Grey Vale responded to my magic, to some degree, now that I held my talisman. This forest was an unknown. "Anyway, if you feel the sudden urge to do anything that seems irrational, it's probably them. Don't go near water, either. That's how nixies and kelpies get you."

"Oh, let's get it over with." Isabel held out one of the knives she'd selected from Vance's weapons room, her hand trembling on the hilt. "We'll deal with whatever we find. They'll all be weak against iron, right?"

"Yep." I ducked under an overhanging branch. "Not the witches, but unless they're working *with* the faeries, that won't be an issue. Which is still a possibility, but since it's the faeries' fault the Hemlock witches are trapped inside the forest, I can't imagine they're the best of friends."

"Exactly," said Isabel. "The Hemlock Coven wouldn't ally with the faeries. Even Lady Harper would have told us if that was the case."

I didn't quite have her level of faith in the scheming old mage. The forest was entirely too reminiscent of the Vale, and another thought entered my mind as we climbed over the sprawling tree roots at the entrance. "And the hunters? They used the witches' glyphs, didn't they? What're the odds of them being on the same side? Maybe the Hemlock witches changed their minds about not wanting power."

"I doubt it," said Vance. "The Hemlock Coven were easily on a level with the strongest mages when they disappeared. They wouldn't need to use weak humans to achieve their goals and would never have the need for bullets like the ones we encountered. They have more efficient ways of killing, from what Lady Harper told me."

"And there's no way to send word of our arrival."

"No," said Vance, "but I'm sure they'll sense our presence, if her claims about their response to intruders is accurate."

Yeah. A shiver ran over me, though part of it was due to the familiar chill that told me this part of the forest had been claimed by Unseelie. "Let's see what they're made of."

With no path to follow, I picked a direction at random

once we'd crossed the swathe of tree roots marking the entrance. Not a beam of sunlight penetrated the gloom; the Winter fae held sway here, and the biting wind made me glad I'd worn my jacket. Trees were coated in frost, and shrivelled leaves crunched beneath my steps. This forest might not be the Grey Vale, but they shared some similarities, with the added confusing of having to guess which tricks were down to the faeries and which were due to the Hemlock Coven reacting to trespassers in their home.

Ten minutes walking in a straight line found us at a dead end. All we'd encountered so far were a nest of miniature trolls, who immediately ran away when I offered to introduce them to Helena, and a bloodthirsty redcap I'd been forced to decapitate. Leaving a trail of blood hadn't been on my plan, especially in an area claimed by the Unseelie, but not even the banshee made an appearance. Most fae were afraid of the blue light radiating from my sword, and the ones we ran into were child's play compared to the horrors of the Grey Vale.

Famous last words, Ivy.

Sure enough, as we rounded a corner, we were plunged into total darkness. "Finally, a challenge."

Vance's voice spoke from just behind me. "I have a light spell, but it isn't working."

"Nor's mine," whispered Isabel.

"Shit." I held up my blade, my body tensing when I saw nothing of the usual blue glow haloing its edges. "Well, I did ask for it."

The forest turned off my talisman? Cursing, I pulled out my phone instead and nearly dropped it when a giggle rang out from nearby.

"Who's there?" I shone my phone's light around, and the banshee came into view, sitting on a tree stump with her bare feet lifted off the ground.

"What are you doing?" I pointed my sword at her, using my other hand to shine my phone light over the ground to check for booby traps..

"I'm offering to be your guide, humans." She bounded upright. "I know you seek the Hemlock Coven."

I tensed. "And just how do you know that?"

"I've been following you ever since you arrived. I suspected you might respond with hostility if I revealed myself to you."

"Yeah, can't imagine why." I swivelled to Vance, my phone's light painting his face half in shadow. "I don't believe her. Do you?"

"I think we should follow her," Isabel whispered.

"What? This is clearly a trap."

"Don't forget she helped us the last time," she murmured. "I think we should take our chances rather than stumbling around in the dark."

True, but the banshee didn't have to launch a direct attack when this place was a deathtrap all on its own. Unlike us, she was clearly familiar with its winding trails and hidden crevices.

Vance spoke. "You will take us to the Hemlock Coven. If I suspect you are misleading us, you will survive long enough to regret that choice, but no more."

"You too?" The banshee admittedly had a better chance of navigating this place than any of us did, but putting our safety in her hands was like sticking my hand into a manticore's mouth and hoping it didn't bite.

"If she's unwise enough to betray us, I'll let you take the first stab at her."

"Well, when you put it like that..." I turned to our grinning companion and resigned myself to giving her the benefit of the doubt. "We'll accept, *if* you agree to lead us where we need to go and not let us go astray."

"I cannot be responsible for any trickery the forest may play on you," she said. "That is beyond my power."

"Right." The forest made me jumpy enough that I'd probably end up decapitating her before we reached the coven regardless of whether she turned out to be on our side or not. "Let's go."

Having a guide didn't make the forest any less of a maze. The darkness persisted, and the banshee didn't seem to care for our comfort as she waded through patches of briar, shimmied between trees that grew far too close together for any of us to fit through, and jumped over ponds that soaked us to the knees. The setup felt distinctly like one of the tests the Grey Vale sometimes threw at unwitting trespassers, but in the Vale, everything glowed with its own silvery light, even in the dark corners. This blackness appeared more like a spell had been placed over the forest to ensure no outside light ever penetrated. Not even my sword, though weirdly, my phone's light still functioned as normal.

"Do the witches live like moles, or do they have a special lair only they can see in?" I tripped over yet another tree root, steadying myself against Vance.

"Were you asking me?" The banshee bounded ahead, for all the world like a little kid at a theme park. "I've never been inside their lair. My kind aren't welcome."

Suspicion reared its head. "So how is it you know your way around their forest?"

"My power brings me to liminal spaces," she said. "The cracks between realms, the dark corners in which we once hid from human eyes."

"Liminal spaces," I said slowly, thinking of the strange between-realm I'd found Fionn sleeping in, where three spirit paths overlapped. Lady Harper had spoken of liminal spaces, too. "Are we inside one of those right now?"

"Of course we are," said the banshee. "The spirit lines hide many secrets, and all the paths awakened when the Sidhe came."

"You weren't even born then." Not that she *talked* like a typical sixteen-year-old.

"All death fae know these things, mortal." She skipped over a fallen branch, laughter trailing in her wake.

"I take it back," said Isabel quietly. "I don't trust her at all."

"Bit late for that now." We'd already placed our trust in her hands when we'd let her take the lead. "We should have checked the spirit line map before we came in here. I bet we walked straight into a key point without noticing."

A place where two spirit lines crossed was a site of immense power, and if the forest existed at a crossroads between realms, it explained how the half-faeries had been able to build such an expansive territory without interceding on the world around them. Their magic existed in a bubble, inside a crack between realms—but so, apparently, did the Hemlock Coven.

Darkness persisted as we walked and made it necessary to put all my attention on my path and not on our slippery companion. Somehow, the banshee was always absent when we ran into one of the forest's tricks, but after we'd sent our foes packing, she was always waiting around a corner with a smile on her mouth as though we shared an amusing secret.

By the time we'd dodged a persistent will o' the wisp, thwarted more fire imps, and narrowly avoided a nest of flesh-eating plants, I was fuming. "Are you leading us into this shit on purpose?"

"No, humans," the banshee said in deceptively bland tones. "The forest is friendlier to the wild fae than it is to your kind."

"Can't you tell them to go away?" said Isabel, who'd left her cool behind somewhere a mile or so back. Her voice was as tense as a wire.

The banshee merely giggled and disappeared around another corner.

As we continued, the trees grew ever closer until their branches formed an arch-like construction over our heads that felt like walking through a tunnel. As the tallest, Vance had to duck under the lowest branches, while Isabel and I squeezed in behind him.

On the other side, luminescent spider webs stretched between the tree branches. My spine prickled at the reminder of a spidery fae lurking in an old train station and feasting on unwitting humans. These webs glowed an odd pale green and formed intricate patterns that at some angles, kind of looked like… well, writing.

Or glyphs.

I stopped. Isabel walked into me. "You okay, Ivy?"

"Does that look like writing to you?" I pointed to the web. "Those are glyphs."

"It's a spell." She extended a hesitant hand towards the mass of swirling webs but stopped short of touching them. "A powerful one."

"I wouldn't advise you to touch that." The banshee's voice rang out from somewhere amid the swathe of webbing.

"I thought not." Isabel withdrew her hand. "Did the coven set up these?"

No answer came from the banshee, but I suspected the answer was 'yes'. We walked a little further, eyes open for any signs of the person responsible for creating these glyphs. We must be close.

I turned back to Isabel—but she wasn't there. Neither was Vance. I whipped around, squinting into the trees. "Er. Banshee? Alison?"

Silence.

"Great." I held still, listening out. Not a sound disturbed the silence, so I walked on, hoping I was heading towards my companions and not away from them. Whether the witches were behind this trickery or not, I'd be wise to follow Faerie logic and assume every path came with a trap, a trick, or a bloodthirsty monster. Or all three.

A high wail cut through the silence, raising the hairs on my arms. The voice cried on and on, strident and terrified. Like a young child.

It's a trick. No child would wander into these woods, but the witches seemingly weren't above using classic faerie mind tricks against their prey.

I kept going until the sound faded into the background, yet I saw no sign of the others, only ancient trees that grew so close together that I I had to walk at an awkward crouch. I held my sword extended in front of me so I didn't walk into any branches. I might not be able to see its light, but its sharp edge would spear anything that tried to jump me.

Soon a light glinted ahead, not luminescent like the webs but reflective, like moonlight on water. I ducked underneath a branch and found the light came from a small pond surrounded by a cluster of gnarled trees. Their ghostly reflections swam in the water as I approached, holding out my sword.

I stumbled. My weapon felt heavier, as though weighed down. My arms ached, my legs burning as though I'd lost all physical strength. My feet touched the edge of the pond, and I caught sight of my reflection.

And stared. The person looking back at me *was* me, but smaller and skinnier, wearing a school uniform I hadn't seen in years.

No wonder I'd struggled to lift Helena: I was me, but younger. Twelve or thirteen. The age I'd been when I was taken to Faerie. The girl's sad eyes watched me, pleading, from the distant past.

I closed my own eyes, breathing hard. Gritting my teeth, I drove the point of my blade towards the pool's surface.

The sword passed through the water like through smoke. My eyes flickered open again. My younger self continued to watch me, standing on a path dappled with grey leaves. The Grey Vale.

I knew before I looked down that when I did, I'd find a carpet of silver beneath my own feet. Another classic faerie trick.

When my head snapped up, the pond disappeared, replaced by a winding path between trees draped in silver and frozen in time. I lifted my blade, no longer struggling to maintain my grip.

My feet began to walk.

Hey! I held back, but my own limbs disobeyed me. My feet moved against my will, as if I'd used a tracking spell to relive someone else's past in full colour and with the sound switched on. I might as well have been a spectator. When I tried to speak, no words escaped my mouth.

Movement in the bushes. I lifted the blade in a hand that definitely *wasn't* mine, larger and gloved in some kind of black material. My arm, too, was covered in what appeared to be armour. I was no longer the kid I'd been in the last illusion, but much taller, my sword lightweight in my hands. Yet its glow told me I was the wielder. Blue light shone, both from the talisman and from my own skin, as I brought the blade down in an arc into the throat of the unfortunate creature that had tried to ambush me. Satisfaction flooded me, but the emotion didn't belong to me. The sudden surge of dark, twisting thoughts that swam through my mind weren't mine either.

Please, no. Please no...

The sword glowed brighter, illuminating the thick blood dripping down the blade. Leaving the beast lying dead on the path, I continued to walk with long, confident strides. At the path's end, a large castle stood in a clearing. Huge, furred beasts prowled at the edges. Hellhounds. Which meant…

Everything that remained of my own awareness shrank into helpless terror. I didn't need to see my reflection to know whose eyes I watched through.

Avalin.

13

I—or rather—Avalin walked past the hellhounds and continued to approach the castle. His fortress was as huge and forbidding as ever, yet somehow less vast than it had seemed to me as a human. Through a Sidhe's eyes, the world was clearer, my senses keen and sharp. I smelled the forest, the ever-present stench of rot mingling with the residue of fear from the human captives in the castle. I heard their agonised screams like they came from right behind me, as my talisman's glow brightened, feeding on their terror and pain.

And I felt the emptiness, the soul-sucking emptiness that persisted no matter how much pain I fed into the blade in my hands.

No. Not me. This was an elaborate trap, however convincing it might be. The question was, how could I escape from this illusion? I must still be in the forest somewhere, but Avalin's thoughts and sensations had overwhelmed me so thoroughly that Ivy might as well have not existed at all. I tried to slam a barrier down in front of Avalin's inner thoughts, but his unpleasant ruminations remained in the background, and I felt the cold sucking at my bones, a constant torturous reminder of what I'd lost.

What *he'd* lost.

Fuck me, this was creepy. Not just being in a Sidhe's mind, but that the witches had managed to conjure up an illusion so convincing as to encompass thoughts as well as sensations. Mostly, I was aware of how *alien* the person whose body I occupied was, and yet how painfully vulnerable he truly was under all the armour and bravado. If this was what it felt like when the magic was stripped from a Sidhe lord, I was eternally glad I'd been born human. The Sidhe of Summer and Winter couldn't have come up with a worse punishment for faeries who broke their laws than stripping away their magic and condemning them to a slow, agonising death. Even the fae cast out into the mortal world didn't suffer as profoundly. Their power waned over time, but it wasn't torn out altogether. Severing a limb would have been less painful.

As I reached the castle, someone else approached from behind. I swung around, lifting my blade to alight upon another male Sidhe, also armoured, also very familiar. His pointed face was framed with dark hair, and his green eyes glittered with amusement.

Holy shit. *Velkas.* Last time I'd seen him he'd been wearing Avalin's armour, stolen from his corpse. Now he wore light-green armour in the style of the Summer Sidhe and carried the life-drinker sword. Glyphs travelled up and down its length, mirroring the sheen of my own sword.

"What are you doing here?" Avalin did *not* sound pleased to see his old friend.

"Looking for you." Velkas rested a hand on the hilt of his sword as two hellhounds came slinking around the side of the castle to stand protectively beside their master. "You're still keeping these monstrosities? You know they don't belong to you."

"They obey me." Avalin rested a hand on a giant hound's head. "They are far more loyal than my fellow nobles."

Velkas grunted. "I thought you'd forgotten about them."

"Forgotten Winter?" Avalin gave a soft laugh. "Its absence fills my very bones."

"Then you'll know what I'm here to ask," said Velkas. "This realm is a poison. I want to get out."

"I've grown fond of it," I said—or rather, Avalin did. "Nobody bothers me here, aside from my pets."

"Really." Velkas's tone was flat. "Is that truly what you want to make of that talisman of yours? Fionn tells me you're using the suffering of lesser mortals to fuel your power, but you're made for more than that. We all are."

"I have no interest in any more of Fionn's games," said Avalin. "I imagine he wants his hellhounds back, and I cannot say I am willing to oblige."

"Are games all you desire?" he said. "What if I were to tell you that Fionn believes he has found a way for us to avenge ourselves upon Winter and Summer?"

"I'd say that it's a nice sentiment," said Avalin. "I have everything I need here."

"Lies do not become you, Lord Avalin," said Velkas. "You must know that you'll succumb to the poison of the Vale in time, or else one of your miserable captives will get the best of you."

"I know you came to recruit me, Lord Velkas." Avalin sounded bored. "I've heard the rumours, and I'm not inter-ested in forming a new Court with the same petty rules and regulations as Winter and Summer."

"There will be no Court." A smile twisted Velkas's mouth. "What Fionn proposes will see the realms themselves shake with the impact and the Courts dissolve into naught but smoke. That talisman of yours will be satiated for centuries to come, and you'll have everything the Winter Court ever denied you."

"I'm listening." The words left my mouth even as horror coursed through me—through Ivy. A reminder that somewhere, I was still here. Still alive.

And witnessing the conception of the invasion.

Heart racing, I leaned forward to better hear Velkas's words, but the view warped and twisted before my eyes. The Vale melted away, and I stood in front of the water's reflective surface once again. As if I'd never left. I dropped my gaze to my reflection, and the face that looked back at me was my own, adult self.

"The power is yours," whispered a voice from over my shoulder. "The magic that was once used to inflict great cruelty bows to you now. But are you sure you're its equal?"

"Yeah, I'm sure." To my intense relief, the words came out in my own voice. I could speak again. "The blade's mine. I won it. Twice over. Let me go."

In the pond's shimmering surface, two more figures appeared behind me. Both were ghostly, transparent, and painfully familiar.

Mum's eyes brimmed with sadness as she looked at the weapon in my hands. "What have they done to you, Ivy?"

My heart twisted. The Grey Vale had spent three years tormenting me with visions of my parents. The Sidhe had used my past as a weapon against me so many times that I'd been forced to lock away all but the most superficial memories of before the invasion. And yet the same tide of bitter emotion swept through me every damn time. I blinked tears from my eyes despite knowing deep within my heart that parents would never see what I'd become, what Faerie had made me.

"Nothing I do will change the past." I spoke the words to

the pond's surface rather than looking at my parents' ghostly faces. "I'm sorry."

"Isn't there?" Mum's voice hitched. "Isn't there a place where nobody truly dies?"

"No." I shook my head. "My parents have never been to the Vale. Whoever you are, they're gone."

"Then die," growled my mother.

Behind my reflection, the two ghosts vanished. In their place stood a large clawed beast with the face of a lion. Giant paws supported its huge furred body, while a crocodile's tail snapped behind and bat wings protruded from its shoulder blades. A chimera.

"Finally something I can stab." Fighting in an enclosed space wasn't ideal, but my body and soul cried out for a real battle. The sword's hilt was slippery in my hands, drenched in sweat, but my grip was steady. *Let's go.*

I kept an eye on the beast's huge mouth as I sidestepped, circling its vast body. The last one I'd battled had breathed fire, but the witches didn't want to set their own forest ablaze, surely.

When its jaw unhinged, I retaliated with a wide swipe, and its teeth snapped down on my sword. *Ow.* My shoulders jarred as I fought to pull the blade free. What the hell were its teeth made of, concrete? Cursing under my breath, I latched onto the sword with both hands and tugged harder. The beast's teeth didn't give

Time to try something new. I pushed instead of pulling, driving the blade against the chimera's teeth. I threw all my weight against the blade, forcing it up into the roof of the beast's mouth.

The chimera uttered a bellow of pain. Thick torrents of blood dripped onto the ground. In its death throes, it lashed out with a paw. Unable to dodge without letting go of my blade, I dropped to a crouch and felt its sharp claws gouge my cheek.

The weight on my sword vanished, and I fell back onto my rear. The beast had vanished as though it was made of smoke, leaving my sword suspended in the air. Breath rasped through my lungs. My cheek stung where the claw had pierced the skin, but when I looked up, I saw a thorny branch was the culprit, and no blood ran from my sword.

"Is it over yet?" I addressed the forest at large. "I'm kind of in a hurry, you know, and I'd appreciate it if you stopped with the cheap tricks."

A long-haired female figure bounded from behind a tree, bare feet splayed on the ground. The banshee. "You survived the Illusionist's Path."

"No thanks to you." I pushed to my feet, glaring at her. "Is this all a game to you?"

"I'm not the one playing games."

I brushed leafy fragments and dirt from my jeans. "Where in hell are Isabel and Vance?"

"I expect your companions are still on the path," she said with a wide smile. "Each of you will be tested individually."

"Including you?"

"I have already proven myself worthy. So have you. Others were not so lucky." She gestured at the surrounding trees.

I looked closer. Skeletal bodies were draped across the branches, bones picked clean. Nausea twisted my gut. I couldn't tell whether they were human or half-faerie, but I hoped their deaths had been painless.

"Yeah, I got it." My mind was still reeling from the vision and the subsequent fight. "How in hell did it know my past? Can the forest read minds?"

"Memories," said the banshee. "Certain experiences leave

an imprint both on us and on the world around us. The forest is capable of reading those memories."

The memories weren't mine, though. They'd been Avalin's, and I'd thought the witches hadn't left the forest since before the invasion. So how—?

The talisman. That was the one connecting factor. Had they read the memory from my *sword?* I couldn't think of any other way they could have possibly seen the inmost thoughts and emotions of a Sidhe Lord who'd surely never entered this forest himself. While I might have been glad that they hadn't read *my* mind, I really didn't like the idea of Avalin being known to a group of ancient witches whose own motives were decidedly murky.

I looked closer at the banshee. Behind her lay a door formed of gnarled wood that stretched between two trees.

"The Hemlock Coven are in there." She darted aside. "Go ahead."

"Hmm." I examined the knotted wood. A symbol was carved onto the door, etched in silvery green.

I sucked in a breath, readied my weapon and opened the door.

14

The space on the other side of the door resembled an overgrown cave. Roots snaked underfoot and faint light shone from the myriad spiderwebs strewn across the walls. *Wait. Not webs.* My heart jumped into my throat when they moved, revealing countless overlapping glyphs shifting and warping around one another like a giant tapestry. My eyes followed the movement and then snapped over to the wall. A head popped out and spoke in a rasping voice.

"You were a fool to come here alone." The head was followed by a short figure who barely came up to my knee.

"I didn't come here alone. My friends are here, and… who *are* you?" Asking 'what are you' wouldn't be wise, but the fur covering the creature's body indicated some kind of shapeshifter. Except most regular shifters didn't make a habit of disguising themselves as walls.

"It's rude to stare." The creature flashed sharp white teeth in a smile. "You're human."

"Yeah, I am. Where are the Hemlock witches?"

"You're lucky," said my companion. "The forest found you worthy of setting foot in the Hemlock witches' domain."

"Doesn't look like anyone's home."

The furred creature chuckled, gesturing to what I thought at first was a leafless tree, sprawling from floor to ceiling. Up close, I realised it wasn't wood but stone, resembling a sculpture that had been carved into a vaguely humanoid shape. The arms were contorted in a manner that made my own limbs twinge in sympathy. A number of other similar structures stood throughout the cave, resembling people who'd been turned to stone in the middle of some ghastly torture. Gnarled hands reached out from arms twisted at unnatural angles and faces sneered from craggy faces.

"What the fuck is this?" Were these people alive? Shit, were they the last people who'd visited the Hemlock witches, and this was to be my fate, too?

"Who is here?" The rasping voice undoubtedly came from the giant stone sculpture.

Dread trickled down my spine. My gaze locked on pitted eyes inset within the stone above a mouth like a pitch-black abyss. *Okay. Not a human. Not a prisoner, either.*

"I'm Ivy Lane." I swallowed against my dry throat. "Are you… a witch?"

"I am Cordelia of the Hemlock Coven, and you are trespassing." Her lips moved like scraping stones. My heart pounded a steady beat against my ribs as her eyes raked me up and down. "Are you the one they're talking about? The girl who conquered a god?"

What *was* she? The woman wasn't just old, she was ancient, more like the Lady of the Tree before she'd restored her youth and vitality than a regular, mortal human who'd lived a long and happy life. Her face was carved of stone in a very literal sense, wrinkles etching long lines across her face.

I'd seen two human prisoners in Avalin's castle put under an artificial ageing spell which made them age to a hundred and they didn't look anywhere near *this* decrepit. I couldn't tell if she merely resembled a rock or if she'd actually grown into it.

After a heartbeat, her words sank in. "What? How do you know me? Did you set up those traps?"

Cordelia's smile cracked the rock like a gaping wound. "The forest tested you, my child, as it does all trespassers."

My body tensed. "Where are my companions?"

Illusions were one thing. Living rocks claiming to be witches were another matter entirely, and now that I'd escaped their trickery only to find myself in a nightmare that rivalled one concocted by the Sidhe, all my worries for the others came roaring back.

"Who did you come here with?" enquired the witch.

"The new leader of the Laurel Coven and the head of the local Mage Lords." I hoped mentioning the two prominent supernatural leaders' titles would make the witches less inclined to allow their forest to eat us alive, but when faced with something as unnatural as this cave, all bets were off.

"The mages," she croaked. "They have no reason to concern themselves with us."

"Do you have any idea what's happening outside the forest?"

"Some. I hear rumours, but this forest is rooted deep in memories and rarely ventures into the present."

"What—what happened to you?" Call me insensitive, but whatever she'd been turned into didn't look in any way human. But she wasn't a faerie either, right?

"What happened to me?" She uttered a gravelly laugh that travelled down to my bones and made me fervently regret asking. "I, and the rest of my coven, were cursed, bound to the forest for the rest of our existence. We considered it a worthy sacrifice to make."

"Ah." I had zero clue whether it would help in the least if I offered my condolences. Likely not. "My allies are out there somewhere. If you're bound to the forest, can you sense where they are?"

"Your friends are alive, child."

The knot in my chest loosened. "Good. We came here because it's an emergency. Someone's killing off supernaturals—" I broke off as the rock shifted and Cordelia's head turned, her pitted eyes examining me thoroughly.

"Interesting," she growled. "You're still human, but something about you is... different."

"You don't say?" Oops. I should probably put my filter back on, but the way her head protruded from the rock was so grotesque that it was hard to focus on anything else. "I'm a human with faerie magic. That's probably weird even by your standards."

"Your magic. Do you use it?"

"Yes. Why?" Come to think of it, my sword's glow had been notably muted since I'd come into the forest. I hadn't tapped into its magic consciously and now did not seem an ideal time to start, but part of me wondered if the forest held some level of resistance against the Sidhe. The Hemlock witches had survived the invasion, hadn't they?

She grinned with teeth like shards of black stone. "Normally, humans who attempt to take on the power of the gods meet unfortunate ends."

Power of the gods? "I won this magic. I made a bargain and took it from the Sidhe lord Avalin. You know that, if you've been poking around in my memories."

"Your talisman carries memories that don't belong to you. You are entangled in magic beyond your lifespan, and yet it undeniably answers to your command. You've even used their language."

"You mean Invocations?"

"Yes… I suspect that the talisman itself aided you in reading them."

I glanced down at the symbols carved on Helena's hilt. That made sense, but it was also clear that the Sidhe lords were far from the only powerful magic users in existence. Take this forest, wrapped in magic so ancient and deadly that even a Sidhe might become entangled in its webs.

"You've asked me questions. Now it's my turn." I pushed ahead before I lost my nerve. "That vision the forest showed me. You saw it, too. Were Avalin and Velkas discussing the invasion? People have wondered how it started for decades."

"The forest remembers," said Cordelia. "We are all marked by history, though humans have a tendency to erase theirs through sheer carelessness."

"And… the Sidhe?" The ancient witches had undoubtedly played a role in the fight, but had they encountered Fionn? Did they know how he'd ended up imprisoned in that tomb, locked in an eternal slumber?

"The Sidhe are more ancient than your human mind can comprehend."

"*You're* human," I said. "Aren't you?"

Cordelia grinned again. "That depends on your definition of human."

I shuddered. These witches weren't faeries, certainly, but their longevity outmatched any regular humans even if it didn't stretch for centuries like the Sidhe. The only person I knew close to their age was… "Lady Harper. You've met."

"Correct."

"You worked… together." I scrambled to get a grip on my spiralling thoughts. "Ah, Lady Harper had a message for you.

She said you were fools to sacrifice as much as you did. And not to assume the past would lie buried."

"That," she said, "is nothing I haven't heard before. Tell her I'm disappointed."

"I'm not your messenger," I said. "The truth is, I came here because the leader of the Laurel Coven was murdered the other day, and now they're trying to kill her replacement. And the leaders of the mages and half-bloods, too."

"How very ambitious," growled Cordelia. "The coven leader was Francine Blackwood, was she not?"

"Yes. They shot her, with a magical bullet that somehow negated whatever spells she was using to protect herself."

"Impossible," she growled. "Unless Francine stopped using the protective spells which have kept our kind safe for centuries, no simple bullet of human creation could have killed her."

"Believe me, it did," I said. "They nearly killed Isabel and me when they took out the wards keeping the faeries out of our house, too. I don't know any spell that can stop witch wards from working like that."

The old witch shook her stone-like head. "Nothing of human creation can harm a coven leader. All of us have protections built into our blood that cannot be undone with mere trickery."

"But—does Isabel, too?"

"The gift passes with the ascension of a witch to the title of coven leader. If your friend was chosen as worthy, the gift now resides in her blood."

"She was chosen," I confirmed, "but the gift, whatever it was, didn't stop the hunters from killing the previous leader. Why?"

"Because they used another means than a simple bullet to reduce her defences first."

"Used… what, exactly?" My blood chilled. "Isabel needs to hear this."

"Greta," the witch growled at a nearby rock. "Find the young witch and bring her here."

The rock moved, revealing the humped back of another witch. Rising upward, the witch bared craggy teeth in a grin before her face withdrew into the rock. *Yikes.* Whatever that was about, I decided not to ask.

"Uh," I said. "You were saying the bullets couldn't have harmed Francine because she was protected. What if they can turn off wards? The hunters did that at my house, and the same with the wards outside the witches' storeroom. That's the place they murdered Francine."

"Yes," Cordelia said in her gravelly voice. "That, I fear, is the result of a force that should never have resurfaced, much less fell into in the hands of foolish humans."

"What force?" Damn. She'd said the protections on a coven leader were immune to anything created by humans. She hadn't mentioned *non*-humans. "We're talking some kind of magical object. Like a…"

"A talisman that once belonged to the Sidhe."

My hands clenched around my own talisman's hilt. "You knew. You knew what was causing this, didn't you?"

"I knew the ring resurfaced, yes," she growled. "Its magic carries a distinct taint that we can sense even within our forest."

"This talisman is a ring, not a sword?"

"Yes, an ancient faerie artefact that was thought lost after the invasion," she replied. "Any magic that comes near the talisman is instantly dissolved. Wards, glyphs… even the power inside that sword you hold in your hands, Ivy."

My mouth dropped open. "It can block my talisman?"

If the ring was also a creation of the Sidhe's, it was no wonder that it had been potent enough to counter the protections on a coven leader. Our flat's wards had stood no chance.

"Yes," said Cordelia. "The ring originally belonged to the Summer Court before it was stolen by someone who never took the title of lord, and who belongs to neither Summer nor Winter."

"Who..." But I knew. The one faerie I'd met who belonged to neither Court and who possessed enough power to challenge both. "Fionn."

15

Cordelia watched me with those deep, pitted eyes. "You know of him, Ivy. The Huntsman and his army."

"Were you the one who sealed him away?" Whoever had imprisoned him in that tomb had been able to use Invocations and also touch iron without ill effect. An impossibility, I thought… until I'd met the Hemlock Coven.

"No, we did not." My shoulders tensed when she leaned forward, her pit-like eyes studying me. "You met him, Ivy, didn't you?"

Ah, shit. If I confessed that I'd been partly responsible for the leader of the Wild Hunt walking free, I might never leave this forest. Calder was more to blame than I was, but the fact remained that I'd let Fionn slip through my fingers together with his army.

The witch laughed, the sound echoing like stones falling into an empty canyon. "Your silence is pointless. I know the Hunt awakened. This forest lies upon a spirit line, and we knew at once that the Huntsman had returned."

"We're on one of *those* spirit lines? Near where the Hunt

rode?" I spun around, as if Fionn and his horsemen might come riding through the forest at any instant. "That'd have been nice to know sooner."

"We are a long way from the key point in which you found him, mortal."

"Might he have been the one to steal the ring?" If so, I would have assumed he'd use it himself, not pass it on to a group of magicless humans. He'd once commanded an army of hellhounds and creepy horsemen who didn't seem to be alive or dead. The hunters were a step down in terms of allies, to say the least. What was his game?

"I know nothing of what became of the ring after the invasion, human," she said, "but I do know that it can negate any spell and break through any ward, no matter its strength."

"You specifically said *after* the invasion. How about before?"

The Sidhe blasted the wards down and killed everyone inside. Vance's voice spoke in my head, and my heart gave a quiver of dread. Was that how the Sidhe had defeated the mages? An item that negated all magic could easily decide the outcome of a war.

Maybe it did.

A chill took hold of me. Nobody was a match for the Sidhe aside from the mages, and they'd been absolutely decimated during the invasion. Four of five Mage Lords had been slaughtered, and with so few surviving witnesses, it was near impossible for anyone to know for sure which Sidhe had been involved. Not Avalin. He'd been too busy kidnapping humans to pay attention.

Fionn, though, had started the invasion. Had killed the Mage Lords. Now, at last, I knew how he'd accomplished his goals.

"You are right to be afraid, child," croaked the old woman.

"The invasion wrought permanent change upon this realm. If the ring has indeed resurfaced, I fear worse may lie ahead."

Fuck. Fionn had presumably lost the ring before he'd been imprisoned, but had the hunters found it by accident or had Fionn handed it over to them himself? If so, why?

"And the Sidhe?" I asked. "Didn't they notice someone stole it? You said the ring was Summer's, once."

"A long time ago," she growled. "It is hardly the first artefact the Sidhe have misplaced."

No kidding. My talisman, once, had presumably belonged to the Courts. And the Sidhe might not have guessed Fionn had brought the ring into the mortal realm either. To most, humans weren't worthy of consideration, while even the half-faeries' Chief wasn't welcome in their realm.

"So how do we get rid of it?" I asked. "Throw it into a fiery volcano?"

Cordelia offered a blank look in response. "If you ask whether the ring can be destroyed, that lies outside of the scope of our knowledge."

That's not good. And a reminder that even the Hemlock witches had limits, and that some secrets were restricted to the Sidhe alone.

The scrape of wood against stone made me turn back to the door. Isabel entered the cave. When she saw me, relief flitted across her face and swiftly morphed into alarm at the sight of the sculpted figure of the ancient witch within the rock.

"You're... you're..." Isabel almost sat down on a rock, then caught herself in time. Good job, because the rock was probably alive.

"Yes," Cordelia growled. "I am Cordelia Hemlock."

Isabel edged closer, her body trembling. "I'm Isabel. Leader of the Laurel Coven."

"You are." The old witch gave Isabel an appraising look. "You're younger than most who are chosen as coven leaders."

"Francine didn't expect to die so soon." Isabel straightened upright to look into the witch's pitted eyes. "Can you help us?"

"That would depend on what you're asking for. My coven is bound to the forest and cannot interfere in human affairs."

"But she knows how the hunters killed Francine," I added. "And how they shut down our wards. They have a talisman, a ring, which can negate any magic. It was stolen from the Summer Court, and I think… I think the Sidhe used it in the invasion."

Isabel gasped. "A—ring?"

"I'm right, aren't I?" I added to Cordelia. "A talisman that can negate anyone's magic is a double-edged sword." Even for Fionn. Maybe that was why he'd handed it over to a bunch of inept humans.

"Clever," growled the witch. "Unfortunately, I cannot say for sure who currently holds the ring. I can only give my suspicions."

"Hang on, fill me in a little," said Isabel. "If the ring belonged to the faeries, how did the hunters get hold of it?"

"No clue, but it's the only thing that might have negated the protective spells Francine had on her," I said. "Also, according to her, you have them, too."

"I do?" asked Isabel uncertainly. "I… I haven't yet. I was told they'd kick in at some point, but… I don't know. I'm also not clear on the effects. Francine never had the chance to tell me."

"If she didn't expect to die soon, she might have been waiting for a later date," said the witch. "You'll find no ordinary spells intended to cause harm will have any effect on you, and you'll have enhanced speed and stamina."

Isabel's eyes rounded. "I thought she used glyphs."

"Glyphs are imperfect and temporary. The coven's protection lives within your very blood."

Isabel spoke hesitantly. "Is it the same with you? Is that why you gave up your life?"

"Very astute," said Cordelia. "The answer, however, is no. Our position came about due to a set of circumstances that I sincerely hope will never be repeated. You'll doubtless face similar dilemmas in your time as coven leader... assuming you live that long."

Isabel's hands fisted at her sides. I wished I could offer her reassurance, but I didn't know the faintest thing about this supposed coven leader protection, nor why it hadn't kicked in for Isabel yet. It was obvious she'd hoped the Hemlock witches would offer her guidance, but these people were far more than witches. The Hemlock Coven had no reason to fear the likes of Fionn coming back.

"There's something else," I said to Cordelia. "The hunters... the people who killed Francine, they left us a message written in code. It's based on your glyphs."

"Did they now?" she asked. "What did the words say, child?"

"They warned of something Lady Harper called the Rite of the Devourer," I said. "On the solstice. Tomorrow."

A ripple travelled up the rock as Cordelia's head protruded, her eyes raking me up and down. "The rite? If these foolish humans intend to attempt the ritual, they will die in the process."

"What exactly does it summon?" I asked. "Lady Harper told us you'd explain."

A chuckle vibrated through the rock, and Isabel and I edged closer to each other.

"That's for the summoner to find out, at their own risk. The ancient witch clans used similar rituals to interact with spirits, but they knew that other *entities* might be listening, too."

"Entities?" Honestly, it was no wonder she and Lady Harper had formed an alliance. They were like two cryptic peas in a single irritating pod. "Like what? Hellhounds? Fae?"

She gave a laugh. "Think bigger… much bigger."

"Gods." My mouth went dry. "We're talking about gods."

Did they know the other god had awakened? If they'd been aware of Fionn's return, they might have sensed the dragon stir, too. The Rite of the Devourer didn't refer to *that* god, though—right?

The old witch surveyed both of us. "The Sidhe's attack upon your realm had many effects, including exposing liminal spaces long forgotten by humans. Eraenar, I imagine, is not the only god to have been disturbed."

Eraenar. She does know.

"It's not him, is it?" My hands curled into fists. "They're summoning a god. As if the instant-kill bullets and magic-destroying ring weren't enough."

"You know which it is, don't you?" Isabel pressed.

"Their attempts will not succeed, and you would both be considerably happier not knowing which entity they seek to expose."

"Try me." My body and mind warred, the desire to know my enemy fetching up against the primal instinct that urged me to get the hell away from anything that strayed remotely close to the word 'god'.

Cordelia said nothing, but the shifting webbing around the cave began to move faster. Glyphs peeled back from the wall, revealing what appeared to be a tunnel leading off the main cave.

Isabel and I trod closer, trying to see inside. Shimmering glyphs covered the opening—which wasn't a tunnel at all but a vast open space of yawning emptiness like a starless sky.

Isabel tripped back, a hand pressed to her mouth. My legs locked into place and a trickle of cold sweat ran down my back. Within the emptiness floated a gigantic, furred head, the size of a small car and covered with thick black fur. Its body, equally vast, was suspended within an abyss wreathed in fog. Icy energy pulsed outward, making my teeth chatter. I had little doubt that the power contained within the sleeping beast could topple mountains and crush cities, yet it slumbered on, oblivious both to us and to the cave of witches whose dwelling concealed its prison.

A whimpering noise came from Isabel. She'd backed against the cave wall, near the door leading out into the forest and away from the monster.

I ran over to her, took her arm, and we ran out of the Hemlock witches' cave.

The door slammed behind us. My breath escaped in a rush, and I steadied myself against a tree without a care for whether it turned out to be a person in disguise. "Holy fuck."

Isabel sank onto a tree root and gulped. "Is that why they're imprisoned in here? Their magic's keeping that... *thing* caged?"

"Looks that way." I shuddered, the imprint of those shifting glyphs replaying against my eyelids. "Guess we aren't getting any help from them. Though if them staying inside the forest is what's stopping that creature waking up and escaping into our world, I'm good with it."

"Yeah, me too." Isabel shuddered. "And—the hunters are trying to reach that monster? With the ritual?"

"You'd think the Hemlock Coven would be able to stop them." We didn't have all the pieces yet, but it was plain to see that the hunters were in way over their heads and meddling with ancient magical forces that no human could possibly be a match for.

Isabel rose upright on shaky legs. "Ah… which is the way out?"

"And where's Vance?" Now that we were out of sight of that monster, worry for Vance took root inside me. The witches had brought Isabel to my side, but Vance wasn't as valuable to them, and they plainly cared little for the mages. Except perhaps for Lady Harper. "Where's that bloody banshee when we need her?"

"When did you last see her?" asked Isabel.

"She's the one who pointed me to this place." I gestured to the door to the Hemlock Coven's cave. "Guess she did know where she was going."

Vance could handle himself, I knew that, but the forest was as inscrutable as ever. Without our guide, I could only guess at the way out, but the Hemlock Coven's professed control over their forest made me certain that if they wanted rid of us, they'd hasten to show us the way out.

"I came this way." Isabel gestured vaguely to the south. "I can remember part of the route, I think."

"Glad one of us does. The trickery had better be over. I'm not getting split up again."

"I don't think the Hemlock witches have any reason to test us again," Isabel said. "I imagine they want us to leave."

"In one piece, hopefully."

Vance. I called his name as I walked, stopping to reach for the glyph on my shoulder. I hesitated, unsure if summoning him to my side would trigger some kind of trickery. If he was still trapped in one of the forest's illusions, he might not even have access to his mage powers.

Screw it. I nudged down my collar and pressed my fingertips to the mark.

"What's that?" Isabel peered at my shoulder. "Oh—you and Vance are linked. I forgot."

"It's not working." The mark was supposed to flare up

when I touched it, but it remained dead, grey as the wards the hunters had taken out. *With the ring.*

"I bet the Hemlocks don't want rival covens using magic in their forest." Isabel reached for my arm and gave a reassuring squeeze. "It's okay. It doesn't mean anything happened to him."

Vance. To distract myself, I recalled Cordelia's comment about Isabel's coven magic. "We haven't updated them recently. The glyphs, I mean. But they aren't permanent, not like a coven leader's marks."

Her expression shadowed. "No. I haven't… I was going to ask Francine how the whole thing works, but we didn't get long enough with her."

"Sorry. I shouldn't have asked so many questions. I hoped we'd get longer."

"It's not your fault," Isabel insisted. "We had to find out if she saw her killers. That was more important than my—my insecurities about being coven leader."

"Bullshit." Now it was my turn to give her arm a squeeze. "You had every right to ask all the questions you wanted, as her successor."

She blinked, her eyes glistening. "I—I don't want to talk about this where the Hemlock witches can hear every word we say."

"Of course." Guilt writhed in my chest as we began walking again. I hadn't meant to pull the scabs off the fresh wounds of Francine's death coupled with Isabel's unexpected ascension to coven leader, but I didn't believe for a minute that she was unequal to the job. Isabel was the best witch I knew. Cordelia didn't count. She and her fellow witches had closed the door on humanity a long time ago.

I quickened my pace when we spied a patch of luminescent light indicated the spiderwebs that marked the area where we'd initially got split up. Seeing movement amid the trees, I pointed my sword at the shifting shadows then lowered the blade.

"Vance." I ran to him, relief crashing down on me as I breathed in his familiar scent and buried my face in his chest.

He stroked my hair. "I knew you'd get yourself into trouble."

"Speak for yourself." Aside from the leaves and twigs tangled in his coat and hair, it didn't look like the forest had done him too much damage. "We need to get out of here."

Vance released me. "Did you already speak to the Hemlock witches?"

"Yeah. You won't believe what we just saw."

"Tell me on the way out," he said. "I can't teleport in here. I tried. We'll have to go the long route."

"I figured."

I filled him in on our conversation with the old witch as we made our way back through the dark trees. I didn't mention the content of the visions I'd seen, not wanting to revisit those images with the forest's inhabitants potentially listening in, but I figured that anyone present here surely knew of the beast that lay sleeping within. Held captive by the Hemlock Coven's magic.

If it had taken the collective power of every witch in the Hemlock Coven to seal the beast away and they'd paid such a high cost, one would think a simple ritual conducted by humans wouldn't have a hope of summoning the same monster into the human world. But if Fionn was behind this scheme, and backed up by a magic-killing ring, the notion seemed a lot more plausible. The witches had all but confirmed he was involved. Though while it would certainly make sense for him to want the supernatural leaders off the playing field, why not use the ring himself? A bunch of non-magical humans with an irrational grudge against the mages were hardly its equal. No, we were still missing a piece or two of the puzzle comprising Fionn's latest scheme.

When I'd finished my account, we fell into silence until the sight of sunbeams coming through the branches spurred us on towards the exit.

"Do you think it is him?" Isabel asked quietly. She'd hardly spoken on the way back, and I couldn't offer a word of comfort on the question of her coven magic. Though it was equally likely she was still freaked out over that massive god. She hadn't got close enough to see the last deity I'd encountered, and I sincerely hoped that whichever hellish dimension that monster was imprisoned in was as far from this realm as humanly possible.

"Fionn?" I asked. "I can't think why he'd target the witches, but this ring… it sounds like it's powerful enough to have taken out our wards. And the Hemlock witches have prior experience with it, so they'd know."

"I bet it blocked all those witches' spells from working, too," Isabel added. "But the hunters didn't have it when we ran into their hideout at the pub. Why?"

"No clue," I said. "I assume only one person can carry it at a time, but I'm not sure how they decide on that. They might have thought they wouldn't need it to take us down."

"The talisman blocks all magic, you said," said Vance. "Does that include faerie magic?"

"Yeah, even my talisman." Which made me wonder if they'd been holding back. The ring must have a certain range, too, because I hadn't noticed my magic behaving oddly when we'd arrived in the flat to deal with those trespassers. "Typical. I have a million more questions now we're out of the forest."

"We're not going back in," Vance said firmly. "We have enough information for the time being. We know the nature of our enemy and their weapon."

True, but a magic-destroying talisman in the hands of a self-proclaimed master of death was a significantly more daunting prospect than a bunch of inept humans, even if their bullets were capable of taking out a supernatural in one shot.

I sighed. "I should have known I was tempting fate when I thought we hadn't had any world-threatening dilemmas for a while. How on earth are we going to explain this one?"

16

"There you are." Lady Harper came out of the living room when Vance, Isabel and I reappeared in the hallway. "I thought you'd perished in the forest."

"Thanks for the vote of confidence." I tugged off my jacket, scattering leaves onto the carpet.

"What…" Isabel held up her phone. "How is it seven in the evening?"

"We lost twelve hours in there?" No wonder I was starving and exhausted. "That's not right. How's that possible?"

"I don't even know," said Isabel wearily. "I need to tell the rest of the coven I'm still alive. They'll be frantic."

"You'll have to stay here tonight," I insisted. "The flat's not completely safe yet."

"No, but at least we know how they turned the wards off," she said. "And I bet that's how they dodged my trapping spell, too. I've spent hours wondering about that one."

"One of the dicks who got out the fire escape must have been carrying it." I thought back. "Strange that they ran.

Maybe they realised they couldn't take on three of us at once, with or without magic."

"They're cowards at heart," said Vance. "They have that in common with the original League. Their formidable weapons are a cover for their deep-seated terror of the supernatural world. Even the presence of the fae inside your flat might have scared them into running."

"They still tried to shoot me on the way out." I scowled. "Oh, shit. The manor's wards…"

"There are guards surrounding the place on all sides. They'd instantly alert us if there was an intruder."

"Good." I kicked my shoes off. "I need food and a shower, in any order."

"Agreed," said Vance. "I'll ask Quentin to bring food while we figure out how to handle this new development."

"As opposed to 'imminent catastrophe'?"

"I was trying for practicality," said Vance.

"I'm with Ivy," said Isabel. "I need to contact the coven. I have a hundred missed calls."

Lady Harper cleared her throat loudly. "And one of you is going to tell me everything, I hope. Did you pass on my message to Cordelia?"

"Yes, I did. Did *you* know there's a giant…" I waved a hand, unable to summon up the words to convey the monstrosity we'd found in the forest.

She gave a laugh that sounded downright evil. "I thought you'd provoke them into showing you."

Fuck you, too. I left Vance to explain and made for the stairs before I lost my temper and pulled out my sword.

Half an hour later, we gathered in the living room over bags of Chinese takeout. Quentin had apparently objected to our disappearing all day and refused to cook, so Vance called the local takeaway instead. Mercifully, Lady Harper had declined to join us.

"I can't believe you actually went into the forest," said Wanda, who'd heard the story from Vance while I'd been in the shower. "How have those witches survived this long?"

"They're stuck." I shovelled fried rice and prawns into my mouth. "Possibly permanently, but it seems more a kind of forced immortality than the sort the Sidhe have." Which sounded like a slow form of torture to me.

Isabel shuddered. "Yeah. Their magic felt different to any witches I've met before. Not just old, but… alien."

"I knew my grandmother used to work with them," Wanda admitted. "She didn't tell me much, just that they had some kind of alliance. But she worked with the other covens, too."

"She was advisor to our coven and never told us," Isabel said. "Francine didn't know, and she would have worked directly with Lady Harper herself."

"She used to be less reticent." Vance gave her an apologetic look. "However, given the nature of the creature their magic keeps imprisoned in the forest, I imagine she was sworn to secrecy."

"Never mind her." Probably I should be less careless with my words when Lady Harper was in the same house, but it was a little hard to be scared of her mind powers when I'd come within sniffing distance of an ancient deity not two hours beforehand. "Honestly, I don't give a crap. Let her keep her secrets. We need to find out who gave the hunters that ring, and I'm guessing it's the dickhead who stole the damn thing in the first place."

"We also need to get that ring away from the hunters," said Isabel. "That's the key to beating them."

"True," Vance agreed. "Since the ring cancels out magic, it's also a potential way for us to track their location. A risky one, but a valid one, too."

"Yeah." I couldn't say I relished the idea of intentionally

walking within range of something that could turn off my talisman, but a sword was a sword whether it was magical or not. "We know they had it at the house…"

"And that its effects must have faded when they ran away," Isabel added. "I was able to use spells against the faeries."

"Yeah, and I used magic to slow my fall when I… er, jumped off the roof." I averted my eyes from Vance's disapproving stare and took another large mouthful of fried rice.

"But what about those malfunctioning spells?" asked Isabel, her forehead pinched. "I assume the person carrying the ring was moving around the witches' part of town, but where did they go?"

"Their real hideout, maybe." I swallowed my mouthful. "Don't forget they had a secret escape route in the basement. The ring might've been in there. We don't know how wide a range it affects."

"No." Vance put his chopsticks aside. "I won't be able to use my abilities to displace it, either."

"Right." I pressed a hand to my forehead. "I never asked if it affects the person carrying it, but shit, maybe that's why it's in the hands of a bunch of dim-witted humans. They can't get hit by the backlash."

"The bullets don't count as magical." Vance nodded slowly. "But if we did manage to get hold of the ring, we'd have to quickly decide how to dispose of it without dispelling our own wards."

"Or neutralising our spells." The ring would have killed that ward in front of the pub if they'd carried it too close. I'd been dead right when I'd called the talisman a double-edged sword. "Hand to hand it is, then. I can do that."

Vance stood. "Yes. I'll warn the other mages so they know what they might be up against if the manor is attacked."

"Are you sure you want everyone to know?" I asked. "I mean, talismans are serious business."

"The mages should be made aware, but we'll refrain from spreading the news to the public," he said. "We haven't put out a warning about the hunters either. The council didn't come to a definitive decision at our last meeting."

"Yeah, and we ended up spending most of today lost in the forest." I put my takeout carton aside. "I'd say it was a productive time, though. We didn't get forced to swear any promises of secrecy or dodgy bargains."

For all their trickery, the Hemlock Coven hadn't ensnared me in any fae-style vows. Nor the banshee, though in hindsight it seemed mildly suspicious that she hadn't asked me for anything in exchange for guiding us to the witches. Hmm.

Vance went to find the other mages, and Wanda followed shortly after. That left me alone with Isabel.

"I have an idea," I told her.

"Oh, no."

"You haven't heard it yet."

"I know what you're like, Ivy."

"We need to corner the hunters first," I said. "We know they're leaving an unavoidable trail now. All we need to do is separate the person who's holding the ring and the others are fair game."

"How?" she asked. "If Vance keeps teleporting to different places until he finds somewhere he can't use his ability, we might catch them, but that'd take hours. Days, even. Tomorrow's the solstice. Isn't that when they're supposed to put their plan in motion?"

"Yeah." I had a hard time believing they had a chance of penetrating the Hemlock Coven's forest, but that didn't mean they wouldn't try. There was the chance the threat had been a ruse to distract our attention, but the presence of the ring alone showed they weren't fucking around. "We need to act as early as possible. You have a coven meeting tomorrow?"

"Not until noon."

"Go there early," I told her. "Pretend the meeting starts first thing in the morning and show up alone. Except it won't be you. I'll wear an illusion that makes me look like your twin, and the mages will be right behind me."

Isabel's mouth twisted. "I don't like it. If they shoot you—"

"I'm immune. You won't get a second chance. Neither will Vance or anyone else."

Isabel sighed and rubbed her eyes. "I'll think about it. I—I have to make another call."

"To your necromancer friend?" I guessed.

"Yes. He's slightly concerned that I disappeared all day."

"Tell him I dragged you off on an errand. Have you told him about me?"

"A little. I think Colby's been telling the other necromancers how amazing you and Vance are."

I snorted. "Better than Lord Evander telling them I'm pond scum. Is he nice, at least?"

"Of course." A pause. "But half the coven hates necromancers."

"Oh." Isabel hadn't dated anyone in a couple of years and although the timing wasn't the greatest, I was all in favour of her getting to have a little fun. Rick seemed a decent guy and having him in her life brought the added bonus of repairing our fractious relationship with the necromancers, but the decision ultimately rested with Isabel alone.

"Yeah. Basically." She sighed. "It's been years since I even *wanted* a serious relationship, and honestly, being the head of the coven means that the others won't raise any objections. I just don't want to screw this up. Either the leadership or this… whatever this thing with Rick is."

"You won't."

"He raises dead people."

"Have you forgotten some of the first dates I've been on?"

Her mouth tugged into a reluctant smile, probably remembering the particularly disastrous occasion in which a harmless trip to the cinema had turned into an encounter with a rogue undead and ended with me pouring salt on a disembodied hand as it tried to strangle my date. Not one of my best moments. "Yeah, well, you have Vance now. You two just… fit. He loves you."

"Yeah. He does. He wouldn't have walked into that deadly forest with me otherwise."

Her smile faded. "I care about you, too. I'm really not sure about this plan."

"It's all we've got at this point," I said. "We can't risk them trying this ritual, and the easiest way to draw them out is to use bait. Besides, they can't see my magic."

I didn't know how obvious the ring's effects would be, but if they wanted to take out Isabel in the same manner that they had Francine, one of them would almost certainly be carrying it. Still didn't explain why they hadn't used it at the pub, but they might not have expected Isabel to come with me. They sure as hell hadn't expected me to bring a team of mages either.

We'd taken them by surprise once. We'd do so again, and this time we'd end them.

"I hope so." She clicked on her phone. "I'll be back in a second."

I flopped back on the sofa, so tired that my eyelids felt weighted. As I drifted, Velkas's face swam before me, his voice echoing. *"What Fionn proposes will see the realms themselves shake with the impact and the Courts dissolve into naught but smoke. That talisman of yours will be satiated for centuries to come, and you'll have everything the Winter Court ever denied you."*

So casual, how he'd plotted the destruction of our realm. As though not a single human who walked upon its surface was worthy of consideration. Nothing mattered more than his own ambitions. If Fionn waited at the end of this road, I would turn that ring on its owner and bury my sword in his throat.

A hand brushed mine. My eyes flickered open to Vance leaning over me. I pushed myself up onto my elbows. "Dozed off for a second there."

"I saw." He delicately brushed a strand of drying hair from my face with one hand. "Isabel told me your plan. Would it help if I thought we could stage an ambush without you risking your neck?"

"There's less risk in it for me," I said.

"I strongly dislike it when you put yourself in harm's way."

"Occupational hazards. I strongly dislike it when you decide to play the hero, too. I have a way to contact you." I tapped his shoulder where the glyph lay.

"The glyphs didn't work in the forest." He touched his fingertip to my shoulder. "I think I should redo them."

"Sure you aren't looking for an excuse to get your hands on me?"

"As if I needed an excuse."

I shivered as his fingertip trailed across my collarbone and leaned in, inhaling the cool scent of him.

"Bad faerie!"

"Shit." I spun on my heel as Erwin pelted across the room. Isabel followed, and there was a lot of cursing and fumbling as the piskie dodged our attempts to catch him.

When Isabel finally caught him by the feet and put him back in his cage, Lady Harper came into the room.

"What's going on?" she demanded. "I'm trying to sleep, and all I can hear is your vulgar shouting."

"Who, me?" I helped Isabel lock the cage. "Sorry, Erwin. We can't have you flying amok around the house."

"No, we can't," Lady Harper snapped. "This has gone on too long already. Get that creature out."

"We'll take him back home when there are fewer people trying to kill us," I informed her. "And when we've prevented the end of the world as we know it. So, you know, a typical week."

Isabel put down the cage and cast a wary look at Lady Harper. "You were an advisor to my coven, weren't you?"

"For a time, yes," she grunted. "Spit it out, child. I know you want to ask me something."

I tensed, readied to intervene if she showed the slightest inclination to use her mage powers on Isabel.

"I—just wondered about the protective spells I should have inherited when I took control of the coven," Isabel said. "I don't have them yet. Do you know when they typically kick in?"

"I'm not a witch," she said. "I was only an advisor. That said, I imagine it varies depending on the coven… and on the witch."

"I have some books that explain the theory," said Vance. "You can help yourself to any of them, if you like."

"Thank you," said Isabel. Her downcast expression me wanted to punch Lady Harper in the nose all over again. I was pretty sure the old witch knew it, too, judging by her smirk as she retreated from the room.

"I'll help," said Wanda, with an apologetic glance in her grandmother's direction. "I know where they are—if Vance hasn't moved them again, that is."

As the two of them left the room, I moved to Vance's side. "*How* are she and Lady Harper related? Even Cordelia Hemlock was more pleasant to talk to than she is."

Vance crossed the room to the sofa, displacing the empty takeout cartons with a casual wave of his hand. "I think Lady Harper partially blames the witches for the losses in the invasion. According to her, they knew the attack was coming ahead of time, although they were unable to prevent the Sidhe's assault."

"They knew?" I joined him on the sofa. "Lady Harper fought in the invasion, didn't she?"

"Yes. I believe she killed two Sidhe lords in person. But she took the loss of her family hard, and she didn't expect to be dragged back into office as an advisor to the Mage Lords when it was clear we'd lost too many members of the council to continue functioning."

"Whoa. She killed two Sidhe?" Without a talisman? Damn. I'd been right when I'd suspected she'd be able to give the Sidhe a run for their money. "In the forest, I saw… I saw Avalin and Velkas discussing the plan. It was Fionn's idea, but I already guessed that part."

"You saw them?" His grey eyes looked into mine, his expression softening. "You didn't say."

"Yeah. I didn't want to, not with the banshee and the faeries listening." I swallowed. "I saw through his eyes. Avalin. I think the forest somehow read the memory from my talisman."

"Accursed forest," said Vance softly. "Tell me. If you want to."

"Not much to tell." I took in a quick breath. "Velkas taunted him and said he was wasting his time capturing humans. I'm not sure how long ago it was. Might have been twenty years ago, might have been a hundred. Also, it was really weird to feel the Grey Vale sucking the life out of him.

No wonder he needed to keep torturing people to feed the talisman."

I cast a glance at the sword leaning against the sofa, deceptively innocuous. I didn't like to think about what it'd been used for before. How many people had suffered and died at the Sidhe lord's hands, because he'd had to feed on their misery to keep himself alive.

Vance's expression darkened. "The scum deserved worse suffering than the Grey Vale inflicted on him."

"He and Fionn didn't care for each other much, but I still don't know why my magic reacted to Fionn the way it did." Nor had I probed into another question that had arisen from Cordelia's words. *Normally, humans who attempt to take on the power of the gods meet unfortunate ends.*

"Ivy?" Vance rested a warm hand on my arm. "Something else on your mind?"

"I reckon some of the talismans contain power that even the Sidhe can't fully control," I said slowly. "Look at the life-drinker, and how the Lady of the Tree kept losing control of its magic even when she'd claimed it as hers."

"And the ring?" Vance lifted a brow. "Maybe that's why Fionn hasn't used it directly. If he *is* behind this scheme, perhaps it drains his own magic so much that he can't use it at all."

"There is that, too." I hadn't considered the ring might be one of them, but it made sense. Now, however, was far from the time for another earth-shattering revelation. "He's using the hunters as an intermediary, but I can't imagine he'd let it go far from his sight."

"We'll figure it out." He conjured up the pen-like instrument he used to draw on the glyph. "Let me redo this."

His hand moved my top from my shoulder, revealing my bra strap and the fading edges of the last glyph. My skin tingled as he reapplied the mark with a careful twist of his hand. Then he passed the pen to me, smiling lightly as I undid the top two buttons of his shirt. His skin was warm to touch, and his eyes were the light grey of a sky before a thunderstorm.

"That okay?" I studied the glyph to check that the pair matched, and he took the pen from me and closed his mouth over mine.

"I like being able to find you," he murmured, drawing back. "In the forest, when I couldn't sense you… I don't want that to happen again."

"You know most people can't do that, don't you?" I said teasingly.

"Yes." He delicately touched the mark on my shoulder again. "You're stuck with me now."

"Pity."

His stubble brushed against my cheek as he leaned in to kiss me. "I think," he murmured, "we should forget about the witches and the forest for tonight."

"I've already forgotten."

His hands brushed my cleavage, teasing my nipples through my shirt. I felt him harden against me, and he made a faint growling noise low in his throat, somewhere between rough and tender. I felt the moment when he let go of the tight self-control he typically held as he transported us straight from the sofa to his bedroom upstairs. The silken covers caressed the bare skin of my back, and my breath escaped as his fingers slid along my legs to the inside of my thighs. The man had skills. I moaned and writhed as his tongue replaced his fingers, each stroke igniting a new flame until I blazed all over.

Need flared in his eyes as I pulled him onto me so that our bodies were aligned, and I gasped aloud as he buried himself in me. I dug my fingernails in as he drove into me harder, faster, until we were gasping in time with one another.

My back arched as a second orgasm crashed down on me, and a second later, he came with my name on his lips.

I lay alongside him and ran my fingers over the glyph on his shoulder. "I'm looking forward to our trip to the coast."

"You're really keen on that idea?"

"Of course."

"Good." He paused, long enough for me to tilt my head to see his face. His mouth curled in a smile, but the hint of a question in his eyes made me wonder if he was working himself up to something. "If staying in your current flat proves problematic, you can always take up permanent residence here. We could come to an arrangement that would allow you to run your business from another premises, if you like, or if Isabel would prefer—"

"Are you asking me to come and live with you?"

Heat crept up my neck. There was no hiding it, naked and inches away from him, though Vance's long-winded approach suggested he'd been nervous to ask. I'd practically lived at the manor for months, but there was a huge difference between staying over and *living* here.

"I am," he said.

Yep. Definitely nervous. Maybe he'd expected me to say no. I'd never lasted this long in a relationship, so I had no benchmark to measure it against. I was fairly sure I wasn't meant to stare at him like he'd asked if I'd like to adopt a troll.

"If you'd prefer, we can wait until the situation is less volatile."

"This is us we're talking about," I said. "If it isn't hunters or witches, it's flesh-eating faeries or undead."

He laughed quietly. "Isabel is welcome to stay in the guest room until your house is safe. I merely thought you might prefer a residence which is better equipped for your needs. Were there always holes in the ceiling?"

"Might've been," I acknowledged. "The landlord's an arse, but rent's cheap so I can't really compare."

"It seems unfair for you to pay rent on a place you don't live in."

"It's also our office." I searched for the right words. "Vance, you know this place is worth more than all the properties my landlord owns put together? I could have a top tier mercenary job like Larsen and never be able to afford to stay here. I know it's not your fault, but it's a little intimidating."

To say the least. The fact that he'd asked me at all was a big deal, because I'd inferred that a fair bit of the attention he'd got both before and after he'd joined the mages' council was from people who wanted to get their hands on his inheritance. Between assassination attempts and the demands of being on the council, he'd had very few long-term partners.

"Sorry, that sounds ungrateful. Can we save the life-changing decisions until after we've dealt with the hunters?"

He stroked my cheek with his palm. "There's absolutely no pressure from me. Make the decision you feel comfortable with. Wanda and some of the other staff have permanent or temporary residence here."

"And Lady Harper." I was glad she was in the opposite end of the house under soundproofing spells so she couldn't hear a word of our conversation, nor the loud sex that had preceded it. "She'd raise hell if I came to live here. More's the pity for her."

"I think my parents would have liked you."

"Even though I'm vulgar and crass?"

"Did Lady Harper call you that?"

"More or less."

"Hmm." He trailed a hand down my side. "I happen to like your vulgar tongue."

"Good." I kissed him, long and deep. "Because I'm planning to make use of it."

17

"I'm really not sure about this plan of yours," said Isabel.

"When has that ever stopped us?" I cracked a grin. "Trust me, I'm prepared."

We'd hashed out the details the previous night, going back and forth over a dozen possible ideas before Isabel had reluctantly agreed that luring out the hunters by pretending to walk to the coven's headquarters alone would be our best way to get them to play along and attack us on our own turf, not theirs. If they thought they were ambushing the coven leader, they'd employ the ring immediately, and we'd pounce.

Isabel had been less thrilled with the notion of me being the bait and not her, but ultimately my argument that I was the only person likely to survive if the ring's carrier also had a gun won out. Magic wouldn't work for any of us, but there were no second chances for anyone except me.

With the illusion spell in place, Isabel and I were now identical twins, down to the chalk marks on our arms and the traces of glitter in our curly hair. Only the faint glow of faerie magic around my skin was a giveaway to any fae who happened to look in my direction.

I was banking on the hunters not bringing any faerie allies. So far, they'd only employed fae to create diversions or cover their traces, but I carried iron just in case they changed tactics again. Otherwise, they'd think I was Isabel until the last possible moment. The instant they revealed the ring, I'd kill its owner and figure out how to safely dispose of it. Far from simple, but having a strategy made everything easier to manage. Vance and Isabel would be on standby to help deal with the other hunters once I'd taken out the main threat.

"Relax your hands," Isabel said. "You look like you're about to stab someone."

"I'll probably have to before the day's over." But she was right. I was standing like Ivy, not Isabel. I unfurled my fists and slouched my shoulders a little. Isabel was four inches shorter than me, which meant I'd had to borrow her clothes, which weren't designed to go with my extensive weapon collection. Isabel's bright attire felt too conspicuous too, but that was the point. I wanted them to see me.

Vance's gaze settled on me. "Are you sure about this, Ivy?"

"Positive." We'd decided against using another illusion spell to make Isabel look like me. Nobody except me could handle the talisman, and I didn't want to risk it reacting badly to someone else mimicking its owner. I didn't think it would, but she'd offered to hang onto the sword until I needed it. I wasn't certain I could keep my power reeled in for long, either, but with a little luck, I wouldn't need to maintain the façade for longer than a minute or two. "Simple as evicting a nest of piskies, right?"

"If you say so." Isabel chewed on her lower lip. "I wish I'd been able to figure out how to tap into my coven leader magic."

"What did I say about beating yourself up over that?" If I

hadn't forced her to go to bed, she'd have stayed up all night poring over Vance's books and racking her mind over why her coven's protective magic hadn't kicked in yet. While it wasn't unusual to take weeks or even longer, I knew Isabel was worried that it was a sign that her coven's magic didn't consider her truly worthy of holding the title of leader.

"I know," she said. "Shana said the same, but—I worry that we made the decision too fast."

"You're still a badass," I said. "Anyway, you *are* worthy. You've proven yourself to the coven a thousand times, *and* you're about to risk life and limb to protect them. I'd say that's more than enough to qualify as coven leader. Trust me."

She managed a smile. "Thanks, Ivy."

Isabel had already let the rest of the coven know the plan and had urged them to spread the rumour that the solstice gathering would take place first thing in the morning and not at noon. The witches had been more than happy to jump on board, and some would already be waiting inside the town hall to ambush any hunters who wandered in. Others would be outside, pretending to be ordinary shoppers.

We'd wondered if the hunters might be planning a simultaneous attack on half-blood territory like yesterday, but Vance had checked with the Chief that there hadn't been any new developments and had reassured him that he'd be a phone call away. Isabel had called her necromancer friend, too, confirming that no hunters had been seen on their side of town, and the mages' patrols hadn't picked up on anyone either.

Otherwise, I was counting on the hunters not passing up an opportunity to target the witches again.

"Ready?" I asked. "I'll keep up the pretence until the last second. You stay close to Vance."

Isabel herself would wear a shadow spell, but the spell

would be negated the instant she went within range of the ring, so we wouldn't have long to use the element of surprise. The upside was that I now knew what to look for. As a talisman, the ring was bound to be distinctive enough to spot, and I had every intention of swiping the hunters' advantage and turning it against them.

Isabel flickered out of existence as she turned on the shadow spell. "Ready."

"Me too."

I took Vance's hand, and we landed on a side street near the town hall. Vance disappeared a second later, Isabel slipped away, and I walked onto the main road in as casual a manner as possible.

I made my way leisurely to the hall, occasionally glancing behind me. Isabel herself would have good reason to watch her back, and it'd look more suspicious for me *not* to be overly cautious. When I reached the hall, I pretended to check the protective wards on the doors. While I didn't know the meanings, I *did* know the wards remained in place and the hunters hadn't come here yet. If the ring was nearby, the wards would switch off instantly.

A thump sounded. I clamped down on my magic's instinctive reaction to the threat and spun around as a hunter dropped from the roof to land in front of me.

Gotcha.

I advanced on my enemy, whipping one of the iron daggers from my sleeve. Ducking an oncoming punch, I slashed open my attacker's sleeve. Two more thuds announced the arrival of more hunters, each dressed in the same black uniform from head to toe.

"Isn't it too hot to be wearing those ridiculous clothes?" Ivy would say that, not Isabel, but they didn't know either of us.

And I would give them hell for targeting my best friend.

The hunter closest to me grabbed for my weapon hand, and I dodged easily, glad they were unable to see the magic surging around my skin. That alone was proof they didn't have the ring—but where was it?

I struck out with my elbow and the hunter fell, choking. I kicked the hunter in the face and heard a pained grunt. Blood seeped from below their mask and I bared my teeth at the others. "You didn't think I'd come unprotected, did you?"

They closed in. I swept one's legs out from underneath and thrust my knife into the other's chest. Their slowed reactions confirmed they were as human as I was—more so, technically—and they weren't even particularly skilled fighters.

Dammit, one of you speak already. Where was that bloody ring? This was not how it was supposed to go. I'd expected a challenge at the very least.

A bullet bounced off the pavement. *That's more like it.* I ran at the gun's owner. My move clearly confused them, because their split second's pause gave me the chance to tackle the person who'd shot me.

We both hit the pavement. I wrenched the gun free from my attacker's grip and turned it on the five newcomers who'd come running out to surround me.

"You're outnumbered, girl," growled a masculine voice from underneath me.

I punched him in the eye. "That's for Francine, you bastard." Another punch. "And that."

Each punch brought a spark of magic that the hunters couldn't see, but that proved they hadn't brought the ring with them after all. I climbed off the limp hunter and faced his allies with an iron knife in one hand and the gun in the other.

"Come and get me."

They did. One fired a gun at me and spun in confusion

when I used my magic-enhanced speed to dart around behind them and drive my knife into their back. The hunter crumpled, and I grabbed the gun from their hands and threw it at another. The weapon hit its target on the temple and the hunter dropped like a stone.

A bullet grazed my arm. The hunter who'd fired took aim again, and the blast of an explosive spell hit the ground. The hunters who were still on their feet scattered with cries of alarm.

Way to go, Isabel. My sword came flying towards me, arcing through the air. I caught the weapon in my right hand, and blue light blazed, bright enough to make them shield their eyes. As magic burst from my skin, I felt the illusion spell slide away. Isabel's clothes tightened as my shoulders widened, stretching the fabric, while my feet stumbled in shoes that no longer fit. Fortunately, my magic was more than enough compensation.

"You aren't the witch," yelped the hunter with the broken nose.

"You don't say?" I trod on his face again and used him as a launchpad into a flying kick that took out another hunter. Another explosive flew overhead and hit a fleeing hunter in the back, sending them sprawling.

Two more attempted to run. I sprinted, leaping over their heads to slam into the pavement in front of them. "Tell me. Why did you want the coven leader?"

"You aren't her." Quick on the uptake, that guy was. His deep voice came from beneath a mask knocked slightly askew and he seemed to have dropped his gun. "You're an impostor."

"And you're a giant shithead." I grabbed him by the scruff of his neck and yanked his mask free to reveal an unmistakably human male face framed by tangled brown hair.

"Tell me where your boss is hiding or I'll cut your throat and use your blood to follow the trail."

"Won't—that won't work."

Why? Because their leader has the ring? The talisman likely negated tracking spells, too, but the prevailing question was why they'd put so little effort into taking me out.

"I'm disappointed." I caught sight of the other hunter trying to flee and stuck the knife into their shoulder without releasing my captive, eliciting a shrill scream. "Why'd your leader send you here without backup?"

The hunter I held squirmed, trying to free himself. He whimpered when brought my blade up to point at his chest, legs folding beneath him. "I surrender."

"You shouldn't have been able to kill Francine," I snarled. "You shouldn't have come after Isabel either. That's why I'm going to make your death especially painful."

He shook his head frantically. "No, we didn't want to kill her. You… she said you were more dangerous."

They didn't want Isabel dead? I'd been the target after all? "And who is 'she'?" Not Fionn.

He gave another head-shake, leaning away from my sword. "It's too late."

"For what?" I pressed the blade harder. "Tell me where to find your leader."

A trickle of blood ran down his neck. "The ritual's already in progress. When they have the coven leader, it'll be complete."

"Not on your life." I drove the blade deeper.

He collapsed with a gurgle.

"Ivy." Isabel spoke from behind me, concealed beneath a shadow spell. "Two of them got away—"

"No, they didn't." Vance appeared in front of me, a blade in each hand. "I took care of them, but not before they took me to their hideout."

"Handy." Wait. "Does that mean they don't have the ring?"

"Apparently not."

I swore. "This guy said the ritual's already in progress."

The hunters' bodies vanished with a wave of Vance's hand. "I put them somewhere they won't cause a disturbance," he said in response to my questioning look.

"Not the manor, I hope." I wiped blood from my sword. "Isabel, you need to hide. If you come with us, you'll be handing yourself over on a platter. He said they need the coven leader to complete the ritual."

"They killed Francine." Her eyes blazed with fury. "I haven't punished them enough for this."

"If I find Francine's killer, I'll save them especially for you. How about that?"

Isabel gnawed on her lower lip. "I… all right."

"I'll be fine." If they didn't have the ring, I could unleash the full might of my talisman against them, stop their ritual, and then turn my attention to the real enemy.

"Yes." Vance stepped up to my side. "If all goes to plan, this will be our last stop."

"Does anything ever go to plan?"

He shot me a smile. "No, but I live in hope."

"Me too." I readied my sword. "Let's go storm an evil villain's lair."

18

The hunters' base was closer than I'd thought, within one of the abandoned parts of the city and uncomfortably close to the park from which I'd left this realm to duel Velkas. Here, nobody had tried to fix the damage from the invasion. A jagged line cut through the centre of the road like the aftermath of an earthquake. Grass and weeds grew in the gaps, around the rusted skeletons of old cars. Even a bus lay banked against the roadside, its blue paint peeling, plants growing wild through the shattered windows. In the old world, I'd watched the same bus drive past my school a hundred times. I closed my eyes for a brief moment then opened them again.

"Ivy?" Vance gave me a quizzical look. "We need to find that house."

"Yeah. I... I used to live near here before the invasion. Haven't been here since. I thought the whole place was trampled."

Last I'd seen, a giant had been rampaging through buildings and tearing humans to pieces. Presumably someone working for the necromancers had been here post-invasion to clear the bodies away and burn them so they wouldn't rise as undead, but they'd left enough debris behind for my mind to conjure a ghostly bus passing by, ferrying latecomers to school.

I shook off the memory as we walked, my gaze travelling along houses that had suffered varying degrees of damage. Vance pointed to one near the end, more intact than the others. The garden in front was a mess of cracked paving stones and the door leading into an alley at its side had been torn from its hinges, but the house itself stood upright with its blue-painted door closed. A curtain fluttered in the window when we drew closer. *This is the place.*

The door was closed but not locked. I took it down with a well-placed kick. Blue light shone from my hands, a reminder that my magic was undeniably functioning. The ring wasn't here. Likely it'd interfere with their ritual.

An open trapdoor clued me in. I'd learned my lesson from last time and stopped short of jumping, instead gathering magic in the palm of my hand. I took aim and sent a blast of vibrant blue through the open hole. Someone screamed.

"Surprise." *Now* I leapt in, soaring several feet down and driving my blade into the spine of the unfortunate hunter who'd been directly beneath.

Someone reached out of the dark and pulled me on top of them. I spat hair out of my mouth and drove my fist into the man I'd landed on. Light from above penetrated the gloom, revealing brick walls enclosing a basement that was otherwise bare of furniture and that contained maybe six or seven hunters, all wearing black clothes but without their masks.

"Thank god for that." I punched the man beneath me again. "It was getting really annoying not being able to tell you apart."

He squirmed, trying to grab his gun. I drove my knee into his crotch and then finished him off with a quick stab. Withdrawing my blade from his chest, I rose upright to get my bearings. The other hunter I'd stabbed lay bleeding on the floor. In the light streaming from above, I glimpsed symbols chalked on the concrete, forming a circle of crudely drawn glyphs. Like a summoning circle.

"Amateurs," I muttered. "Which of you is the leader?"

A figure moved into the light. The black-haired woman who'd feigned being a witch in distress gave me a thin-lipped scowl. No signs remained of her prior injuries and she wasn't limping. She must have used a healing spell.

"Me," she said. "You're trespassing in my home."

I burst out laughing. "Sure, it's not like you did the same to me. Or called me pretending to be a witch in distress. Oh, and *murdered the head of the Laurel Coven*. Fuck you."

I shot magic from my palm, a stream of blue energy flooding the darkness. The hunters ducked for cover. One attempted to climb the ladder, but I hit him in the legs with another blast of magic and caused him to tumble down onto his companions. This group wasn't any more skilled than the last one and the tight space worked against them. I drove my blade through two at once and turned to their leader. She'd frozen, fear etched on her face.

"Well?" I said to her. "Which of you killed Francine Black-wood? I've promised my best friend I'll save them for her."

"You're not her."

"No shit." God, these people were pathetic. "I bet Francine's turning her grave knowing she was killed by a bunch of fucking nobodies. Hopefully, she'll get another shot at you in the afterlife."

"I killed her." She pulled out a gun and pointed at me. "And even the faerie killer doesn't get a second chance."

"Wrong." I put on an enhanced burst of speed and dodged the bullet, making a mental note to incapacitate but not kill her. I'd meant what I'd said to Isabel and besides, I needed to find out who was really calling the shots. This bunch of amateurs was a far cry from the organised force they were supposed to be, but the ring was somewhere, and I'd bet my sword the person who held it had a plan to enact the ritual if the hunters failed.

My blade bit out, slicing the legs of another hunter attempting to flee up the ladder. Blue light blazed, its brightness a warning that there was a faerie nearby. "Out of interest, which faerie was leaving messages on your behalf?"

She tried to shoot me instead. I dodged and slammed a kick into her chest, and she stumbled, gasping for breath. Then, inexplicably, she smiled.

The wall behind me exploded. Dust filled my eyes and mouth and a huge arm locked around me, lifting me off the ground. More dust rained on my head as I twisted, trying to see what held me. Through the haze, I glimpsed a huge hulking figure that could only be a full-blooded troll. Its huge head barely fit under the ceiling, and it'd blasted a sizeable chunk out of the wall on its way in.

"Did you have this thing chained up inside the wall?" I choked, my hands trying to pry off the troll's meaty arms, but it was like trying to lift an anvil. The troll held me up as though unsure where to throw me. My sword arm was crushed against my back, and when I tried to free myself, pain wrenched my shoulder. Ow.

The woman straightened up, though she moved slowly enough for me to be certain I'd cracked a rib or two. It'd been a hell of a good kick. The flicker of a smile touched the hunter's mouth as the blue light of a healing spell enveloped her body.

"You're part witch?" I guessed. "I knew one of you must be."

"I regret it," she said coldly.

"More than killing Francine?" I extended my free arm,

trying to reach the weapon in my limp hand. Trolls were slow on the uptake, but I needed to move fast before the hunters' leader pointed her gun at a body part that wouldn't heal regardless of any immunity to those bullets I might possess.

"I killed Francine because she was in our way. Her notions of cooperation between the magical races would have ground ordinary humans further into the dust."

"You're the one terrorising innocent people. And you aren't exactly working with ordinary humans." I gave a pointed jerk of my head towards the beast that held me and another wave of pain radiated from my shoulder. "Why the hell did you decide joining a bunch of wannabe vigilantes was a good life plan? There's no barrier to entry in the witch covens."

"You wouldn't understand. Humans have been down-trodden by supernaturals for far too long."

"*I'm* human. Maybe you're just pathetic."

The troll shook me again. I yelled as the bones in my arm jarred, blinking tears from my eye, but the movement had inadvertently moved my other hand close enough to grab the hilt of my sword.

Magic burst from my body as my sword came free in my hand. I whirled and stabbed the troll, sinking the blade through the lumpy skin of its neck. Viscous blue-tinted faerie blood spattered the concrete.

"No." The leading hunter backed up against the far wall, her eyes on the dusty chalk markings on the floor that I'd all but forgotten about. "You fool. That's a—"

"Summoning circle." And I'd got troll blood in it. "Don't pin this one on me. This is your fucking fault."

The basement shook under a tremendous crash. I backed towards the ladder as more rumbling thuds ensued from above, like giant steps upon the floor. What in hell was going on up there? *Shit, I left Vance outside.*

Through the trapdoor, I glimpsed the biggest foot I'd ever seen, bigger even than the troll's. *Fuck me, that's a giant.*

That explained why nobody had moved back to this part of the city. The giant's vast body wouldn't even fit into the basement, but with each of its steps, more dust and plaster rained down on our heads. If I stayed down here much longer, the ceiling would collapse on our heads, and while I didn't much care if the hunters' leader got buried alive, I couldn't say I'd be a fan of the experience.

And Vance was still somewhere up there, too. Since he hadn't come after me, I could only conclude that he'd run into trouble elsewhere in the house. Giant-sized trouble.

As I reached for the ladder, white lights began to glow on the floor around the summoning circle. *Oh, shit.*

A deafening roar from upstairs was followed by a thump that rained yet more plaster dust on our heads. I raised my hands to shield myself and the faint blue glow of my magic illuminated the outline of the female hunter fleeing up the ladder. I needed to get out, too, but leaving a half-formed ritual swimming in faerie blood was even more unwise than letting the hunters' leader escape.

A chunk of ceiling fell down. *Okay, never mind.*

My hand closed around the cold metal of the ladder and I pulled myself up, shoulders aching, eyes stinging from the dust. Seeing the giant wasn't directly above me, I jumped the rest of the way and crashed into the hunters' leader, sending both of us sprawling onto the floor. Further down the hallway, Vance's blade sliced into the giant's legs. No wonder it was stomping hard enough to knock the basement ceiling in.

"Hey, Vance," I called hoarsely. "Need a hand?"

Vance's blades flashed out again and he glanced over his shoulder. Blood soaked his white shirt, but the blue tint told me it belonged to the giant, not him. The hunter pinned beneath me tried to get up, but I drove my knee into her stomach and she doubled over with a gasp.

A horrible noise came from the trapdoor we'd just vacated, sounding a little like a cross between a fight between street cats and a giant crow.

"No," moaned the hunter. "Let go of me. Before…"

A wrenching cry came from below. Sharp claws dug into the hall carpet as something pulled itself up through the trapdoor, something covered in black feathers edged with red as though dipped in blood. Its wings were the reverse, red and jagged and with inky black membranes. Eyes black as pitch shone above a cruel, curved beak, and I instinctively averted my gaze in case the beast could create the same immobilising fear-effect as a hellhound. Whatever it was, its body was at least seven feet long and its claws longer than my arms.

As it lunged, I rolled sideways and a piercing claw stabbed the hunters' leader through the chest. The hunter-witch screamed, high and loud, as the claws ripped her body clean in two. Her innards spilled on the floor and through the open trapdoor. I gagged, backing down the hallway towards Vance.

"Ivy." His arm came around my shoulder, steadying me. "The giant's paralysed. I'm guessing that creature's magic affects other fae."

"What *is* it?" I glanced behind me, confirming that the giant stood slackly in the doorway, its eyes fixed on the monster and its stumpy legs streaming blood from a dozen deep cuts inflicted by Vance's swords.

"Whatever it is, this house will collapse on us if we aren't careful."

"Yeah." Slight problem: the clawed monster was between us and the way out. Batlike wings extended to block the front door, and with the giant behind us, we were hemmed in.

As a second bird-shaped monstrosity began to tear its way loose from the trapdoor, Vance took my arm and we vanished, reappearing in the front garden. The house trembled, indicating the giant had shaken off the monster's spell, unless it was the arrival of more beasts further damaging the foundations.

"I called backup," Vance said out of the corner of his mouth. "Where's that summoning circle?"

"In the basement. I don't think we can destroy it from here." *But if we don't, they'll keep coming.* "Also, the ring's not in the house, but I'm guessing you already figured that out."

The first beast flew out of the house, the gory remains of the hunter's body still embedded on its front claws. I swung my blade, leaving a deep gouge in its talon. At least whatever unnatural magic it possessed didn't repel my sword, but how many of those beasts were inside whatever hellish dimension had opened in that basement? A chorus of more shrieks and cries came from the house, grating and inhuman.

"Vance, please tell me your backup's almost here." I launched upward, using magic to boost my speed, and my sword folded into the beast's neck. Feathered skin and flesh gave way as its head tumbled free, but the burning pain in my shoulder told me I still needed a healing spell.

The second monster emerged from the house as I landed, its beak snapping inches from my hand. I stabbed upwards and let Vance finish the creature off so I could swiftly grab a healing spell. I sighed as light enveloped my shoulder and the ache disappeared. Now I could fight effectively with both hands again, I grabbed an iron dagger from the inside pocket of Isabel's jacket and threw it at a third monster. I'd never even seen this particular branch of faeries before, but the death-like stench rolling off them carried a chilling familiarity. *They're from the Vale.*

"Was she the boss?" Vance indicated the remnants of the female hunter in the hallway.

"Yep. Not sure she even knew what she was summoning."

Vance finished off his opponent with a strike to its throat. Black scales sheathed his arms, his shifter form taking the reins to match this new threat. The third beast took flight with my knife still embedded in its side, but I leaped to meet it in mid-air, slashing at a diagonal angle to sever its head from its neck. I landed as the beaked head flew to the side in a spray of blood.

"I've never even seen faeries of this sort before. Do you recognise them?"

Vance moved to sheathe his claws in another monstrosity, ripping off its head. I risked a glance at him when he didn't respond to my question. His mouth was pressed tight, his grey eyes angry. "I remember seeing them in the invasion."

The door frame collapsed in a shower of dust and wooden splinters. My magic reacted on instinct, conjuring a shield to block the damage from hitting me. Two more beasts emerged, wings unfurling behind their shoulders.

I turned the shield into a blast of magic that knocked them backwards. If they'd been human, it'd have taken their heads off, but the beasts were made of stronger stuff. Their bodies struck the house wall, and a roaring came from within. The giant must be trying to escape but had found itself entrapped in a house full of monsters. The summoning circle had dragged dozens of these creatures out of whichever hell they inhabited, and I had the strong suspicion that these creatures fed on death. In other words, the more I killed, the more I'd draw into this realm.

"We need to take down the summoning circle." I brought

my blade up to its hilt in a feathered chest. "I'd have thought having a house collapse on it would be enough."

"Apparently not," Vance growled, ripping into the second beast with his claws.

The rumbling noise of a car came from the roadside. Relief mingled with trepidation as a group of mages came running up to join us in the fight.

"Don't look those creatures in the eyes," Vance ordered them. "Take them out by any means necessary."

The giant roared again. Drake, who was in the lead, fell back a few steps. "What *is* that?"

"A giant," I told him. "Big, nasty, but less dangerous than these fuckers. And it's kinda stuck in the house."

"Oh, fun."

A bird-creature burst into flame as Drake directed the fire to eat at the creature's wings, eliciting a high-pitched screeching noise. I decapitated the monster, putting it out of its misery.

"The beasts are coming out of a summoning circle," Vance told the others. "It's buried in the house, and it needs to be destroyed in order to stop this."

"You want to go *into* the house?" Drake sent another fire-ball at another winged beast, which crumpled in front of the open door.

Vance displaced the air to knock a second one downward and his knife sank into the bird's eye. Its death rattle mingled with the increasingly frustrated yells from the giant.

I drove my blast into another bird-monster's chest. "I'll clear the way to the circle. Once it's closed, these fuckers will stop coming."

"What?" Vance flashed me an alarmed look. "Ivy—"

I ran in through the open door, calling up a magical shield to repel the flying pieces of wood and brick as the giant tore its way through the remains of the house. I could see its hunched shape at the end of the hallway, cowering away from the monsters.

"Sorry mate, but I can't have you knocking the roof on my head." I leapt forward, stuck my sword into its eye and twisted, hard. As its body sagged, I stabbed it in the other eye for good measure.

Another screeching monster pulled its way out of the trapdoor and flew straight at me. I spun around, lifting my blade, but its claw exploded into gore before it made contact. Blinking the glare from my eyes, I looked around in disbelief. That was one of Isabel's explosives.

"Hey, Ivy." Isabel herself ran into the house, a pointed explosive in each hand. "I see you're causing property damage again."

"Isabel. I told you to stay behind."

"I know." She threw another explosive into the monster's face, and I finished it off with a stab to its neck. Isabel's foot nudged a severed hand lying on the floor. "Whoa. Did they kill the hunters?"

She'd spotted the grisly remains of their leader.

"Yeah. Sorry... they got to Francine's murderer before you did."

Her eyes shone, and she ducked her head. "That's a far nastier way to die than I could have come up with myself. What *are* those things?"

"There's a summoning circle in the basement, and I'm sure it can only be taken apart by a witch."

That was when the floor gave way. My magic reacted, forming a shield beneath our feet, as the floorboards folded inwards. Vance appeared between us and a heartbeat later, we landed in the front garden. Not a moment too soon. Behind us, a wrenching crash shook the house, roof tiles sliding free and clattering onto the ground.

"It's a giant sinkhole!" yelped Isabel. "Look."

"Holy shit."

The lower floor was sliding downward into the ground. The upstairs portion of the house also descended as the foundations buckled. A glow emanated from the area where the basement had been, as if the summoning circle was somehow sucking the house *into* it.

Three more bird-creatures emerged from the mess and flew upward at speed. I drew back, prepared to jump—but my sword gave a sudden aggressive hum, and a spasm of disconnected anger shot through me. I jerked back, dread curling around my spine. My magic had only responded with that level of fury when I'd been around one person. *Fionn.*

"Where are you?" I asked aloud, but no answer came.

"Ivy!" Isabel flung an explosive up at the beasts, showering us with gore. Drake's flames bit into another, while Vance's swords flashed. More dark shapes stirred in the house's ruins. If we didn't shut the circle down, they'd swarm across the city. Worse, I was fairly sure the circle led directly into the Grey Vale, and whichever dark corner these creatures had been banished to.

Was that why I could sense Fionn? I sure as hell couldn't *see* him, but being Sidhe, using glamour was second nature to him.

We have to close the circle first. That's our priority.

By now, the house had all but disappeared into the haze of shimmering lights, which had noticeably expanded, covering an area as large as the lower floor.

Isabel ran up alongside me, throwing a knife at a retreating bird-creature. "I'm not sure I can get rid of that circle. We might need the necromancers—"

A bullet snapped through the air. Isabel jerked back, a choking noise escaping her mouth.

"No…" I ran in time to catch her in my arms. Blood foun-

tained from the wound in her shoulder. Not a fatal shot…
but it would be.

This can't be happening. Isabel can't be dying. She's supposed to have protective wards…

Numb, I gently lowered Isabel to the ground and scanned wildly for the attacker. Where had the shot come from? There weren't any hunters.

The sound of hoof-steps clattered on the road. The fighting ceased, and even the monsters turned to regard the horse riding out of nowhere, and the armoured rider upon its back.

"What would you give to heal her?" Fionn called to me. "Tell me, Ivy."

19

Fionn rode up to the doorstep and dismounted his black horse, his feet touching down beside me. He wore different armour to last time, grey with a silver sheen like the realm he came from, and loose and flowing to allow maximum movement. His dark-blue eyes shone with an inhuman glow, and a visceral shock of fury jolted through the sword in my hands. My magic recognised the enemy and wanted to destroy him, but I refused to let go of Isabel. She'd gone still, quiet, greyness already fanning down her arm from where she'd been shot.

"I have to admit," Fionn said, "I much prefer it when you're wearing your own face, Ivy."

Through numb lips, I said, "Stay out of this."

I reached in my pocket for a healing spell. Delaying even a minute would cost Isabel her life, but I knew before the flash of blue light fizzled to nothing that it would have no effect.

"Don't bother," he said. "None of your spells will work."

"You..." He'd picked up a hunter's gun and shot her, knowing that it was the one wound that nothing could heal even if he didn't have the ring. I didn't see it—he carried nothing in his hands, and his sword was sheathed in silver and black at his waist—but I had a hard time focusing on him when my entire body was ablaze in anger. "I hope you rot in the hell you created, you fucking piece of shit."

In a fluid movement, Fionn stood beside me, his hands placed on Isabel's injured shoulder. "I'm going to dismiss that insult as an outburst of grief and anger and give you another chance to make the right choice, Ivy. You know there's no cure other than mine."

"You're lying if you say you can cure her at all." Didn't the ring affect him, too? I felt his gaze boring into me, his fathoms-deep eyes promising he'd give me everything I wanted... but what would he want in exchange? My talisman? Or both of them? I had little doubt that whatever he planned involved untold destruction in which humanity would be little more than a footnote.

Then again, what was the alternative? Even if I locked away my heart—even if I did the unthinkable and challenged him instead of accepting a deal—I was far from prepared for a one-to-one duel with the leader of the Wild Hunt. Aka, the person who'd been responsible for the death of half the human population on the planet. How could I ever have entertained the idea that I stood fighting chance against him, with or without the ring?

A screeching cry drew my gaze to where Vance fought one of the monstrosities Fionn had summoned. Bits of bloodied wings flew left and right and he threw the creature's beaked head aside, blood staining his claws to the elbows.

Fionn laughed. "He's like an animal, your mage. I can see why you like him."

"Stay the fuck away from us," I growled at him. "Let Isabel go."

The flicker of a smile touched his mouth. "I'm keeping her alive, Ivy. If I let her go, she'll die."

Horror hit my heart. *No.*

"These bullets are instruments of torture. Personally, I find them crude, but whatever it takes to reach one's goal…"

"What do you want from me?"

"Merely your cooperation. I believe you're familiar with faerie vows, correct?"

"Yes. I won't hand over my talismans."

"You think I want Avalin's old relics?" He gave my sword a dismissive look. "I have no use for the life-drinker, either. I have everything I need, thanks to these trusting humans. My own magic is far superior to yours. And hers."

"Tell me what you want from me." I tried desperately to keep my tone even, but Isabel's life was literally in his hands.

Vance moved, but I caught his eye and shook my head a fraction. Anger flashed in his grey eyes as he looked at Fionn holding Isabel, correctly grasping the situation. Nobody could intervene. This was on me.

"A favour, to be called upon at the time of my choosing."

"I've played this game before. It won't end well for you."

"You have?" He tilted his head. "With Avalin, am I right? Don't worry yourself. I'm not so easily fooled."

Not with Avalin. With the Lady of the Tree. Which at least proved he didn't know *all* my secrets, nor how I'd obtained the life-drinker. "I don't give a shit. Heal Isabel and you'll get your favour."

"Swear on it."

"I swear that I'll offer you one favour, as long as you heal Isabel… and never threaten my friends again."

"No. You will give me one favour, in exchange for my healing your friend."

"Fine," I ground out. "That's our deal."

A white glow folded around Isabel's shoulder, and the

grey lines shrank away until nothing remained but unblemished skin.

"There." He lifted Isabel and placed her on her feet. She swayed a little, but held her balance.

I ran to her side as Isabel's foot lashed out and slammed into Fionn's leg. He stumbled back, the faintest trace of surprise crossing his face.

"That's for the invasion, you prick."

I nearly laughed, but stopped when Fionn bared his teeth in a grin. "You have intriguing friends, Ivy."

"Yeah, and you'll never be one of them, no matter how many times you try and trick cooperation out of me." I pointed Helena at him. "You and I will finish this before you ever get to force me to fulfil my end of our bargain."

He laughed. "Unfortunately, I have to decline. I have business to attend to—"

Vance tackled him from behind. I hadn't even seen him move. His claws didn't make a dent in his armour, but I took advantage of Fionn's distraction to swing my blade at his chest.

The end glanced off his armour, and a screeching cry was our only warning before several more winged beasts descended behind Vance.

"Careful," said Fionn. "I saved the witch because I need her. I won't do the same for you, Mage Lord."

"None of that," I said warningly. "I take it these monsters are yours as well?"

"The furies are mine, yes. Someone sealed them in a distant corner of the Grey Vale. Such indignity for those majestic creatures to suffer."

"Your allies are lying in pieces thanks to your charming monsters." Furies, he'd called them. Appropriate. "Got your memories back yet?"

"Wouldn't you like to know." His eyes gleamed dangerously. "I owe you nothing, Ivy Lane. You owe *me* a favour, and yet you attacked me anyway. I'd be more careful."

"You coerced me," I said. "Like with those hunters. Why them? You could have your pick of the scum of the earth to serve you and you picked those pathetic nobodies."

"They were easy prey. Desperate humans, living on the outskirts, craving a solution to the hierarchy wherein the magically inclined gain all and those less fortunate are left to rot." He gave a dismissive shrug, an amused glint in his eyes. "Given your own history, I'm surprised *you* caved to the mages so easily, Ivy… though I can imagine being the lover of this one comes with enough advantages to yourself to keep them close at hand."

Fury rose, mingling with the rage pounding through the weapon in my hands. "Make one comment on our relationship again and I'll use your brain matter to paint the road."

Vance made a motion towards Fionn, but the Sidhe lord beckoned to the furies hovering in the air. The beasts descended, drawing closer around Vance with their claws outstretched and cruel beaks ready for the kill.

Fionn laughed. "I'm not in the least bit interested in your petty human games. You make little sense to me. So quick to divide, and yet so quick to unite under a rallying cause. Humans want leadership and direction and then grouch about the unfairness that inevitably results. The mages, who see half-bloods and other supernaturals as an asset, cannot give a voice to those without any magic at all. That's why the humans will never support you, in the end. The half-bloods will be next to join me. They feel misjudged and abandoned, and who can blame them?"

"Sorry to disappoint you, but humans and half-bloods don't want the likes of you in charge. On account of how you *murdered* so many of them in the invasion." I glared at him.

"I'm through with your crap. You murdered the coven leader, too, didn't you?"

"Now, I wasn't the perpetrator," he said. "My foolish allies were a little too enthusiastic in their methods, but no matter. Your friend will do as a sacrifice instead."

Isabel made a faint noise. I moved in front of her protectively, but Fionn laughed.

"There's no need, Ivy," he said. "The Rite of the Devourer requires the lifeblood of a witch to reach its full potential. Your friend has already given her part."

Isabel gasped. I followed her gaze to the blood on the paving stones. *Her* blood, which had leaked from her shoulder when she'd been shot.

Lifeblood. Shit.

I reached for a cleansing spell. A rumbling noise travelled underfoot, and as I sought to catch my balance, the light of the summoning circle crept further outward. Towards the blood on the ground… and us.

"Don't worry." Fionn tilted his head. "You still have a little time, though that might change if you try to attack me again. In the meantime, I have a question for you, Ivy."

"What?" I ground out.

"I'm curious. You have a talisman that many others would kill to possess, yet you choose to live under the power of the mages. Why?"

"I don't want to rule over anyone, in this realm or otherwise. You're wasting your time if you think you can recruit me willingly."

"What if I told you this realm will expire in less than a day?"

My gaze dropped to the trail of blood leading up to the house. "I'd say challenge accepted. Fuck you."

"Oh, it's not the ritual." His smile widened. "Haven't you guessed?"

I narrowed my eyes at him. "If you're about to order me to rain terror down on this realm with that vow you forced me to make, I'll slit your throat like I did his."

"Watching you try would be highly entertaining," he mused, "but there's a strong chance you'd be killed in the aftermath, and I still need you."

"For what?"

He grinned. "To be my partner, of course. I'm sure you know that it's lonely over in the Grey Vale."

Ugh. "We met for all of half an hour, if that. You also tried to kill me and destroy my world. Oh, and you weren't even supposed to wake up in the first place."

"Yes, due to Avalin's persistent offspring being allowed to roam long after he expired," he said. "It's funny how one simple mistake can have so many dire consequences, isn't it? These poor misguided humans only wanted their circumstances to change. It's too bad they put their faith in the wrong person. Not unlike yourself."

"What are you saying?" Vance growled. "Ivy wants nothing to do with you."

"She can speak for herself," said Fionn.

"Don't start pretending to be on my side," I said warningly. "What's the point in all this, then? Are you actually going to use the ritual or are you stalling so you can talk me into an early grave instead?"

"The ritual wasn't your main plan," said Isabel slowly. "It was a ruse. You just wanted us to fixate Ivy's attention on trying to solve your riddle. Right?"

"Right you are, but I'd have thought Ivy here would have made the connection after her experiences in the forest."

"What?" Then it hit me. "The ring? What—you have it with you, don't you?"

He laughed. Loudly.

"What have you done?" Dread trickled down my spine,

and my sword vibrated with fury. Another indication that he didn't have the ring. In the panic of Isabel's near-miss, I'd utterly forgotten.

"If you did your research thoroughly, you'll know the talisman negates all magic it comes into contact with," he said. "And that it cannot be countered or destroyed."

"What did you do, drop it outside the manor?" There weren't many people there aside from Lady Harper and Wanda, but he wanted to wipe out the leaders of the supernatural communities. Two were here. The necromancers didn't have one. That left… "Half-blood territory?"

"Not quite. Go on, try again."

Vance interrupted by sheathing his blade in the nearest fury's throat. Blood spurted, and Fionn spun around, an irritated expression on his face. "Really. Didn't anyone ever teach you it's rude to interrupt? I would have thought the Mage Lord would know better."

"Tell me where the fucking ring is." If Fionn didn't have it, I could use magic to its full extent. And if I took him down, it wouldn't matter how many dangerous artefacts he'd got his hands on, nor how many heinous schemes he'd concocted in the six months that had elapsed since I'd last seen him.

My gaze connected with Vance's and we exchanged a nod. His claws readied to dig into Fionn's neck.

"I wouldn't." Fionn addressed Vance. "I'm only keeping you alive because I find you rather entertaining, but it won't be for long. Soon this realm will perish, and Ivy will have to choose whether to come with me or expire along with it."

My mind raced. *Not quite,* he'd said. Not half-blood territory, but…

Oh no. The forest.

If the talisman had ended up in the Hemlock Coven's forest, what effect would it have on their magic? They'd been a force to be reckoned with, a match even for the Sidhe, but the talisman destroyed *all* magic it came into contact with. Such as the power keeping that monster contained and preventing it from breaking into this realm. *The Devourer.* The same beast his dim-witted followers had been trying to summon with the ritual… a ritual he hadn't needed, in the end.

"Well?" said Fionn.

"How?" My throat caught on the word, unable to say more, but Fionn's eyes gleamed, grasping my meaning.

"You worked it out." His face split into a delighted smile. "Did you know you planted the ring yourself, Ivy? You took the talisman into the witches' lair."

My heart plunged somewhere below the earth. "What?"

He laughed. "I suppose I cannot blame you for not recognising the talisman even when it was right in front of you. You're still human, for all your unique quirks."

I racked my mind. I hadn't seen a ring. I definitely would have remembered, but the forest had been pitch-black and draped in the witches' illusions. Who was to say what else I'd missed? "You couldn't be bothered to put the ring into the forest yourself, so you made *me* do it for you? What was the point in using the hunters, then?"

"As a backup, of course," he said. "And I never said I made *you* carry the talisman. I rather think it would have given the game away, don't you?"

"Who—?" I broke off. "The banshee."

We'd thought our magic was malfunctioning due to the effects of the Hemlock Coven's magic testing us. Our light spells had shut off, and even my talisman's light had died, but my phone's torchlight had been fully functional and I hadn't even thought it strange. The Hemlock Coven's own magic had been intact, admittedly, but the banshee… *the little shit.* Had she been carrying the ring the whole time?

"My little harbinger." He laughed again. "She was happy to make the sacrifice."

"I'll sacrifice her, all right." Never mind the banshee. We needed to get hold of that talisman before it burned through the protections keeping that giant monster from devouring the earth. Fionn would be more than happy to talk to the literal end of the world. I needed to take him down.

I fired magic from both palms, aiming one at his front, the other behind. He effortlessly raised a hand and repelled my first attack. The second, glamoured, slipped by his defences, and made him stagger, just a fraction.

"So you *have* been practising since our last encounter. I did wonder."

"Don't patronise me." Damn, he was strong. Hitting him with magic barely winded him. Of course, we were also in the mortal realm. Neither of us was at our strongest here.

Fionn lifted a hand, and threads of vibrant blue magic shot towards me, twisting like vines and wrapping around my back. I dodged and slashed, but one caught me by the waist, yanking me up into the air. I hovered upside-down, taking aim. Fionn had no idea that for the past few months, I'd trained with someone who could levitate me off the ground almost every day. I was more than ready.

I rotated, upside-down, and magic burst from my hands and knocked him right into the path of Vance's claws. The threads of Fionn's magic released me and I flipped over, landing on my feet as Vance sheathed his claws in Fionn's back. This time they penetrated through the gaps in his armour. Blood spurted, thick and tinted blue. Fionn laughed, a guttural choking sound, and spun with dizzying speed. I screamed a warning, too late. Vance hit the floor with a force that shook the ground.

"Bastard!"

Fionn didn't look great himself. Blood dripped as he staggered forward a few steps, a manic grin stretching his mouth. I raised my sword and readied myself to give into the anger pulsing from the blade through my body, from Avalin's magic to me. It wanted to tear him limb from limb.

"Meet me in the Grey Vale, Ivy."

Fionn's horse galloped over the garden wall, and Fionn swung onto its back. How he could even move while bleeding so much was a mystery, but his grin remained in place as the horse turned towards the house, and the summoning circle within. Fionn vanished into the swirling circle of lights, laughter echoing in his wake.

"Vance." I lowered the sword, willing the fury seething through my veins to calm down. "Are you okay?"

He groaned, rolling to his front. My heart plummeted at the sight of all the blood, but the blue tinge gave it away as faerie blood, not his. I reached for a healing spell and threw it to him, then applied one to myself.

"Thank you." Vance's claws had disappeared when he'd been knocked down, and he pushed to his feet, his clothes torn and bloody. "Where did he go?"

"No clue." I swore. "Isabel?"

"Here," she said faintly, crouched behind the remains of a wrecked car.

"Do you need a healing spell?"

She straightened upright. "No, he healed me, all right. But he summoned…" She gestured to the circle of lights with a shaky hand.

"It's not your fault," I said. "He set us up. Besides, he tricked all of us."

"Into leaving the ring in the forest." Her mouth thinned. "I can't believe the Hemlock witches didn't notice."

"Him and that bloody banshee." I turned to Vance. "I can't believe none of us figured it out, either. I thought I couldn't use my magic because of the forest's trickery. Not because that devious banshee double-crossed us."

"She seems to have switched sides since our last encounter." Anger reverberated through his voice. "Fionn won her over."

"She's a death fae. I imagine she felt more of an affinity for the master of death than for the likes of me." I hadn't exactly been trusting of her, but she'd proven all too recently why my instincts had been dead on the mark. "Fionn will be back. He'll be healing up in the Grey Vale, but he wants me on his side too badly to walk away this time. While he's gone, we need to close that summoning circle."

The forest might be in peril, but the ritual was designed to summon the same creature the Hemlock Coven's magic was protecting. Fionn wanted us to split our attention, to ensure his plan succeeded.

"I'll do it," said Isabel. "The rest of the coven members are on their way. They should be here any moment now."

Screeching cries rang out from the summoning circle, heralding the arrival of a fresh group of furies. "And so's someone else."

Fionn's arrival had brought the fight to a standstill and pushed the other mages into retreat, but they returned to face the new threat. We might outnumber the enemy, but when Isabel tried to get close to the house, a new monstrosity tore itself loose from the summoning circle and bore down on her.

I moved in to help, not daring to leave for the forest despite my knowledge of the ticking clock hanging over my head. The circle was too dangerous to leave unchecked, and a fresh wave of oncoming furies forced the mages to pull back to keep them from escaping into the neighbouring streets.

"Isabel!" The shout came from across the road, where Shana

ran to engage one of the furies. An explosive spell flew from her hand and hit its target like a firework, blowing the fury's outstretched claw clean off. Another blast took off its head, and a dozen more coven members ran in to join her, including Chloe. All were armed to the teeth with iron and spells.

"Need help?" Shana called. "Sorry we took so long to get here. We found some stragglers hanging around the town hall."

"You fought the hunters?" Isabel gestured towards the house. "Be careful. Those monsters are death fae—don't look directly in their eyes. And watch those claws!"

Three more furies swooped on the newcomers, and a series of explosive spells flew upward and set off concussive blasts in midair. I'd never seen the coven members fight as a team before, but I was impressed at how well they managed to coordinate their spells. Isabel fell back from the house to let them catch up to her. When the witches reached the other side of the road, they all stared in horror at the vibrant lights visible through the ruins of the house and the monsters stirring within.

"Is that… necromancy?" Chloe asked uncertainly. "I've never seen a circle *that* big."

"It's a ritual," Isabel said. "Intended to summon much worse than those creatures. We have to shut it down."

"Something worse than those monsters?" Shana sounded faint.

"Much worse."

A fury burst sideways from the wreckage and flew at the newcomers, its claws seizing a younger witch around the waist.

"Hey!" Isabel ran behind and drove a knife into the fury's foot. The blade stuck fast, and though the fury released its target, its claws swung towards Isabel.

The world slowed. I ran, putting on a burst of speed, and

yet I could already see the claws bursting through Isabel's chest, already see her lifeblood spilling out again. A scream tore from my lips.

Light shone, pouring out of Isabel's arms until her body became a golden pillar. I gawped as the fury's claws bounced clean off her and it flew sideways into the path of my oncoming blade. I sliced off its head and landed beside Isabel, staring at the new symbols glimmering on her skin. No, not *on* her skin, but beneath the surface, emanating a radiant glow.

"It's my coven leader magic." She looked down at herself in wonder. "Cordelia was right."

"Isabel." Shana ran behind her, faltering. "I'm sorry. I should have been faster. That monster—"

"I'm fine." Isabel smiled widely. 'Better than fine."

"I told you the magic would choose you as worthy." I shot her a grin. "Let's finish these dickheads off."

We faced the oncoming furies with renewed enthusiasm. The other witches closed ranks around Isabel, some of them eyeing the glyphs on her arms with admiration and awe. As radiant as she might be, a sobering reality was that the same magic hadn't been able to save Francine, and the ring needed to be dealt with. Once we'd got rid of the summoning circle.

Isabel tried to enter the house and was once again pushed back by a new group of screeching furies.

I caught Vance's eye. "For the witches to get inside the house, someone needs to take out the furies the instant they appear. Can the mages get any closer?"

He dipped his head in acknowledgement and moved to consult with Drake and the other mages. They spread out and took up positions around the house, ready to strike at any fury that rose from the ruins with fire and lightning and anything else they could throw.

With the path clear, Isabel managed to get close enough

to the house to throw an explosive spell directly inside. Shards of debris blew in all directions, and I'd have been worried for the neighbouring houses if they hadn't already been in a worse state than this one. The blast took out a chunk of the front wall that had been blocking the way to the swirling vortex fuelled by the circle within the ruin of the basement.

"Careful," I warned as Isabel climbed onto a piece of broken wall to better reach the summoning circle. The eye of the storm, in an almost literal sense.

A fury rose from within the circle but was repelled by the glow radiating from the glyphs on Isabel's arms. As it veered away, I brought my blade to the hilt into the fury's eye and kicked its body out of the witches' path. The others joined Isabel, picking their way closer to the summoning circle while the mages fired off attacks at any fury that tried to ambush them on the way.

"Ready!" Isabel called. "Everyone spread out. Cover the whole circle."

The witches moved around the circle's edges, and Isabel watched, concerned, as the they clambered over the house's ruins to reach the far corners of the circle without falling into its depths.

When everyone was in place, they began chanting, I didn't know the words, but a shiver rose to my skin at the echoing chant that sounded as though it came from more people than their small group. The glyphs on Isabel's arms gleamed even brighter, the glow expanding to the witches on each side of her. Similar glyphs sprang up on Shana's arms, then Chloe, and then each other witch as the effect spread around the circle's perimeter. My hair stood on end at the power humming in the air, and the next fury that attempted to rise from the circle fell back, pushed by a shimmering golden barrier. By the collective power of the coven's magic.

Whoa.

The swirling vortex shrank in on itself, the circle of lights dimming in the brighter glow of the coven's magic. With a wrenching crack, the summoning circle collapsed like the front of a car colliding with a brick wall. I raised my hands to shield myself from the flying chunks of brick and glass, but there was no need. The golden barrier around the witches remained in place and not a single piece of debris broke past their shield. Not until the circle was gone, the house reduced to harmless rubble.

The light faded, the golden barrier dissipating as the glyphs on each witch's arms faded one by one. Isabel was last, and a faint shimmer lingered on her skin as she jumped down from the ruins.

"Done." Isabel flashed me a triumphant smile. "Those furies won't be bothering anyone again."

"Nice." I high-fived her, grinning. "You never mentioned a coven leader could do *that*."

"They don't usually get to fight monsters from the void in their first week as leader," Shana said, clambering down from the wreckage of the garden wall. "Fuck, that was amazing."

"Yes, it was."

For a moment I let myself get swept up in the coven's triumph, sharing hugs and high fives with the other members. The mages joined in, too, and I even saw Chloe and Vance exchange cordial words as well. There really was nothing like fighting a world-destroying monster to bring people together.

And yet. The ritual might have been cut off, but that didn't mean Fionn's scheme was at an end, and the forest remained in imminent danger.

While I hated to burst the bubble of her victory, I beckoned Isabel aside. "We need to go. Fionn's still around, and the forest…"

"I know," she said. "We have to stop that ring."

"There's another backup team waiting at the manor," Vance said. "I'll have them drive to the forest right away."

"Don't forget they'll need weapons that aren't magic," I warned. "We'll need iron, and a lot of it."

"Agreed." Vance nodded to Isabel. "I can't take the entire coven with us, but it's up to you if you want to come to the forest."

"I'll stay," she said. "I need to check on the rest of the coven. Some of those hunters might've stuck around."

"Fionn might have had more than one group attempting the ritual," I added. "Be careful, okay?"

"I will." She lifted her arm to display the new array of gleaming glyphs. "Besides, I have added protection now."

Yeah. Her newfound shield would defend her against anything, save for the ring, and I indented to deal with *that* myself.

I hugged her. "If the world doesn't end, you'll know I've won."

"Reassuring." A steely glint appeared in her eyes. "You'd better take him down, Ivy."

"I'll stab him twice for you, if I can."

Vance and I disappeared, landing back in the manor. While he ran to the weapons room, I replaced Isabel's blood-stained clothes with my own, shrugging on my leather jacket and stashing iron daggers in the pockets. If the worst happened and the ring cancelled out my magic, no faerie could beat iron. Not even Fionn... I hoped.

A shriek rang down the corridor as I was lacing up my boots.

"Bad faerie!" screamed Erwin.

"Where?" I grabbed my sword—which had ignited in bright blue. Ah, hell.

A familiar screeching noise from outside the manor. *Furies.*

20

"We didn't get all of them?" I ran outside, into the front garden, and spied three winged shapes circling above the manner. Some of the furies must have escaped the hunters' house. That or there was a second nest of monsters elsewhere.

Shit, we don't have time for this.

I ran outside and along the garden path to the manor's entrance. The furies swooped down, and I shot magic from my palm, knocking one of the beasts out of the sky. Vance appeared behind me and his blade slashed at a second fury in midair. His shifter claws were out again, the black scales stained in blood.

"Bad faerie!" Erwin zig-zagged over my head and threw a spell up at the third fury, which missed wildly and caused a section of the hedge to catch alight. From his other hand dangled a spiked weapon. Where in hell he'd got hold of a mace, I had no clue, much less how he managed to keep hold of it while flying around like a demented ping-pong ball.

Vance hastily displaced the burning hedge before it set anything else on fire, too. Erwin continued to zip around haphazardly, and though the furies swiped at him, he moved too fast for them to catch.

"Ivy!" He flew to my side, damn near hitting me in the face with the spiky weapon. "Protect you!"

"Okay, but—be careful."

Another fury dived at me and I stabbed it through the foot, severing its claws. As the fury fell, I beckoned to the piskie. "Erwin, have you seen a massive evil faerie on a horse anywhere?"

Fionn had claimed he'd be waiting in the Vale, but if the furies were any indication, he wouldn't make it easy for me to reach the forest before the ring obliterated all the defences keeping that beast contained.

"Bad screaming faerie!" he shrieked, swinging the mace so wildly that he nearly knocked himself out of the air.

"Who… the banshee?" Was she around? She and I needed to have a conversation. A short and bloody one.

"Get out of here, you scum!" roared Lady Harper.

With a loud crack, three of the furies collided in mid-air in an explosion of gore, claws ripping and tearing Whoa. She hadn't even used a weapon, but the furies plainly no longer recognised their own allies. With their wings ripped to ribbons, they tumbled out of the air, and Vance and I finished all three of them off.

"What the devil is going on?" Lady Harper screamed at me.

"Faeries," I said. "You haven't seen a massive guy in armour, have you?"

"No," she growled. "What now?"

"Erm." No point in underplaying the issue. "Fionn left a magic-repelling ring in the middle of the Hemlock Coven's forest. I assume Vance told you the ring is a talisman that used to belong to the Sidhe, and that it can destroy any magic that comes near it. Including the spells keeping the creature underneath the forest caged in."

I was also assuming Vance had told her about the monster, too, but for all I knew, she'd already been aware, given her history with the Hemlock Coven.

Lady Harper swore at the top of her voice. A crack splintered the air, and the decapitated body of a fury fell on top of me. I yelped and shook myself to dislodge its twitching claws and fraying wings.

I kicked the fury's corpse aside. "The hell was that for?"

"This mess has your name written all over it, Ivy Lane."

"Seriously?" Nobody threw a dead body at me, even if they were right. "Fionn's a master trickster. If you want to blame anyone, blame the Hemlocks for not noticing the ring was in their forest. Or the banshee for putting it there in the first place. It's bad enough the Chief will blame—oh, *fuck*."

"The Chief." Vance tossed another dying fury aside and ran to my side. "We have to warn him first. If the worst happens, his territory will be the first to get hit."

"You think he'll believe us?"

If he didn't, it was his funeral. Though for all I knew, the effects of the ring had already spread beyond the forest and into the magic that sustained the half-faeries' territory. We didn't have any time to waste.

Vance tossed me a healing spell, which I caught in a hand. "What's this for?"

"Backup," he replied. "I know the ring negates all spells, but we won't be able to return for supplies."

"True."

I had my sword and three daggers. While my talisman alone would suffice, beating Fionn would be a tall order even when I *did* have access to my magic. I'd get rid of the ring first and deal with him when the threat of the world being destroyed by a giant god was less imminent.

Vance caught my eye. "Ready?"

"As I'll ever be."

The smell of rot filled my nostrils as soon as we landed inside half-blood territory. I coughed, rubbing the sting from my eyes. And stared. The grass had yellowed, and flowers wilted in their beds. Rotten leaves littered the paths, blackened as though scorched in fire. Between lay thousands of tiny carcasses. Even the insects were dying. The sound of shrieking, growling, and despairing cries filled the air.

The effect must have spread from the forest, as I'd feared. With no magic to sustain it, the whole of half-blood territory would collapse. Soon.

"I'll warn the Chief." Vance moved towards a small dwelling that I belatedly recognised as the Chief's house. Such was the miserable state of the surrounding forest that I hadn't realised where we'd landed. "I'm guessing he'll be hiding inside."

"Mage Lord." The door opened a crack, revealing the Chief, who looked as withered as the forest did. His green eyes had dulled to grey, and his staff might as well have been a walking-stick. "I do hope you've come with an explanation."

"Not one you'll like," I said.

The Chief wrenched the door fully open. "Are *you* responsible for this?"

"No," said Vance. "You're being affected by a talisman that negates all magic, including yours. It's infecting your territory from within. We're intending to remove it, but I'd advise you to get your people out first, before they suffer any more ill effects."

"You're lying," he spat. "You want this territory for yourself."

I burst out laughing. "Are you kidding me?"

No, he wasn't. Eyes bulging, he raved at us. "You've

wanted to be one of us ever since you stole the magic you hardly deserve—"

"You're talking crap," I cut in. "Listen to yourself. We don't care about your territory, but if you want to live to see the dawn, I'd get as far away from that forest as possible. That talisman belongs to the leader of the Wild Hunt. Know who that is?"

He gaped at me. "The Wild Hunt were responsible for ferrying the souls of faeries lost in battle over in their own realm. That's hardly relevant."

"Their leader certainly fucking is," I said. "Fionn is homicidal, deranged, and has decided to drop a magic-killing talisman right on top of an enchantment keeping an ancient god contained. Which also happens to overlap with your territory."

The Chief's mouth twisted into a grimace. "What absolute *nonsense*—"

"Do you think *I* did that?" I indicated the rotting flowers dangling from the ceiling inside the hallway. "There are ancient protections on that forest coming undone beneath your feet. Vance and I are going in to stop it either way, but I thought I should warn you to get out in case we fail."

The Chief sagged against the wall. "We can't evacuate," he said weakly. "It's not feasible… the others will never agree…"

"Taive." A dark-skinned half-Sidhe with silvery eyes stepped into view. Killian, the Chief's partner, who I'd seen at the house during my previous visit, placed a consoling hand on the Chief's arm and murmured, "I don't think it's wise to stay. If she's right…"

"I am," I said. "You don't think I *want* everyone in here rendered homeless? I want as few people as possible to die. The ring destroys any magic it comes into contact with, and I can't promise we'll manage to get it out before this place collapses around your ears."

The Chief's eyes bulged. "You're talking about Summer's ring?"

"You know it?"

"Every half-Sidhe descended from Summer nobility knows of the legendary ring that was stolen from the heart of the Summer Court."

I blinked. "The heart of the Summer Court? How did it not destroy... you know what, never mind. I'll file that away with my questions for whoever created the damn thing in the first place. Seems like a disaster waiting to happen."

"We do not question the wisdom of the Erlking."

I raised a brow. "Yeah, well, asking questions might have solved a lot of your current problems. Anyway, I'm sure you can survive outside your territory for a bit. Isn't it the solstice, so Seelie faeries are at the height of their power?"

The Chief blew out a breath. "You are correct, but if my people lose their homes as a result of this, I expect compensation, Mage Lord."

"Naturally," said Vance. "Tell your people to make haste, but I would advise you to refrain from mentioning the name of the person responsible until we have dealt with his incursion."

The Chief's mouth worked. "Is there no reasoning with this... Fionn?"

"I'd like to see you try reasoning with Fionn. Trust me, he makes the Lady of the Tree look like a calm, rational person."

"Fine," snarled the Chief. "Get on with it, then."

Vance and I vanished, this time landing in the spot where we'd entered the Hemlock witches' forest the last time. Dead trees greeted us, rotting carcasses with roots sprawled like the legs of a giant spider's corpse. Their branches enclosed us the moment we stepped inside, cutting out the light. I shivered, raising my sword to let the blue light penetrate the dark. My magic was still working. The ring wasn't close, not yet.

"Can you use your ability?" I whispered to Vance.

"I can try." Vance placed a hand on my arm.

We vanished, reappearing deeper in the woods. The low light levels suggested we'd landed near the place with the glowing cobwebs. When I lifted my head to look at Vance, he wasn't there. In his place stood Fionn, one hand casually resting on a tree trunk and a wide smile on his face.

"Thought you were in the Vale." My heart gave a disjoined thump. "Bit risky coming here in person, isn't it? The ring affects you, too. Am I right?"

"I wanted to once again make you an offer," he said. "You're too late to save your realm. Come with me instead. Join me, and ride with the Wild Hunt."

"What does destroying this realm even achieve?" I knew reasoning with him was as futile as playing chess with a troll, but I couldn't help myself. "You have free run of the Vale and haven't had your magic ripped away like the other outcasts. You don't need to come back and torment humans. Let us live."

"Now, the humans aren't entirely blameless," he said. "This one agrees with me. Don't you?"

The banshee crept out of the dark, her thick dark hair tangled with branches, and her eyes fixed on her bare feet. Lifting her head, she nodded. "I do."

21

"Isn't she wonderful?" said Fionn. "Her kind were thought to be extinct. Harbinger faeries are viewed with superstition even amongst the other Unseelie. The Sidhe are so *touchy* when it comes to acknowledging the inevitable end of their extended existence."

He talks about them as though he isn't one. "You used to collect their souls, didn't you?"

"For a price." His teeth flashed white. "I much prefer my new position."

"What, an eternal pain in my arse?" I glared at the banshee, whose eyes were on her feet again. While some of that might be guilt, I was more inclined to think she was scared of Fionn. She stood more rigidly than usual, and displayed none of her usual flippancy. My anger at her betrayal had nothing on the sheer rage pulsing from my magic as it sought to rip Fionn to pieces. "Where the hell is Vance?"

"Your mage is where you left him," he said. "This coven's magic is powerful enough to alter reality in a way I thought only the Sidhe and their kin were capable of. It's rather impressive."

"Yeah, we humans aren't as powerless as you think. Do you know anything about the Hemlock Coven, or are they just another obstacle in your way?"

"They are no threat to me." He spoke in a flat tone, all traces of humour disappearing. "Soon, they will cease to matter altogether."

"Were they the ones who imprisoned you?" I already knew the answer was no, but from the irritated twitch in his jaw, he was still as much in the dark over how he'd ended up in that tomb as ever. "Or were you hoping the forest's magic would bring your lost memories back? Is that what this is about? It must really piss you off to know someone got the best of you and not be able to remember who it was or how they did it."

"I'd advise you not to push me, Ivy," he said. "I've tolerated you up until now because you're the most uniquely fascinating human I've met, and I would dearly love you to join me as an ally. That may change."

"You're doing a stellar job of convincing me to sign up." I rested a hand on my sword's hilt, debating. If I attacked, he'd knock me down. If I stalled, the forest would be eroded and the beast hidden beneath would tear its way into this realm.

Getting the ring out had to be the priority, but we weren't close, not yet. My magic's rage persisted, tendrils rising upward and reaching towards Fionn. He didn't react, perhaps knowing my power would have no effect on him.

"I know why you like the Mage Lord," said Fionn. "You look up to him because he's so accomplished at keeping his shifter side contained, the same as you do with your magic. Despite wielding two of our talismans, you still run from what you are, what you could be."

"I'm not running. I haven't done that in a long time." That

much I knew. "Not everyone craves world domination, Fionn. Fear has nothing to do with it."

Sure, I was scared for my friends, for Vance, for the world at large, but fear of my own magic didn't even factor into the equation.

"Actions speak louder than words, Ivy Lane," he said. "You haven't set foot in the Grey Vale since I was freed from my prison. Either you're lazy and unwilling to accept responsibility for the power you wield… or you're afraid."

I gave him a flat stare. "Or maybe the Vale is a shithole that doesn't even have adequate plumbing."

He gave a laugh. "So fierce… so evasive."

"Believe whatever you want," I said. "I never wanted this power, but now it's mine, I'll use it on my terms. You don't have to live in Faerie to use your magic. I'm human, and this realm is my home."

"You must know you don't belong here," he said. "Do you know what a gift you'd bring to the Grey Vale? Most faeries there are dying, stripped of their powers. You're young and whole, magic burning within your very bones. You can do more than survive there: you can rule."

"Did you not hear me say I've no intention of ruling anything?" I spat at him. "Give it up, Fionn. I'm nothing like you."

"Maybe I didn't make myself clear," he said. "You're human, but magic altered your very nature. The fact that you can traverse realms without losing your humanity proves that. You and I are very alike indeed."

"Then why does my magic want to rip off your fucking face?" The power burned beneath my skin, demanding to be unleashed. Maybe I had been holding back. Avoiding the Grey Vale, certainly, but by extension, avoiding using my magic to its full extent because I knew that at its core, the talisman had no distinction between friend and foe. Like

Avalin himself, my magic was a bottomless pit that no amount of suffering would be enough to satiate. The two had been suited, but even Fionn had seen the limits of the insular world he'd lived in. To Avalin, the talisman was all that had existed.

Me? I had far more to live for. I didn't depend upon the talisman for my own survival. More crucially, I knew I didn't need to inflict suffering on others to achieve my goals.

That didn't make me a coward. It made me human.

"Does it?" He smiled. "Why not allow your power the freedom it craves?"

"Oh, believe me, I've been waiting." Blue energy poured from my hands, fusing with my blade as I ran at him.

Talons blocked my path. The banshee leapt into the way, her mouth opening into a deafening scream that hammered against my eardrums and knocked my entire body off balance. I reeled, my ears burning, cursing myself for ever believing she wouldn't join Fionn at the first opportunity.

"I should have killed you sooner." I kicked out, knocked her onto her back and pressed the sword to her throat. Its light blazed, drawing in her fear as well as mine.

A soft laugh drew my gaze to Fionn. He smiled at me, and his eyes asked the question, *Are you really going to kill someone I coerced into helping me? A changeling like you?*

I changed trajectory and lunged at Fionn instead. He drew out his own sword, no longer laughing, as my magic collided with him like a high-speed car crash. He staggered a little, but his blade caught the brunt of the hit. He returned with another strike, almost lazy, easy to block. Toying with me.

I'm not playing this game again.

I slashed at his legs, attempting to sever the arteries above his knees. My blade bounced off his armour. I didn't know what material it was made of, but that shit was strong, and even my talisman didn't make a dent in the plating. I swung again and his blade caught mine. Despite

his childish games, he was undeniably a skilled swordsman. He'd had a thousand years of practise, after all.

I couldn't beat him on skill alone, but trickery was still on the table, and I did have some advantages here. For one, I'd bet he couldn't regrow limbs like he had in the Grey Vale when I'd busted his hand open. He might be toying with me, but he must know that outside of his own domain, I'd be able to do him some permanent damage. Especially if the ring's effects caught up to us.

"What're you stalling for?" I brought my blade up in a diagonal slash which narrowly missed slicing his nose off. "Did you want to fight me without magic? The ring's effects will catch up to us soon, and we both know you could have killed me by now, if you wanted to. If you're as powerful as you claim to be."

"Now, you know why I don't want you dead. The sad thing about mortals is that they don't come with second chances."

"Neither will you." I brought my blade up to his neck, and he punched me in the chest. Pain exploded through my whole body, and I slammed down on my back, the wind knocked from my lungs. *Damn. This is where armour would come in handy.*

Sucking in air, I rolled over and fired magic from both hands. The banshee got in the way and went flying with another shrill scream, her back hitting a tree.

"Not like you to hide behind your servants, Fionn," I wheezed, pushing to my feet. My chest ached sharply, warning he'd broken a rib or two when he'd hit me. I usually didn't regret wearing lightweight clothes without armour that would slow me down, but damn, that hurt.

As I readied myself to lunge, fresh pain bloomed up my

side. My gaze dropped to a bloody streak soaking through my top from the protruding hilt of a knife. *Ah, shit.*

"I'm disappointed you fell for the same trick twice, Ivy." Threads of magic spun from his hand, twisting the knife. I screamed.

Magic blazed around me, drawing on my pain as well as its incessant anger. I sent a blast at Fionn, my vision blurring, and grasped the knife hilt in my hand. I pulled it out, sending another bolt of pain through my core. He hadn't hit any internal organs, but the wound was too deep to heal without a spell… or without going into the Grey Vale, where my healing abilities would be stronger. And where I'd be at his mercy.

Fionn's mouth tilted up. "You don't need this realm, Ivy. Neither of us do."

"I'm not like you." I coughed the words. "I was born here."

"And you were reborn in the Vale, beyond the reaches of Death itself." An alien gleam shone from his eyes. "I am far older than any creature in this realm. My harbingers and I can endure beyond death, and you would do well to remember that, Ivy."

My side throbbed. The pain fed into my magic, the glow burning bright as ever, but the same agony prevented me from moving. Blood seeped from the wound, leaking into the forest floor.

Fionn lunged forward and stabbed me in the chest.

My body froze, impaled on his blade. He smiled knowingly, and my vision blurred even further. This wound, I knew, would be fatal. Already greyness filtered in, the veil beckoning. No healing spell would save me now.

"Come with me," he whispered. "Come to the Vale."

The last shreds of my consciousness brought a reminder that the Vale might be Fionn's domain, but it was mine, too, in part. My magic was drawn there, and coupled with its incessant desire to destroy him, that might be enough to give me an edge.

Death loomed closer, grey and endless, beckoning me to slip out of my body and join the spirits on the other side. I resisted, drawing on all the willpower that remained. To reach the Vale, I needed to pass through the realms, body and spirit both, and it would be the first time I'd done so without the Ley Line as a base. Two spirit lines intersected within the forest, though, and as I'd learned already, all the paths led to the Vale.

With the last ounce of strength in my limbs, I reached forward and locked my fingers around Fionn's ankle. My vision flickered as my spirit tried to leave my body, but I fought back. *I'm going there in one piece or not at all.* Like it or not, Fionn was right: my very nature had been changed when I'd claimed Avalin's magic and his talisman along with it. Part of me belonged to both realms. It always would, as long as I existed.

Fionn laughed, cold and triumphant, as the two of us were borne into the grey.

22

Consciousness returned. I sucked in a breath, relief flooding my body from head to toe as the pain washed out of me. My eyes flickered open to see magic circling me in a faint blue glow, mingling with the grey light smothering the path of the Grey Vale. With the pain gone, my body filled with rejuvenating energy—but Fionn was nowhere to be seen.

Damn. I'd hoped to bring him with me, but I stood alone on the path, with no sign of my enemy. Why force me into the Vale if he didn't want me to fight him? Or had he just wanted me out of the forest, to leave a clear path for the ring to wreak destruction on the world?

I have to get out... but my rational mind told me that if I did, he'd simply stab me again and force me to return here to save my own skin. For whatever reason, he wanted me here. Against my best efforts, a flicker of the old fear stirred. Though the Vale's paths were open to me, I still felt out of my depth when it came to navigating this place, and I had far too many bad memories associated with its dark corners and crevices to ever fully be rid of them.

Fionn, by contrast, had been wandering around here for weeks. Or maybe months or years, depending on how time had passed in Faerie. He'd had long enough to craft his own domain and shape it to his will.

I can do the same, I told myself, beginning to walk. The Vale would oblige, provided I stayed in the neutral zone and didn't wander into another Sidhe's domain. *Take me to somewhere I can find a way to kill Fionn. Take me to a way to stop him.*

An Invocation might work, but he was far more resilient than a regular Sidhe. Even whoever had imprisoned him all those years ago hadn't finished the job. Maybe another forgetfulness spell would work, except the first one hadn't stopped Fionn from reawakening with the same murderous instincts he'd had prior to being locked in that tomb.

There *was* the sleeping spell that I'd used on the god. Maybe the same one had been used on Fionn, too, but I didn't know it by heart. I'd spoken the words by instinct, aided by the magic living within my talisman.

I'll do it again. I couldn't afford to doubt myself now. He had to be taken out of commission one way or another, and so did the ring.

Come on, Grey Vale, I thought. *My magic is bound to you. Show me a way to beat Fionn.*

I rounded a corner and came to a halt. Fionn himself stood not ten metres away, waiting expectantly.

Faerie, you total dick.

Of course the fucker had the same world-altering power that I did, and when his was pitted against mine, his won out. Looking at him, I realised I hadn't appreciated just how much the mortal realm toned down the sheer raw, uncontrolled energy. In the Vale, he looked even taller, bigger, more *present* than before. The blade in his hand burned brightly, but then, so did mine, a blazing blue beacon in my hands.

So be it. Magic poured through my veins, humming in my ears like a second heartbeat. Searing anger bursting from my skin like a tidal wave and crashed down on Fionn in a raging torrent, bright enough to dazzle my own eyes. I squinted, seeing him stagger a little, but I might as well have thrown a paperclip at him. Not a scratch marked that armour.

"Now, your magic can't kill me, Ivy. You should have worked that out by now."

The flicker of a smile crossed his face, though compared to his playful mood earlier, he was all business. "Let us finish this."

He lifted his blade, and I did likewise, no longer fearing any damage to myself. Here, I could heal any injury.

I feinted then struck, sweeping at his armoured legs. He sprang back, catlike, and I moved in pursuit. My hand grabbed for his sword hand but failed to lock before he brought his blade up towards my chest. I leapt aside, the edge snagging my jacket but failing to reach its mark. Good, because being able to survive a fatal wound didn't mean I enjoyed being stabbed.

I renewed my attack, meeting him blow for blow. I was sure he was holding back, at least a little, but blocking his strikes brought me some level of satisfaction all the same.

"You could wield any talisman you like," I said, my words punctuated by the clash of blade on blade. "I understand why you don't want mine, because you and Avalin didn't like each other, but that ring would take down anyone who opposed you. Why throw it away?" I got past his guard, but my sword bounced off his armoured chest. "Unless… are you *trying* to get rid of it?"

He hesitated for a millisecond, a tiny reaction I wouldn't have noticed if my magic wasn't on high alert, enhancing all my senses.

I thrust upwards and pierced a hole through the armour

on his left arm, then stabbed deeper, drawing a stream of blood. *Gotcha.* However tough he might be, he had weak spots like everyone else. Like the ring.

"Shit, I'm right, aren't I?" In fact, had he brought me here because the ring muted his own powers? Was his intention to let the ring destroy my realm and leave Faerie untouched? The talisman might have aided the Sidhe in the invasion, but it might easily have been their undoing as well. Cordelia had hinted as much. In addition to removing our realm from the picture, leaving the ring behind would ensure it was never used against him again.

If I was right, and he was willing to put the entirety of humanity at risk from that sleeping god's wrath in order to be rid of the ring, Fionn was a fucking coward.

His next strike skimmed my shoulder, the point coming within inches of my neck as I blocked. My mind whirled, threatening to derail my focus. If the ring was indeed his weakness, wielding it against him might be the edge I needed to win. The slight problem, of course, was that the ring would also shut down my magic. I might not even be able to use my powers to cross realms and return to the Vale... though that raised the question of how it'd ended up in the mortal realm in the first place. Someone had brought it here from Faerie, right?

"I'm curious." I blocked another strike, my teeth rattling at the jarring crash. "Who found the ring first? You, or the hunters? I bet it hurt your pride that some weak humans have an advantage over you. If they used the ring, would one of those bullets be able to take you out?"

"No." He tried to kick me in the chest again. I pivoted aside and slashed at the backs of his legs. Yet again, my blade glanced off his armour. "I'm far more than a Sidhe, Ivy. I am a god."

"Did anyone ever tell you your ego's probably bigger than this whole realm?"

He laughed and slashed at my ribs. I dodged the blow—barely—and renewed my own attack.

"But you're still afraid of the ring." I pushed on. "You know it can unravel your magic, the same as anyone else. You aren't immune. And without magic, what are you, really?"

"You're making guesses based on half-knowledge and lies, Ivy." He blocked my strike and went on the assault again, words punctuating blows that I narrowly deflected. "If you had come to the Grey Vale and sought the answers yourself, you would have much more knowledge to draw on. You'd know all about the talismans, including the ring, and including your own."

"You must know you're wasting your time trying to recruit me willingly. I'm not as pathetic as those hunters."

"Or her?" He beckoned, and the banshee shuffled into view. Evidently, he'd dragged her along for the ride, and from the stark terror on her face, she hadn't come willingly either. In fact, he might have forced her into a vow like he'd done to me.

"You know," I said between strikes, "death is far from the worst possible fate. I think you know that, too. You're far more scared that someone will trap you again, erase your memories and shut you in a box. Aren't you?"

"Careful, Ivy." He blocked my next stab with a slash that would have cut the blade in two if it had been an ordinary sword.

"Or what, you'll try to kill me?" He wasn't, though. He was letting me put up a fight, refraining from dealing any fatal blows and focusing on blocking mine instead. Sure, I could heal, but so could he, and my magic would ensure I didn't tire at the rate of a regular person. "Or bind me to your will so I'll never turn against you. And you have the nerve to call *me* a coward."

A snarl escaped him. He fought harder, wilder, and though blood streamed from cuts to my arms and legs, they healed as fast as his own. I became more reckless in my own strikes, seeking out every joint in his armour, every gap through which I might land a blow. I'd made him bleed once. If I were to get him incapacitated and then hop back into my own realm, grab the ring and use it against him, I might have a chance at victory. It was my last remaining idea.

With a wrenching crash, part of his front armour came free, clattering onto the path.

Despite the rage simmering in Fionn's eyes, a smidgen of what might have been respect shone through. "Imagine what we could achieve together, Ivy. Truly, no other individual has come close to demonstrating the fortitude to stand at my side."

I ignored him and put on a burst of magic-enhanced speed to leap into a flying kick. My boot slammed into his chest and caused him to stagger. I landed, drove my blade into his exposed chest and twisted, hard.

Healing light sprang up in an instant, but I held the blade in place and willed all the rage and pain inside me to fuel its wrath. Biting deeper. *Come on.*

His blade hand twitched. I released my own sword with one hand and reached for his weapon hand to pry his fingers from the hilt.

Sharp pain speared my hand, as though I'd thrust it into a furnace. I let go of his blade with a gasp, and healing light spread over my palm as I struggled to keep my grip on my own weapon.

Fionn's shoulders shook with laughter. More blood bubbled from the wound in his chest. "You didn't think you could steal my talisman, did you?"

"Thought it was worth a try." I twisted my sword hilt, burying the weapon deeper. His blood trickled onto my fingers.

His sword hand flicked upward and the blade sank into my ribs.

Not again.

The banshee screamed. Not just in terror, but the keening note I'd heard the first time I'd seen her. When she knew someone would die.

Spots burst behind my eyes. My grip slipped on my blade hilt. His didn't. The instant I let go, his wound would heal, but so would mine, and I would bleed out before he drew his last breath. Blue light shone where his blade pierced my side, my healing ability trying to knit the muscle and skin back together.

The banshee leapt on Fionn, talons digging into his shoulders. I fell back, gasping as the blade came free and my healing power kicked in. Fionn snarled and writhed, and my sword slid out of his chest, too. *Shit.*

Alison's eyes locked with mine. "Go, human! I'll hold him."

The wound in my side was already sealing, but his wound was vanishing, too, while he fought to push the banshee off him.

I closed my eyes, willing my body to pass back into the mortal world. Between one blink and the next, the Grey Vale became the Hemlock Coven's forest. Dying trees crowded on either side of me and the stench of rot in the air made it hard to breathe.

I launched into a run, leaping over roots, skirting branches. Tendrils of smoke swirled around the trees, snagging at me like brambles. Wait. That wasn't smoke but webbing, formed of interlocking glyphs. Their luminescence had faded notably, but they were still intact, still glowing faintly. It wasn't too late…

I skidded to a halt. Fionn sat upon a vast tree root, his armour back in place. Behind him, more weblike glyphs spiralled away into the air, revealing a gap like a large window. On the other side of that window lay the abyss where the sleeping monster dwelt, the glyphs keeping it encased gradually leaking away.

"I wouldn't take another step, Ivy."

23

"The threads are unravelling," Fionn went on. "The Devourer will soon wake."

Oh, shit. I'd assumed Fionn wouldn't get too close to the ring, but evidently, he'd decided it was worth the risk to taunt me one final time. I didn't dare move, my attention riveted on the swirling glyphs, the thousands of overlapping threads keeping the creature caged.

All unravelling, one by one.

The beast slept on, oblivious. The Rite of the Devourer hadn't succeeded in awakening the monster, but Fionn hadn't needed it. If the magic of the forest collapsed, there was a very real chance that we'd be looking at Armageddon on a level that made the invasion look like a relaxing country walk.

"Want me to push you in?" I took a step forward, and I bit down on a gasp as Helena burned against my hands. Blue light swirled from the blade, drawn into the abyss, as though my magic was being pried loose from my skin. *Stop that. Stop it.*

"You can try." Fionn gave a broad smile.

"The Devourer, is it?" Who had given the creature that title? More to the point, why wasn't it affecting Fionn in the same way? With each second, more threads of magic tugged loose from me, drawn into the deep. "What does it devour?"

"Everything." A glint shone in his eyes. "It will devour the ring along with the rest of the world."

"You're that insecure about your one weakness?"

"Your world will be erased." His mouth twisted, half in anger, half amusement. "Forgotten. Like you."

"You're the one standing in front of the abyss."

"I fear nothing, Ivy," he said. "I wonder where your treacherous little friend is?"

"Who, the banshee?" He'd thrown her off, but I'd expected him to. I'd known I wouldn't have long, but where was the ring? That wasn't responsible for the prickling at my skin, the sensation of my magic being pried loose from me. The ring didn't *destroy* magic, just negated it. The Devourer was another entity altogether.

"You know she was never your ally, right?" Out of the corner of my eye, I scanned the forest for any signs of the ring, any clues that might point to the force pulling the glyphs out of the abyss. "You don't have allies, Fionn, you have people you've coerced and threatened." My voice grew stronger as his murderous expression grew more pronounced. Magic itched to burst from my hands, but I held back, knowing the pit would simply suck the power from my bones until nothing remained. Once those spells unravelled fully, the ring would be insignificant.

If the ring was strong enough to even bring the master of death to his knees, the Devourer would obliterate him. He'd willingly taken the risk, more than happy to sacrifice a realm of humans to achieve his goal.

And if I tried to get in his way, he'd either feed me to the

Devourer or invoke the vow I'd sworn and force me to watch the monster devour my world.

"You're reduced to mere taunts because you know that no actions remain for you," he said. "You've lost."

"Again. You're standing on the edge of a pit into the abyss." Why? To ensure I didn't miss the moment when the last thread unravelled and the beast escaped into this realm?

I'd bet my sword that was his plan. Fionn had to win at everything, and like every faerie, he wanted the last word. He'd stay until the final thread of the witches' spell unravelled, then grab me and haul us both to the Grey Vale an instant after I watched my world fall apart. He didn't want my talisman or even my magic. He only wanted…

"Did you know this forest holds memories?" I asked. "I saw a vision of Avalin and Velkas. It was very enlightening."

"I care not for the past, only the future."

"Sure about that?" I gave him an appraising look. "Honestly, I don't give a shit how many of Avalin's memories the forest shows me. It's never gonna make me like the guy. I have to say I wonder how you two ended up hating each other so much in the end, though. It sounded like he was willing to work with you."

"Tell me what the forest showed you."

Aha. I knew his curiosity would get the better of him. "Velkas was trying to convince Avalin to join your team and invade the mortal world. Do you remember either of them? That forgetfulness Invocation must have been pretty powerful. Pity we'll never know who did it. If there are more memories hidden here in the forest, it'd be a shame to throw them away."

Fury flitted across his face, and my blood turned to water. "I will not be manipulated.

I call in my favour. Ivy Lane, if you won't stand at my side willingly, then you will obey me from this point forward.

That is the favour I ask of you, and I command that you stay there."

The words hit me like a whip. My legs locked into place. My body angled itself towards him.

He'd overturned my will. There was no winning now.

"I don't think so," growled Fionn. He wasn't looking at me, but over my shoulder, at…

Vance. He walked towards us, the threads of magic parting on either side of him as though drawn by a magnet. Or rather, repelled, driven from the small object Vance held in his outstretched hand.

He found the ring.

Fionn's mouth twisted in a feral expression. "Put that down, Mage Lord."

Aha. The vow still held my legs in place, but I managed a grin. "Shouldn't have taken your eyes off the prize, Fionn."

"The realms can't survive without one another," Vance said to Fionn. "Even the Sidhe know that, and we share a common cause in preventing the likes of you from enacting terror upon this realm."

"Don't speak of what you don't understand, Mage Lord," said Fionn. "I've lived through a thousand or more of your lifetimes."

"So has that beast."

No kidding. Even in the last few minutes, the opening to the pit had widened, revealing a greyness that more closely resembled Death than either the mortal or faerie realms.

In fact, if I threw the ring in there, would the abyss keep it contained? Despite the ring's close proximity, my own magic was still visible, blue threads leaking into the pit despite the presence of the ring.

The Devourer destroyed *everything.* The ring included.

Renewed determination seized me. I caught Vance's eye. *Let's take him out first.*

Fionn's blade swung at Vance, but he caught its edge in one clawed hand. The other still held the ring. He couldn't use his displacing ability, but evidently holding the talisman didn't stop him from shifting. That didn't count as magic, not in the same sense.

In fact, my own enhanced speed and stamina remained intact, as did my ability to cross between realms. That magic was a part of me, woven into my very blood and bones. And I felt it stir, longing to strike him down. The muting power of the talisman pulsed out, quietening the thunder in my blood, but not stilling it altogether.

There was just the pesky matter of the vow he'd forced me to swear, which held me rooted to the spot. Unable to move.

Fionn and Vance collided, grappling with one another. I held my breath as they slammed into the forest floor and rolled over, perilously close to the hole. Crimson and blue blood spattered the ground, and a thrill of horror went through me. Even if the vow hadn't held me in place, I couldn't so much as move without risking knocking them both in. If this went on, either the creature would wake up, or they'd fall into the abyss and would both be lost together.

A scream ripped from my throat when Fionn threw Vance off him. He staggered, fetching up against a weblike mat of glyphs. Shock filtered into his expression. *Did they... save him?*

Fionn, too, stared at the glyphs for an instant, befuddlement crossing his face. A bright gleam told me Vance had dropped the ring on the forest floor. At my feet. *Aha.*

I dropped to a crouch and my fingers curled around the ring. I gasped, unprepared for the cold sucking sensation that instantly muted the rage pulsing from my talisman. I held tighter. Felt the threads of his command loosen. A smile came to my mouth. "That's better."

Fionn leaned in and I rammed my shoulder upward into his chin. He staggered, and Vance hit him with a backhand that made him stumble, his face bleeding. I drove forward with my own blade, pushing him up to the edge of the abyss.

Fionn seized my wrist and pulled me closer as he began to fall. Green light spiralled around us, glyphs of protective magic unravelling. Repelled by the ring. With a cry half enraged, half triumphant, Fionn fell backwards, pulling me with him into the abyss.

A brief moment of terror had us suspended in the air above the giant form of the sleeping beast. Fionn's wide eyes hovered before mine, then the world turned to grey smoke, and Fionn and I fell into the Grey Vale.

Damn. I'd had an inkling that crossing between realms wasn't the same as using a spell or even a talisman. Fionn and I were both bound to this place, though with the ring clenched in my hand, I felt none of the usual heightening of my senses that came with my magic connecting with the realm it had come from. No boost of rejuvenating energy sustained me; instead, exhaustion tugged at my limbs.

Fionn staggered back from me, absent of his usual grace. With the talisman draining our magic, neither of us was at full strength. While I'd wanted to leave him and the ring to rot in the abyss along with the monster, I'd settle for beating the shit out of him.

Fionn laughed harshly. "You risked a lot on a gamble, human."

"Oh, it wasn't a gamble," I said, panting. "The ring repels magic, not our own nature."

"You still think you can outdo me, human?" He sounded almost breathless. "That sword you wield might have altered your body enough that you can shift between realms, but nothing more. While you hold the ring, you will be unable to heal. There won't be any second chances this time."

"Try me." I slid the ring onto my finger and moved both hands to the sword hilt to block his oncoming strike.

A dull clang echoed through my body as my sword met his. Without magic humming through the blade, Helena felt more like a regular sword than a talisman, but still a deadly sharp one. Each tiny wound he inflicted on me burned with twice the pain, but the same went for the ones I inflicted on him. He was naturally faster and stronger, but he seemed to be weakening at the same rate I did.

"Want this?" I let the ring slip off my finger, then tugged it back on again, fending off his attacks as I did so. As though he couldn't help it, his eyes were drawn to the movement of the ring. His one weakness. He wanted to destroy it more than he wanted me dead.

I released my grip on the ring. It fell to the forest floor, and his split second of distraction spared me from a fatal blow. His blade sank into my shoulder instead of my chest.

Pain thumped from the wound, sharpening when he yanked the blade free and reached for the ring. In his moment of distraction, I groped into jacket and pulled out one of my daggers. The iron weapons might have had limited use when he could still heal at super-speed, but without his magic, a mere sliver could cause some serious pain.

Fionn's hand closed around the ring. I stabbed downward, my blade shearing his bare hand. An unmistakeable hint of fear flashed in his eyes as he rose upright. His blade swung, aimed at my dagger hand, but I blocked with ease. My shoulder burned with pain, my grip sliding down the sword hilt, but sweat glistened on his forehead, too. The hand that held the ring hung limp at his side, and I glimpsed a greyish tint spreading where I'd struck him with iron.

I was right.

My whole body ached. Crimson droplets scattered on the ground. My breath seared my lungs as I caught his next attack on the edge of my sword. My shoulder screamed, and the sword slid free from my grip.

As he moved in for the kill, I buried my dagger in his neck.

He let out an awful, animal howl. Choked. Gasped out a breath, trying to speak, maybe. Whatever he wanted to say, I didn't need to hear it.

My legs gave out. I fell, too, my shoulder a torrent of pain. Gasping, I pushed onto my knees, my vision flickering. Fionn was in a far worse state. His eyes were half-open, shot through with greyish lines.

I reached for his limp wrist with the hand that still held the dagger. No pulse answered. Hardly daring to breathe, I felt for a heartbeat next. Nothing. From the mangled state of his throat, there was no way he should be alive, and yet... he'd called himself the master of death.

No wonder he'd feared the ring deeply enough to burn down my whole realm over it. His talisman lay harmlessly at his side, and this time it didn't burn me as I fumbled my hand over the hilt. Before I could get a grip, though, the hilt gave way, falling apart in my hands.

As I watched, disbelieving, the entire blade crumbled to fragments—and so did its owner. Skin flaked from Fionn's grey-tinged face and from the open wound in his neck, spreading southward. His armour peeled back like snakeskin, also disintegrating as its owner did. Every last inch of Fionn fell apart, flaking like burned paper that became dust, and then nothingness.

Holy shit. Was that normal? I didn't think Velkas had fallen apart in the same way when he'd died—and his talisman certainly hadn't—but it saved me the bother of figuring out how to ensure nobody stole either for their own nefarious purposes.

Right then, my injuries decided to reassert themselves. My vision grew fuzzy at the edges. My shoulder screamed.

Don't pass out now. Get out of here first. And take that cursed ring with you, too.

The ring lay where he'd held it, glinting on the forest floor. I reached out, my hand closing around the cool metal.

Undeniably, the place in which that sleeping beast was contained was the only option to ensure the ring stayed gone. Abandoning it in here might not have adverse effects on the Vale itself, a place already stripped of its magic, but I'd learned the hard way that leaving a talisman unattended would only come back to bite me.

Hand clenched tightly around the ring, I willed my body to pass from the Vale into the mortal realm.

My knees scraped against tree roots. The abyss filled one side of my vision, draped in threads that had already repaired themselves in the short time since Fionn and I had left. The instant I landed, the webbing shrank away from me. I held out the ring in a shaky hand, over the the unseen barrier between the forest and the place where the beast slumbered. A place beyond life and death. The ring gleamed in the light of the glyphs peeling back to expose the sleeping monster. Its destructive magic would swallow up the ring while it slept on, oblivious.

I flipped my hand over. The ring floated more than fell, spiralling towards the still-sleeping beast. My vision flickered, but I held still, watching the small shape vanish like a stone sinking into deep water. My heart stuttered when the beast's eyelid gave the briefest twitch—then the threads of green light folded in again, and all was still.

"Ivy!"

Hands grasped my shoulders, pulling me back from the edge. Magic flooded me, thick and dizzying, magic I hadn't even noticed was being drawn away into the abyss.

Vance's face swam above me. "Ivy. Is Fionn—"

"Dead." *I think.*

I tried to say more, to add that killing a death god might not be as simple as destroying his physical body, and that I had to go back to the Vale and check his ghost hadn't lingered.

Darkness claimed me first.

24

I blinked awake on a sofa. That seemed to be happening a lot recently.

I flexed my hands, checking everything was working. My clothes were stained with enough blood to make me wonder how there was any left inside me.

"You really ought to get out of the habit of coming within a hair's breadth of certain death," said Vance.

"Nice to see you, too." I rolled onto my side. Though I wasn't in pain, my body felt utterly drained, as if I'd face-planted onto the life-drinker sword. "No, really. Thanks for getting me out of there."

"The Hemlock witches helped."

"They're okay, then?" I pushed upright and smiled at Isabel, who occupied the nearby armchair and offered a relieved smile in return.

"I would assume they are," Vance answered. "The forest was repairing itself, the last I saw."

"And the furies?" I studied Isabel. Her clothes were torn and bloody, but if it was her own blood, she must have used a healing spell. Belatedly I recalled the glyphs that had awoken during the fight and protected her from certain death, but they must have faded now the danger was over.

"We took them down," she said. "The mages helped. Drake set a fair few of them on fire."

"Good."

"And… the ring?" Isabel asked warily. "Vance said it was gone for good?".

"I threw it into the abyss." I slumped against the cushions, fighting a fresh wave of exhaustion. "Ah… how's the Chief?"

"The Chief wasn't happy that he was forced to call an evacuation only to reverse it within the hour," Vance said. "He doesn't realise how close he came to his territory being utterly wiped out. Some of the mages were injured, but nothing serious enough to require more than a healing spell. I think you were stabbed more times than the rest put together."

I winced. "Yeah. That'd be because the ring stopped me healing myself. You should see the other guy."

"Oh, Ivy." Isabel came over and hugged me, carefully, as if wary of my injuries. "You left him? He's dead for sure?"

"Fionn?" I hugged her back, and shifted into a proper sitting position. "Yeah. Iron poisoning. He kinda… disintegrated, to be honest. So did his talisman. I'd have brought it back with me otherwise. Learned my lesson about leaving dangerous talismans behind in Faerie."

"I didn't know talismans could do that," Vance said. "I thought they usually endured beyond their owners' deaths."

"So did I, but maybe Fionn really didn't want anyone else to claim his sword." Not like I could ask. "Honestly, it's a relief. I was starting to run out of space for all these talismans."

"The ring, too," Isabel said. "He wanted to destroy it all along?"

"Yeah. I don't think he ever intended to fight me *with* the ring. He wanted it gone, and if he could take out the entire human race in the process, so much the better." A shiver racked my body. "He wanted me to join him in the Grey Vale while the world went to hell."

Vance rested a hand on my shoulder. "I'm glad you stopped him."

"With help. Where'd you find the ring, anyway?"

"Deep in the woods. I wouldn't have found it if I hadn't seen the glyphs moving around and pointing me in the right direction. I think the Hemlock witches were trying to help."

"Nice of them." My vision had begun to swim again. I leaned back against the cushions and closed my eyes. "Might be because of Lady Harper. You know. Their history."

Whatever *that* was.

"Might be," said Isabel. "I'm going to speak to the coven again. Will you be okay?"

"Sure," I mumbled. "Thank them for me."

Vance spoke, but I didn't hear the words. Safe in his arms, I closed my eyes and let the world fade away.

———

I slept through the rest of the day and night and woke up in the early hours of the morning with my body aching from my awkward sleeping position on the sofa. Grimacing at the sour taste in my mouth, I reached for a glass of water someone had left on the nearby table and drank half in one go.

"Are you awake, Ivy?" Isabel looked at me sideways from the armchair, eyes half-lidded from sleep.

"What're you sleeping down here for?"

"Keeping an eye on you. Vance just went to check on the overnight guard. He didn't want to move you while you were asleep."

I pushed a handful of matted hair over my shoulder. "You aren't hurt, are you?"

"Nothing a healing spell didn't take care of."

"You shouldn't have stayed with me. The coven needs you."

"I've been with them, too," she said. "And I'll head there later today."

"Good." I tilted my head. "And your necromancer friend? Rick?"

A flush darkened her cheeks. "Him, too. We'll talk, and then... who knows."

"Hey, you deserve some fun. Vance and I are probably going away for a few weeks. He mentioned he has a house on the coast."

"Of course he does." Isabel gave me a knowing look. "Has he asked you to move in here yet?"

"To the manor?" Ah. "Yes, actually. I didn't give him an answer yet, but I know our flat's a hazard zone. You deserve somewhere way nicer."

"Actually..." She paused. "Francine left me some money. She also left her house to the coven, but the money's enough to put a deposit on a new flat. It'd be great if I could find one big enough for us to move our office there. I think our old place is cursed with bad luck."

"You're probably right." Or rather, *I* was. I'd been Fionn's target in the end. Everything else had been him playing twisted games with mortals. He might claim to be unique among Sidhe, but he was wrong. Once I'd taken away his advantage, iron had finished him like anyone else.

Are you sure? A nagging voice in my mind remained. He'd called himself a god, and while he undoubtedly had more in common with a Sidhe than with that creature sleeping in the abyss, the master of death might have a trick or two left. On the other hand, I'd seen him fall apart. The same way I'd seen the ring fall into the abyss. Our realm would survive another day.

A sudden current of magic surged through the air, raising the hairs on the back of my neck.

I bolted upright and grabbed my sword. "There's a faerie."

"What?" Isabel leapt out of the armchair.

Vance rushed into the room. "Someone's outside—Ivy, stay back. Don't forget you're injured."

"I'm fine, and I'm not letting the faeries into your home." I hurried after Vance into the hall. He reached the door in swift strides and opened it.

On the front lawn gathered a number of figures on horse-back. My heart gave a violent jolt. I lifted my blade. *Is this Fionn's final act of vengeance?* They'd got right through the wards—the *iron* wards.

Vance stalked towards them. "What is the meaning of this?"

My jaw hit the floor. Five riders sat astride large horses, but otherwise, they bore no resemblance to the Wild Hunt. They didn't wear dark armour or masks, but were clothed in silver-green attire with gold trimmings, light pouring from them as though they'd brought the sun down from the heavens to grace their presence.

Holy crap. They could only be Sidhe knights of the Seelie Court.

One of them locked onto me with green eyes, more vibrant than any living thing in this realm. Golden locks framed his pointed face. He spoke in a melodic tone. "What are you doing with that talisman, human?"

Oh. Oh *no.* My magic, vibrant blue as any from the Winter Court, was impossible to hide. My sword, too, could never have passed for anything other than the property of a Sidhe noble. But who *were* these people? They didn't know me. Nor I them. The Sidhe had addressed me in English, but his accent was hard to place and when I looked at his face, I had the sense of trying to keep my gaze on a hummingbird's rapidly beating wings. Almost as though his appearance was shifting and changing, or else my human eyes were struggling to grasp something that shouldn't be looked upon by mortal vision.

My tongue unstuck itself from the roof of my mouth. "It's mine."

"You are not one of the Unseelie," said the knight. "You're human."

"Yes, I am. Who are you?"

"I am Lord Raivan, ambassador for the Seelie Court, and I have come to request that you return the talisman you stole."

My mouth went dry. "I won the magic from a Sidhe lord who was exiled from the Unseelie Court." There was no point in hiding the truth. I'd broken no rules by claiming the talismans, to my knowledge.

"Not that talisman," said the Seelie knight. "A valuable ring that belongs to the Summer King."

What? "Er… didn't it go missing before I was even born?"

Never mind the specifics. The ring was lost, somewhere in that sleeping god's prison. The Sidhe would never get it back.

"Perhaps," said Sidhe. "I am here to request the return of the talisman to its rightful owner."

"You're too late." *He can't want the ring. Can he?* "Someone else stole it, not me. Have you ever heard of a realm called the Grey Vale? It's where your exiles end up. There are lords over there who wanted to challenge your courts. Do you know the name… Avalin?"

"No," said the Seelie knight.

"He's the one I won this talisman from." It made sense that the Summer Sidhe wouldn't know Avalin, because he'd never belonged to their court, but it'd be doubly hard to argue my case if they were completely oblivious to anything their exiled kin were doing. "The one responsible for stealing the ring, and trying to destroy this realm, was the former leader of the Wild Hunt. You can't tell me you don't know who *he* is."

"The Huntsman hasn't been heard of in our Court in centuries."

Oh, hell. To the Sidhe, human time passed so quickly as to not be worth noting. We were alive one second and dead the next. No wonder none of them had come back since the invasion. Twenty years was a blink to them.

"Yeah, well. He destroyed the ring. It's gone." Mostly true, and probably the sole version of the story that might spare me from a grisly end.

"Gone?"

How much does he really know? None of them had mentioned that Fionn had been sealed away. The forgetfulness rune affected everyone, the Sidhe included. Whether or not they'd been here in this realm, these people might have zero recollection of his fate.

"Yeah, gone." No point in dancing around the reality, and it was their own damn fault for letting the exiles steal their valuables in the first place. "You know, if you want to avoid a repeat of the invasion, I'd suggest paying a little more attention to where you send exiles. Quite a few of them want to kill you."

"Do not presume to argue with me, human," said the Seelie knight. "We are here on the orders of the Seelie King, and if it turns out you are hiding the talisman from us, your lives will be forfeit. Your name?"

"Ivy Lane," I told him. "And I'm not kidding. The Grey Vale's exiles invaded this realm—"

A dazzling flash of green light engulfed the lawn, and the Seelie knights vanished as swiftly as they'd arrived.

I remained rooted to the spot, unable to move. Even Vance was rendered speechless, his attention fixed on the lawn. I could have sworn the grass shone brighter in the spot where their horses had been standing. *Did that just happen?*

Isabel stepped out of the doorway. "Who *was* that?"

"I think," I said, "we just got an official warning from the Summer Court."

"For what?"

"The ring. They want it back."

"The one you threw into the abyss?"

"That one. Yeah." I leaned on the door frame, my knees buckling. "They might've waited until I was properly dressed. Or, you know, not come at all."

"Why now?" Isabel asked in a hushed voice. "I mean… why was this what drew their attention?"

"Because they care more about their missing magical trinkets than our realm being devoured by an ancient god." I sent a rude gesture towards the spot where they'd disappeared. "I realise they probably have no idea who the Hemlock witches are or what they're protecting, but you're right. *Why* now?"

"Evidently, some rumour made it back to the Summer Court," Vance said. "I imagine the ring's reappearance had ripple effects across the realms."

"Did they not even notice Fionn running amok between the Vale and Earth?" I scowled. "They're a little behind the times, to say the least."

"If they didn't know who Avalin was, I imagine they aren't important enough to have been told the details of Fionn's attempt to take power," Vance said. "They didn't even know he stole the ring from Summer in the first place."

"Shit, you're right." Powerful or not, those Sidhe must have been on the lowest rung of the ladder compared to the other lords who ruled the Courts. That would also explain why they'd been selected for the menial task of passing messages to humans. Pity for them. "I didn't consider that destroying the ring might cause issues. If they find out the truth, we'll have the Seelie King parked on the lawn next. At least then I might be able to have a proper conversation with someone in a position to do something about the Vale's exiles."

"I guess so," said Isabel dubiously. "Doesn't this place have iron wards all over it?"

"The lawn doesn't." The Sidhe hadn't entered through the gates. They'd crossed realms right there in the middle of the mages' garden without touching any iron at all. "I should return the favour. See how they like it when a human materialises in their kitchen."

Isabel gave me an alarmed look. "*Can* you do that?"

"Nah, I can only cross into the Vale." A sigh lodged in my chest. "Couldn't they have asked about the life-drinker instead? I still have that one, and I'm pretty sure Velkas stole it from Summer. What's with the Sidhe and their habit of creating talismans from the gods' magic and then losing them?"

Isabel gasped aloud. "From *what* magic?"

"I thought I told you." I rubbed my eyes. "The life-drinker contains part of that dragon shifter god's power. It's not the same as a regular old blade. I think the ring was the same. Most talismans can't destroy other magic. The Sidhe would wipe each other out if they did."

"You mean it contains the power of a god instead of that of a Sidhe." Vance nodded.

Isabel's mouth opened and closed. "And... *your* talisman?"

"Yeah." I'd suspected so for a while. "It makes sense. Avalin claimed it while he was in the Vale, which is where the Sidhe exiled their gods. He didn't get it from Winter."

"I think you're right," Vance said, in tones entirely too calm for the situation. "That's how you were able to use its power in conjunction with the life-drinker to bind that shifter god."

"And… Fionn?" Isabel said. "*He* wasn't a god."

"Nope." I'd watched his talisman fall to pieces before my eyes, and yet doubts remained, beneath the relief of him being gone, lodged deep in my mind like craftily hidden thorns. "I need to go back to the Vale later to make sure he's not still hanging about as a ghost."

"God, I hope not." Isabel shuddered. "Oh—whatever happened to that banshee?"

"Huh. Good question." I'd forgotten her, in the wake of everything else, but I didn't recall her following me back into the forest. "You know, I think she might have been left behind in the Grey Vale. Fionn coerced her into working for him, but I think she's better off there than here."

"Agreed," Isabel said. "Don't go near the Vale until you've properly recovered, Ivy. You lost half the blood in your body."

"Means I still have half left."

"Ivy." Vance caught my arm and steered me back into the house. "We don't need you keeling over."

"Hey, I didn't even use an Invocation this time." I spoke lightly, but I knew what a close call I'd had. We all did. "We need to go and see the witches again at some point. Once they've got over the shock of Fionn nearly destroying their forest."

"And the Chief," Vance added. "I wonder if he had a visit from Summer, too?"

"If not, he'll be pissed off at us." I reached the living room and found Quentin had slipped in at some point and left us breakfast, including a plate piled high with pancakes. "Hell, yes. That's more like it."

I grabbed a plate and piled it high, while Vance went to check on his fellow mages. That left Isabel and me, and I was more than happy to relax and enjoy a delicious breakfast while revelling in the simple delight that nobody was trying to kill either of us.

Isabel, by contrast, picked at her food. Her eyes were shadowed, and I wondered if she'd had any time to talk to the coven since the battle.

"Are you okay?" I asked. "You're officially coven leader now. No more doubts."

She smiled. "Yeah. I mean, it still scares the shit out of me, but when my power activated, it felt *right*. Like I stepped into Francine's shoes for real."

"Told you so." I shoved more pancake into my mouth. "Go on, eat the free food and enjoy the victory."

Vance returned and grabbed a plate from the table. "You made quick work of those pancakes, Ivy."

"Hey, I lost half the blood in my body," I said indistinctly through a mouthful. "I'm sure Quentin will bring more, though. He must have sneaked in here quietly. He's like a four-foot-tall ghost."

"I think he was avoiding the Sidhe."

"Hmm." I didn't blame him for that in the least. "What about the Chief? I thought he might've called. Since, you know, he has a mobile phone now."

"He does," said Vance. "He didn't call me, though. I imagine he's busy cleaning up the aftermath of evacuating his territory."

"You know, maybe building the territory on top of the Hemlock witches' forest wasn't the best idea his people have had."

"No." Vance sat down next to me. "Did you plan to tell him?"

"About the big world-destroying monster living on top of his territory?" I asked. "Seems like the sort of thing he should probably know."

"Agreed." Isabel was on her feet, her phone in her hand. "I need to go and meet the coven. They're planning a party to celebrate our victory and my official acceptance as coven leader. See you later?"

"If you're making cookies, save some for me." I waved at her as she left. "I'm glad the coven pulled through. That was some serious magic."

"Coven leaders are widely respected across the supernatural world for a reason." Vance watched the door close behind her. "I'm glad she was able to access her powers."

"Thanks for loaning her the books. I'm sure they helped."

"Perhaps, but magic often only reveals its true capabilities when pushed to its limits," he said. "Speaking of which, have you always been able to move between realms even when you aren't anywhere near the Ley Line?"

"Apparently." I put down my fork. "There are spirit lines across the whole city, and every liminal space is a potential crossover point."

Fionn had been right about one thing: I'd neglected to explore the true extent of my powers. I might not *like* going to Faerie, but keeping an eye on the Vale was undeniably the best way to anticipate any further trouble, and without Fionn hiding in there, the prospect was much less daunting.

When Vance frowned at me, I added, "Would you be okay with that? Using my magic to cross realms, I mean? It's not like Fionn's there waiting to pounce, not anymore."

"We'll discuss the subject later, when you've recovered."

I leaned back in my seat. "I've recovered just fine. I'm ready for that holiday."

"I thought so." He tilted his head on one side. "Did you consider my other question?"

"And decide whether I'll come and live in your fancy manor? Yes. On the condition that Drake draws me a map. I still get lost every time I go to the upper floor."

Vance's eyes lit up as he smiled at me. "I sometimes lose track of the stairs."

"That's because you teleport everywhere." I brushed crumbs off my lap and was reminded of the bloodstains all over my jeans. "I can't believe I met an entourage from the Seelie Court while dressed like this."

"Aside from the blood, I think you look fantastic."

"You would." I flashed him a grin. "Isabel and I need to move our business to another premises, but once we have that set up, we'll get our long-deserved break. Assuming nothing else tries to destroy the city beforehand."

"I'll give us a fifty-fifty chance."

"That's pushing it. Depends how the Chief reacts to the news that his people came here, and he missed them."

"Yes," Vance said. "There is that."

"Someone has to give him the bad news." The quicker we got the inevitable temper tantrum over with, the better. "Want me to do it? Or should we flip a coin?"

ABOUT THE AUTHOR

Emma is the New York Times and USA Today Bestselling author of the Changeling Chronicles urban fantasy series.

Emma spent her childhood creating imaginary worlds to compensate for a disappointingly average reality, so it was probably inevitable that she ended up writing fantasy novels. When she's not immersed in her own fictional universes, Emma can be found with her head in a book or wandering around the world in search of adventure.

Find out more about Emma's books at www. emmaladams.com.